For all those who are suffering or have suffered mental and physical abuse from whoever.

David Johnson

THE ENEMY AT HOME

AUSTIN MACAULEY PUBLISHERS™

LONDON ∗ CAMBRIDGE ∗ NEW YORK ∗ SHARJAH

A CIP catalogue record for this title is available from the British Library.

ISBN 9781398445567 (Paperback)
ISBN 9781398445574 (ePub e-book)

www.austinmacauley.com

First Published 2022
Austin Macauley Publishers Ltd®
1 Canada Square
Canary Wharf
London
E14 5AA

1907

It was a beautiful, warm summers day as Jack signalled with his stick for his patrol to move quietly into position at the foot of the steep, grassy slope that rose before them. Apart from the buzz and hum of the many insects, there was hardly a sound as the patrol lay there waiting for their next order.

Jack and his best friend, Harold, had scouted the ground ahead earlier and knew that at the top of the slope was a broad, woodland track. Some muffled whispering had enabled them to locate the enemy, a Boer patrol, which had taken up position in the trees on the far side of the track. Jack had decided that there was no alternative but to launch a frontal attack and as an experienced officer, he knew that timing would be everything.

Battles could be decided by attention to the smallest details and Jack had ensured that his patrol had eaten before moving up to their initial position because he was fairly sure, based on previous experience, that their enemy would not be so prepared or disciplined. It was Harold's job to ensure that the chaps remained quiet and lay patiently, knowing that the enemy would start to get restless as their stomachs craved their lunch. Jack knew because they had fought this particular Boer patrol before that one or two of them would mark the end of their bread and cheese or whatever it was they ate, by loud belches that would put the sound of an artillery salvo to shame. The plan was to attack at the sound of the first belch echoing through the trees.

Suddenly, there it was. That first belch accompanied by some muffled laughter and with a wave of his arm, Jack signalled for his chaps to move silently forward to just below the crest of the slope with each of them carrying a weapon of their own choice. He had to concede that they were a motley bunch which he proudly referred to as his irregulars, largely because they wore whatever was to hand when they got up that morning. Jack, for example, proudly wore an old pith helmet, whereas, the others were either bare headed or wore an assortment of peaked or flat caps. Everyone was under strict orders to stay down so that the

Boers did not spot them. There was an inevitable tension amongst the chaps and it was important at this moment that Jack conveyed to them calmness, certainty and confidence of leadership.

He gripped the small, silver whistle that hung around his neck and moved it to his lips and when he was sure that they were ready, he gave a sharp blast to launch the attack. The patrol rose as one with a blood curdling cry and charged over the crest of the slope.

They moved fast, bending low to avoid the bullets they imagined flying past them as they rushed across the track. Suddenly, there was a shout followed by a scream and looking to his right, Jack saw Harold running to where one of the chaps, inevitably Proctor again, was now spread-eagled on the ground next to a young girl who was on all fours. It was Sis.

The attack ground to a halt as everyone including the Boers, who had by now trooped out of the trees opposite, gathered around the prone figures or more accurately Sis, as nobody was prepared to show any interest in Proctor, who sat alone inspecting a fresh set of grazes on his hands, arms and legs and with nobody prepared to act as a medic. Inevitably, Jack did not enjoy the evident amusement of the erstwhile Boers.

Meanwhile, Harold was gently helping Sis to her feet as a red-faced Jack arrived. "What's she doing here? Didn't I tell her to stay away? She knew we didn't want her here."

Jack glared at Sis, who he could see was trying hard not to cry despite having been winded by Proctor. At this precise moment, although she hated her big brother, she was rather enjoying the attentions of Harold who had volunteered to see her home having said that she could lean on his arm.

Sis had been determined not to be left out of what the boys were doing and so she had set out to find the site of that morning's battle and, having heard Jack and Harold talking, she knew roughly where everyone had headed. Sis was ten years of age, one year younger than her brother, with a mass of blond curly hair and she always wanted to join in with the boys, which was why she had found herself inadvertently standing in the middle of the track when Jack's irregulars had started their attack. The next thing she knew, she was being knocked down by Billy Proctor.

Jack, a born leader if ever there was one, looked around red-faced and angry. "Come on. We'll go back. There's no point continuing the game now, is there? We'll call it a draw."

The two groups happily mingled as they headed back down the track with Proctor limping along at the back. After a short while, they came around a bend and perhaps only young boys could have failed to be impressed by the view of the market town of Acaster, spread out below them with its one broad road in and out of the town. Jack walked at the front, angrily swishing his stick from side to side and determined not to look around at the others. He was angry with his sister, who, as far as he was concerned, always spoilt everything, angry at Harold for walking with her rather than with him and just plain angry as he sensed that some of the others would be smirking and laughing at his expense.

When they reached the town, everybody split up and went their separate ways but not before setting a time and place for tomorrow's battle, their favourite activity during the long summer days. While these negotiations proceeded in hushed whispers, Jack had ordered Sis to stand well away, so that she could not overhear the plans being hatched. He half-wondered whether they could introduce the idea of a spy into the proceedings and then if Sis interrupted their game again, she could be seized and tied to a tree to be dealt with later and if he had his way much later.

Harold was not in the least concerned about tomorrow and kept looking across at Sis, who always seemed to be slyly looking back at him when he did so. If Jack noticed this, then he paid it no attention because it was totally beyond his comprehension why any boy, least of all Harold, could be remotely interested in any girl, especially his sister.

1964

St Benedict's Church was one of the oldest churches in the south of England with parts of the structure dating back to Anglo-Saxon times and was far larger than perhaps its location justified. The church, a grey stone building, stood in the centre of Acaster and overlooked a small park to its front while to one side was an adjoining cemetery and on the other stood the small Town Hall. Acaster boasted more public houses along its High Street than most towns of a comparable size and it was said that nobody ever needed to walk or stagger further than 100 yards to find one. Over the years, the town had started to spread out on either side of the High Street and its population had grown accordingly but it had still retained its charm and the feel of a market town.

Today, the church was full for the funeral of Bill Brown, a much-loved figure in the community and those who couldn't get into the church lined the road outside that passed between the church and the park to pay their respects. His son, Jack Brown, who was the much-respected Acaster estate manager, had attended many funerals over the years of family, friends and estate workers and like any sane person, he hated them. All funerals were inevitably and he felt deliberately sad affairs and he had on many occasions shed tears at the funerals of those he had hardly known. Jack, therefore, knew that today would be a sad occasion for many of those present but this time not for him.

The coffin, which was made of dark, polished oak with three sets of handles down its sides, had been met at the church's fifteenth-century door by Reverend James with the words: "Blessed are those who mourn, for they will be comforted." The pall bearers, solid looking men from the town's undertaker, Samuel Melling and Son, had then carried the coffin down the aisle between the packed rows of black-dressed mourners, who craned their necks for a glimpse as it passed and placed it carefully on a cloth covered trestle table at the foot of the steps to the altar. A simple wreath had then been placed on top of the coffin along with a police helmet and a set of medals.

Jack, staring at the stained-glass windows above and behind the altar, vaguely heard the words spoken by Reverend James, who, over the years, had become a friend of the family.

"We have come here today to remember before God, our brother, William Brown to give thanks for his life, to commend him to God, our merciful redeemer and judge to commit his body to be buried and to comfort one another in our grief."

As the service continued, Jack sat and stood as the dictates of the moment demanded but his mind was elsewhere as his wife, Edith, was only too aware through the tension she felt in the hand that held her own. Jack stared straight ahead and throughout the service he never once looked to his left where his father's coffin lay.

Eventually, after what seemed an eternity, Reverend James rose to deliver the eulogy on behalf of the family. Some in the congregation may have thought it strange that Jack was not carrying out this duty, having heard him deliver the eulogy at other funerals but others would have noted his taut posture as he sat in the front pew and concluded that emotion had got the better of him – and to some extent it had.

"Although, we all feel sad today. I really wanted to say a few words on behalf of the family to celebrate the life of Bill Brown, who so recently reached the age of 89 – not that he would ever have admitted to that!

"Bill's story began on 10 March 1875 and he enjoyed a happy childhood with his sister, Joan, his brothers, Donald and Colin, and his parents, Emily and Harry. Harry was a butcher and Friday nights in the Brown household always saw the scullery full of meat, orders waiting to be collected and a serious card school going on in the front room which could and very often did last all night. Unsurprisingly then, Bill retained a love of meat and of playing cards, invariably winning and like his father enjoyed a bet on the horses, particularly the Derby and the Grand National.

"Bill joined the Army in 1893 and by the time he was sent to South Africa during the Second Boer War, he was already a corporal. You won't be surprised to know that he served with distinction but he was unfortunately wounded at the Battle of Tweebosch in 1902. That wound was to his foot and, much to his frustration, it led to his discharge from the army and it later rendered him unfit for service in the First World War.

11

"No longer able to serve in the Army, Bill joined the Sussex Constabulary and before long he was promoted to sergeant and found himself posted to Acaster. Bill was a popular member of the community and was known to be a stickler for upholding the law, whoever and whatever the consequences. He finally retired from the police in 1930 but went on to be one of the founder members of Acaster's Home Guard during the Second World War.

"Bill met Alice when she nursed him for a time in the military hospital at Capetown. Alice was a member of the Princess Christian's Army Nursing Service, having trained at a London hospital. The happy couple married on 22 January 1895. Jack was born in 1897 and Sis followed in 1898. When they settled in Acaster, Alice polished and cleaned the family home to within an inch of its life and any time left over was devoted to this church, its flower arrangements and its choir.

"After 21 years of marriage, Alice sadly died in 1916 and Bill never fully recovered from her loss and never settled down with anyone again – although many tried to tempt him.

"Despite this, Bill continued to play his darts and bowls and had the trophies to prove it! I am sure that Bill will be remembered with great fondness and appreciation at our bowls club, where he worked hard in his spells as captain and chairman. When Bill took over the chairmanship of Acaster Bowls Club, it was struggling for members but under Bill, the club grew and its members enjoyed success in the competitions entered and representing the county.

"The family would like to thank the many carers who looked after Bill and enabled him to maintain the independence that was so important to him. They would also like to thank Dr Lyons and the staff of Acaster Cottage Hospital, who helped Bill to cope with the ailments that afflicted his final years.

"Bill loved his family and we should celebrate a life that encompassed being a son, a brother, a husband, a father and a father-in-law. He would never admit it but he missed Sis when she and Harold moved to Canada and settled in Toronto. Sadly, this meant that he and Alice never saw their grandchildren, Simon and Kate.

"So, yes, we are sad that Bill has died but I think it is with great affection that we celebrate a life that spanned. . . Sorry, Bill, 89 years and when we leave here, his family and friends will look forward to sharing more memories of Bill over a sandwich and a cup of tea or perhaps something a little stronger at the Stag.

"Bill, you will never be forgotten."

Jack had not reacted to anything that Reverend James had said and continued to sit there staring straight ahead. It was Edith who had to nudge him to stand for the final hymn and prayer and then leading the congregation as they followed the coffin as it was carried from the church and through a small gate into the adjacent cemetery for the burial.

"We have entrusted our brother, William, to God's mercy,
And now we commit his body to the ground,
Earth to earth, ashes to ashes, dust to dust,
In sure and certain hope of the resurrection to eternal life,
Through our Lord Jesus Christ,
Who will transform our frail bodies,
That they may be conformed to his glorious body,
Who died was buried and rose again for us,
To Him be glory for ever. Amen."

Finally with the service was over, people started to commiserate and shake Jack and Edith's hands before heading off, with those invited to sandwiches and drinks making for the Stag's Head. Edith told him that it was time that they went too but Jack said that he wanted a moment and would join her soon.

He turned back to the grave and stood on the green matting staring down at the coffin with a few handfuls of soil scattered on its lid together with a few single flowers, impervious to the grave digger 'Mole' Jenkins, who stood a little way off patiently leaning on his shovel with an ever-present cigarette dangling from his lip, ready to go to work as soon as everyone had left. Jack was a strong, vigorous man in his late 60s, known for his kindness and good humour, however, as he stood there, his eyes displayed different feelings, true feelings at that moment of anger and disgust towards the object of his attention. It was as he muttered, "Rot in hell, you old bastard," that he sensed he was not alone and turned to find Sam, who was first and foremost a family friend but also on this occasion the undertaker, standing next to him holding his father's police helmet and medals.

"Sorry, I didn't mean to overhear but strong words, Jack. I confess I was confused by your demeanour in church and perhaps even more so now that I have heard what you just said."

"Sorry about that, Sam. But it had to be said. I know others will disagree but I think there should be some honesty about today – and what I wanted to say I could never have got Reverend James to include in his eulogy. Call me a coward but I felt I needed to say things to him now that he is in his box that I never said to his face when he was alive. That might seem cowardly but this was my last chance after all."

Sam looked at him, concern evident on his face. "You know, I have always thought that there was something going on in your family. It just seems so strange that Sis has not come over from Canada – I don't even remember seeing a wreath from her."

"You won't see anything from Sis. Something going on in my family – you don't know the half of it."

"I think, on this day of all days, that it would do you good to get whatever it is off your chest, particularly as you feel there should be some honesty today. Talk about it, draw a line under it and then move on. What about staying on for a drink after everyone's left the Stag? I've got nothing to rush away for, not unless old Stan up at the cottages decides today is his time to go."

"I don't know, Sam. Maybe it should all stay where it is, crated up at the back of my mind…"

"Think about it. In the meantime, what about these?"

"I don't want them."

"Well, what about Sis?"

"She won't want them either. How about putting them down there on top of the coffin?"

Sam looked at Jack. "Well, if you're sure?"

Jack nodded and watched as Sam put the medals inside the helmet and turned to 'Mole' and asked to borrow his shovel. With the helmet strap hooked over the handle, Sam carefully lowered it onto the coffin and returned the shovel to 'Mole' and then he and Jack stood back as the old man started to cover the coffin with the heavy soil.

It had started to rain by the time the two men made their way to the Stag, which was an old, black and white coaching inn that seemed to preside over one end of the town. Jack was pleased to see friends and family there but he found their commiserations trying and, if he was honest, not a little tedious. Eventually, there was just Edith, Jack and Sam left, surrounded by the remains of the gathering namely used glasses, overflowing ashtrays, plates of uneaten sandwiches and pork pies scattered over the many tables. Sam had a quiet word with Edith and so once they had cleared up the plates and stacked all the used glasses on one table. She was primed to say that she was tired and would go home and leave them to it.

To start with the two men sat in silence, staring at their pints in the backroom of the pub, where the walls were covered in honours boards for the pub's darts and dominoes teams, unaware that Edith had spoken to the landlord, Don Blackman on the way out to ask that they be left alone and that she would come back first thing in the morning to sort the room out. Maybe it was the alcohol but eventually, without prompting, Jack began to talk.

"I can't forgive that old bastard for what he did in 19…"

1913

It was the day of the Acaster Summer Fair and the town woke up to a perfect June morning of blue skies and sunshine. Harold and I had been given that Saturday morning off from our work on the Acaster Estate and so we and our friends were up early to help set up the stalls, put up the bunting, marquees, tents, sideshows and fairground rides in the park opposite the church. We enjoyed helping but enjoyed even more the few coppers we earned from the showmen we helped.

We were helping to secure the guy ropes for the large horticultural marquee with Harold holding the metal stakes while another friend swung the mallet. My job was to secure the ropes and I looked at Harold and putting on a stern voice said, "Now pay attention and mind your fingers, otherwise you will have to learn to wipe your arse with your other hand."

The banter between us continued as you would expect between two best friends and then I saw my father, Sergeant Bill Brown, patrolling the green. I was always struck by the difference between my father's public face immaculately turned out as ever in his police uniform, who stopped to exchange small talk with those he passed, cheekily smiling as he tried one of Mrs Fawcett's small meat pies and the man I knew at home.

My family lived in the police house in Acaster. It was a detached house that was set back from the road and the only thing that differentiated it from its neighbours was the blue police sign on the wall by the front door. Those wishing to see Father would sit on the uncomfortable chairs in the hall and wait their turn to outline their concerns to him in the front room, which was austere, with its walls covered in dark wood panelling on which various documents were pinned and furnished with a desk and chair, two chairs for visitors and a single green filing cabinet which was kept locked at all times. The room also had a small open fireplace and Father was always determined to keep a fire burning from the beginning of November until the end of February. On the very rare occasions, that someone was arrested and needed to be detained overnight, there was a room in the cellar with a small truckle bed and a bucket, where they could be accommodated. Father worked long days of 12-hour shifts but he never worked on a Sunday, a day of rest, a necessity given the number of public houses and the trouble that occurred on a Saturday night, that enabled him to be seen with his family at St Benedict's for Holy Communion.

Sis and I had our bedrooms on the first floor. My bedroom was at the top of the stairs and had a view out over the rear garden and the fields beyond, while Sis had a room on the left of the small landing that led to the stairs up to our parents' bedroom on the floor above – a room we were forbidden by Father to ever enter.

The house was run with military precision by Father and I was afforded little if any leeway, while Sis on the other hand was Father's favourite and had him wrapped around her little finger. Unlike Sis, who might occasionally be expected to help Mum, I had my chores to do including cleaning out the fireplaces, fetching the coal and laying the fires and working the mangle and if I didn't meet Father's exacting standards, then the ritual that followed was always painfully the same.

"Jack, Jack! Get in here now!" He would roar.

I would enter the scullery to find Father standing there with his police belt in his hand. The irony of which I only saw as I got older. My mum would be standing pressing herself as far into the corner as possible with her face pale and a handkerchief held to her mouth to stifle her sobs – this scene had been played out enough times for Father to no longer need to growl at her to be quiet. A chair would be ominously placed in the middle of the floor and not for me to sit on.

As I got older, Father stopped bothering to tell me what I had done as it was assumed that I would know and so I had learnt to bend over the back of the chair to receive as many as six lashes of the belt across my backside with each blow accompanied by small gasps from Mum. Depending on the misdemeanour or Father's mood, the blows could be with the belt or the buckle itself.

As I got older, I had become determined not to give Father the satisfaction of seeing me cry, knowing that a lack of tears would infuriate him more and so when the beating had finished, I would turn and stumble from the scullery without a sound. In the early days, Mum had tried to follow me only to be angrily restrained by Father, who would be standing there red-faced, eyes bulging and bathed in perspiration. It would be left to Sis to come to me with a cool, damp cloth which she laid across my buttocks as I lay face down on my bed after I had shuffled down my trousers. I never appreciated my sister's kindness, preferring instead to focus on Father's favouritism and the embarrassment, not of her seeing me with my trousers down but of her seeing me with tears in my eyes once I had returned to my room.

On too many occasions, I had lay awake in my bed and heard Father shouting at Mum, followed by the sound of the scrape of moving furniture and thumps, sometimes from the bedroom on the floor above or down below in the scullery, followed by her sobbing. I had seen my share of women on a Saturday or a Sunday with black eyes, cut lips and facial bruises having been struck by a drunken husband on his return from the pub but I had never seen any wounds on Mum's face. And yet, I knew Father was knocking her about. I finally solved this puzzle and why on occasions Mum winced when she moved, when I heard Father giving some advice to a young police constable who had been sent to work in Acaster.

"If you have to hit 'em, either with your fist or your truncheon, then just make sure you don't hit 'em about the face. It's much better to hit 'em on the diagonal from shoulder to groin. Any bruises won't be so obvious and are easier to blame on other causes. It's quite surprising how many people walk into things around here. Clumsy buggers!"

When I was no longer a young boy, I had spoken to Mum about what was going on and I was taken aback when she blamed herself and gave all sorts of reasons to excuse Father's behaviour.

"Please, Jack, promise me that you won't say anything to him or try to intervene. It will only make things worse. Your father's a good man. He can't help himself. He has his standards and just gets easily wound up – I try so hard not to upset him and so must you. Look, I'll try harder to please him but promise me you won't do or say anything to him."

It was only the desperation in her voice that made a lasting impression on me and caused me to make the promise Mum so desperately sought.

***

I certainly never spoke to Mum about the nights when I had heard Father's heavy tread on the stairs and on the landing that stopped outside Sis's room. One night, intrigued, I crept out of my room and along the landing to see if Sis was ill. When I reached the door to Sis's room, I peered around the door frame and saw Father sitting on her bed and stroking her head. Father had his braces hanging loosely around his waist and Sis was just lying there looking up but not at Father.

"Is she ill, Father?"

It was as if the spell that held Father and Sis in some form of family tableau, lit by the candle on the bedside table was immediately broken by the sound of my words and both looked towards the door before Father stood up and left the room to return to his own bedroom taking the candle with him. He never said a word to me as he roughly brushed passed me in the doorway, his face a picture of anger and frustration.

I was unsure what to do or say to my sister but Sis made it easy for me by turning her back on me without speaking and so I closed her door and went back to my own bed, troubled by what I had seen although none the wiser.

***

The fair was to be officially opened at one o'clock by the town's mayor, Councillor Pressley, together with Lord Acaster and as the morning progressed, more and more people came to the green to help ensure that all was ready such as the local butcher, Tom Jones, who had arrived early that morning to set up and start the pig roast and Will Young was there too with his trays of freshly baked bread and already the tantalising aromas were teasing the noses of those present. The fair followed the same format every year under the firm hand of its organising committee and any dissenting or modernising voices were silenced by the diehards reciting the amount of money raised each year for good causes.

It was at the fair that I finally had to accept that Harold was interested in my sister. I had seen how Harold always seemed to be able to sense my sister's presence and his head would suddenly swivel around and his eyes would search her out. Sis for her part made it plain that she no longer saw Harold as a boy who played war games with her brother but as a sturdy and good-looking young man.

Later that morning, Sis had brought some cakes that Mum had baked to be sold on the church stall and Harold, holding yet another stake, this time for me to hammer into the ground, had almost lost a finger as his concentration switched to watching her rather than on what I was doing.

"Harold! What the hell – pay attention, you idiot!"

Harold grunted and I, following his gaze, saw Sis standing by a stall that was selling ribbons and looking across at us. Muttering to myself, I prepared to drive the next stake into the ground and, to Harold's surprise, did so with far more force than was perhaps justified.

***

The fair always attracted a lot of people from the town and the surrounding area and Harold, I and our friends enjoyed wandering around and egging each other on. There was laughter as our volley of wooden balls failed to dislodge a single coconut. None of us were able to throw a ring over a bottle and so thankfully did not have to consider what to do with any goldfish that we may have won. We stood at the back of the small crowd at the Punch and Judy show, children at the front, enjoying the predictable story but also some of the jokes included for the ears of the adults. We took part in the tug of war competition but narrowly lost to a team of regulars from the Stag which had benefited from the rotund figure of Reverend Stoddart anchoring their efforts.

With the fair officially opened, I saw Mum and Sis walking arm in arm like two sisters around the stalls and sideshows and Mum waved when she saw me and came across to say hello to me and my friends. I loved my mum and always felt happy to see her as did my friends. Given that Mum hated violence and conflict, I could only smile at the irony of her standing in front of the ornate façade of the travelling boxing booth with its images of boxers through the ages.

On a raised stage, a small, wizened old man wearing a multi-coloured jacket and a somewhat battered top hat, a cigar stub in the corner of his mouth began vigorously banging a side drum held by an even smaller boy who flinched with every strike before introducing the line of boxers who stood behind him. Some of the boxers were young and shuffled their feet nervously while the veterans, with faces and ears a testimony to a life of fighting, stood still and surveyed the gathering crowd with a look of amused contempt on their faces. The small man spoke in a soft, Southern Irish accent that weaved a persuasive spell over those who were listening.

"Roll up! Roll up! Where are the brave boys of Acaster prepared to put on these boxing gloves, as worn by that great British heavyweight Jack Palmer, and fight with one of these beauties? Where are the sportsmen amongst you? If you win, then you win a pound. That's right, one pound. Now, here's a brave chap. Put these gloves on my lad and then you can follow me to the ring."

The man putting the gloves on with the help of the small boy, who by now had put down his drum, was not a local man but clearly a plant but, nevertheless, those that had gathered were interested and paid their money before entering the tent and getting their first sight of the boxing ring bathed in an oily light with its slack ropes and brightly coloured, padded corners. The tent was oppressively warm on this hot summer's afternoon but the crowd was happy to stand there and cheer on the challengers who were a mixture of the unskilled looking to impress their wives and girlfriends. Some, who had clearly drunk too much and were as a result full of bravado, and others who fancied the life of a fighter and were out to see if they were good enough.

The first fight was over quickly with the plant going down after a bit of dancing around. It had to be said, a theatrical slap rather than a punch. As the first real challenger was having the gloves put on by the small boy, the small man was in the corner telling his boxer to take it easy and not hurt his opponent too much in case it put others off from taking up the challenge. The fights that followed were of variable length and quality but the crowd was royally entertained by what they were watching.

The small man, cigar stub still in the corner of his mouth, was still encouraging men to come and have a go and we began daring each other to take up the challenge. Harold was the first to step forward with a broad smile on his face and I went with him to the ringside, the better to cheer on my friend. With his gloves on and his shirt off, Harold took on an old pro who although bigger than him was much slower and was soon sweating profusely. To roars from the crowd, Harold had his opponent swinging his arms around as though to ward off an angry wasp and breathing heavily as the younger man darted around the ring landing some useful, stinging punches.

It was then that I spotted Sis standing on the other side of the ring and I could see that her face was flushed with excitement. Harold was enjoying himself and was clearly on top of his opponent when Sis, no longer able to contain herself, shouted out, "Go on! Hit him, Harold!"

Harold, on this occasion, had been totally unaware that Sis was there but her shout was enough to momentarily distract him and as he glanced to his right to look for her, his opponent seized the opportunity to land a punch to the side of his face. It was a blow that ensured that there was no way back and Harold crumpled to the floor where he was then counted out, much to the relief of the small man. The crowd cheered his bravery but were disappointed with the outcome and as Harold was helped from the ring, I saw Father laughing as he shook his head surrounded by his cronies from the pub. To gales of laughter, Father was using his hands to demonstrate to those around him the difference between a punch and a slap.

I remember feeling so angry with Father that when the small man asked if there was a final challenger, I instantly climbed into the ring and held my hands out for the gloves to be put on. I stood in my corner and looked across at my opponent, a young man of much the same size and build as myself. Although I had had a few fights over the years, this was a new experience for me. My opponent was as wary of me as I was of him and so we circled around each other looking for an opening and then I found myself on the floor, my eyes watering and struggling for breath following a vicious blow to my diaphragm. The small man was instantly leaning over me and counting. If I close my eyes, I can still smell his cigar breath.

"One…two…three…four…five…"

It was then that I heard Father's shout of, "Come on, Jack. Get up, Son. It was just a slap!" This was followed by the unmistakeable sound of laughter.

At the count of 'six' and much to the small man's disappointment, I staggered to my feet, leaning back on the ropes. What followed, I believe, was more vicious than anything witnessed so far that afternoon, as I willed myself to stand and then began what amounted to an all-out assault on a clearly surprised opponent who was totally unprepared for a situation where I was clearly willing to take a punch as long as I landed several in return. I was oblivious to the other's punches as I set about overwhelming the man in front of me with a barrage of blows to his head and ribcage. Finally, I landed a punch that sent the other man to the floor where he sensibly stayed despite the small man uttering all sorts of threats and curses under his breath as he counted him out, "…ten!"

The small man stood in the middle of the ring and declared me the winner holding my arm in the air and presented me with my prize purse of one pound. Unbeknown to the locals, who cheered, I got the prize I most wanted when I turned to see Father leaving the tent and having to feign pride as people sought to congratulate him for having such a fine, strong boy.

I left the ring and happily accepted the congratulations of friends and neighbours but I was anxious to find Harold. This was to be a further moment when I had to accept that something more than a passing acquaintance was developing between my friend and my sister. I found Harold sitting in the shade of a small tent opposite the boxing booth, surrounded by our friends and a concerned Sis who was dabbing at his face with a wet cloth. Harold had a very swollen eye and a small cut on the bridge of his nose that oozed blood but I could see that he was well enough to be enjoying all the attention. Ironically, it was me who had won my fight, that looked far worse with swollen lips, a cut on my cheek and a rapidly swelling eye but my sister never so much as glanced at me. Eventually, Harold graciously agreed with a cheeky wink in my direction that he felt sufficiently recovered to allow Sis and I to help him home.

***

Harold's father, James, who had been an estate worker, had died some years ago after a short illness and Mrs Smith, who had never remarried, had remained in an estate cottage, thanks to Lord Acaster's kindness. Mrs Smith was still an attractive woman that many men had tried hard to entice back up the aisle or failing that at least into bed but all had received short shrift for their efforts. She was fiercely protective of her son but realised and at the same time also struggled with the concept that she had to let him live his life without smothering him if he was to become a man. When we appeared on her doorstep that afternoon and explained what had happened, she berated Harold for his stupidity and in turn me for allowing him to do such a stupid thing. Harold smiled sheepishly at us as his mother led him into the hall and firmly closed the door with the heel of her shoe on his friends without saying another word.

I was beginning to ache too much as a result of my fight to even think about teasing my sister about Harold as we walked back to the fair to enjoy what was left of the day. Gradually, as summer turned to autumn, Harold and Sis became accepted as girlfriend and boyfriend, even by me. I was at first dismayed that Harold preferred to sit with Sis at the dances in the Church Hall and at the Youth Club rather than laugh and joke with his mates all the time but gradually I accepted it and was pleased to see my friend happy. The two of us still worked together and got involved in a few scrapes but Harold was less carefree and more serious as the year progressed.

We had been best friends for as long as we could remember and we both felt totally comfortable in each other's company but there was one exception because

I never felt able to engage Harold in banter let alone a discussion about his feelings towards Sis, which even I could see ran deep. Whereas I never felt able to tease Harold, as her big brother, I enjoyed any opportunity to tease Sis who would blush and look visibly discomforted. I was her brother and what were big brothers for after all if not to make a younger sibling embarrassed?

***

Our parents reacted to the developing relationship between Sis and Harold as I had expected. Our mum was pleased and when Father wasn't around, she would sit and talk to Sis and was always pleased to see Harold when he knocked on the back door. Father, however, could not accept that his favourite was growing up and that there was a young pretender challenging his position as the dominant male in her life. He never acknowledged what was happening but it was obvious that he was struggling to accept it. I lost count of the number of times Father brought up Harold being knocked down in the boxing booth by what he never failed to describe as a slap, which was also a dig at me as well. He did this both when Harold was within earshot and when he wasn't and although Harold laughed it off every time, the cheeks on my sister's face would turn red although she never uttered a word.

One evening with the scullery lit by the gas mantles ranged around the walls and with the rain tapping on the windows, we had just finished eating our supper and Sis was helping Mum clear the plates from the table. The meal had ended with more comments from Father about Harold's lack of manliness. "Went down like a girl" was one such comment and as on previous occasions, I could see that Father sitting in his favourite armchair by the hearth and cleaning out his pipe was desperate for some sort of response in order to excuse an escalation of the tension surrounding the situation. While Mum shook her head and held her handkerchief to her mouth and Sis flushed as she cleared the table, I finally reached the point where I could no longer bite my tongue.

"Give it a rest, for God's sake, Father!"

Father turned and looked at me with a practiced squint refined over many years so as to put fear into whoever stood in front of him. However, on this occasion, it did not work.

"What did you just say to me?"

I repeated what I had said deliberately and slowly as if I was talking to a child or an idiot.

"I said give it a rest, Father. We've heard it all before and it wasn't even funny the first time."

Father, who was using a spill to clean out his pipe, slowly and methodically knocked the ash into the hearth before slowly placing both in the ash tray on the arm of his chair. He looked steadily up at me as I now stood in front of him and with a slow deliberation, while maintaining eye contact, rose from his chair. However, I was no longer prepared to be intimidated either by size or inclination.

"Pack it in. You will show me some respect, you young bugger!"

"Or what, Father?"

"And you can stop calling me 'Father' in that tone of voice."

I could hear Mum telling us both to calm down while Sis had sat down as if resigned to witnessing what she now sensed had become inevitable.

"What's the matter – old man? Is that better? Not taking your belt off to me then? It's not the same when you are no longer the biggest or the strongest? You see, whatever you do to me, you'll get back with plenty of interest and while I'm at it, I will make you pay for all the times you have clouted our mum."

Sis looked horrified as she glanced across at our mum who seemed to burrow as far back into the wall behind her as she could while Father, with veins now standing out across his forehead and his jaw clenched, took a step towards me but then thought better of it.

"Get out! Get out of this house now! Nobody, least of all you, speaks to me like that in my own home." He spat at me. "Get out!" Father went to the door and took down his coat and began to put it on before turning and pointing at me.

"I'm off down the Stag to have a drink with my mates – real men! Make sure you are not here when I get back. In fact, make sure you are never here when I get back, do you understand?"

Without waiting for an answer, Father left slamming the door behind him and once silence had fallen for a second or two, I heard Mum, who was behind me begin to sob and as I turned towards her, I could only too well both see and sense her agitation.

"Jack. Quickly now, go after him. Apologise to him. Quickly now! Quickly!"

"Never, Mum! He's a disgrace and a bully – you know that. He should be the one to apologise after the beatings he has given you and me over the years."

"No, no, he's a good man, Jack. He just has a bit of a temper, that's all. He works so hard and we mustn't upset him and then he's fine."

I gave Mum a hug. "Mum, if that's what you want to believe and you want to blame yourself, then so be it. However, we both know what he is. Perhaps it's better if I go."

Sis had not yet spoken but she came across and gave me and our mum a hug. Between tears, she asked me where I would go.

"Don't worry about me. I'll find somewhere."

"I'm sorry, Jack. I have always accepted the good with Dad and ignored the rest. I thought it was just normal father and daughter stuff and I was even able to excuse him for the beatings he gave you. If I never said anything to him about you, then I should have said something about Harold – I love him. If Dad thinks that he can put me in a position where I will choose him over Harold, then he is wrong. And Mum, I never knew he hit you. Honestly, I didn't. I never heard it or saw it."

Our mum may have been upset but she had clearly heard what Sis had said. "What do you mean normal father and daughter stuff? What's he been doing to you?"

"Nothing, Mum! Nothing! It's fine, honestly. Don't worry about it."

The three of us stood silently and then Sis looked at me.

"Go to Mrs Smith. I am sure she will take you in and Harold will be pleased to have you around. I'll look after Mum. I'll stand up to Dad. He wouldn't ever hit me."

I looked at my sister who seemed to have woken up from some form of stupor and was now more animated than I had ever seen her.

"Don't worry. If I find out that he has hit you or Mum, then I won't be able to help myself – and he knows it now."

Mum urged me to go and pack my bag as she had a real fear that Father would make it his business to return early from the pub, fuelled by several pints and the encouragement of his cronies and looking for trouble. I did not have too much to pack and after a last hug from Mum and Sis, left the family home for what I fully expected to be the last time.

1914

I had quickly settled into living with Harold and his mother. Harold and Mrs Smith lived in a small end terraced-cottage, which was located at the far end of the High Street from the Police House. Just beyond the terrace of cottages lay the entrance to the Acaster Estate.

When Ester Smith opened her front door, she did not seem at all surprised to find me on her doorstep with my bag in my hand, nor when I asked if I could come in and she never asked the reason for me leaving home that night. Harold, who although concerned for me, was also delighted to see me and the spare bed in his room was quickly made up for me and without the need for any explanation. I had become part of the Smith household. Jack and I would leave early for our work on the estate, fuelled by a mug of hot tea and a piece of hot buttered toast prepared by Mrs Smith, who also left us hunks of bread and cheese wrapped up in a cloth, in the hall by our coats and caps, to have during the day.

As the days turned into weeks and the weeks into months, Sis, Mum and I became very adept at meeting up well away from Father. Sometimes, Mum would come to the estate and spend time with me as I ate the lunch prepared by Mrs Smith. It was in those moments that I could see the pain in her eyes as she watched me eat food that she, my mother, had not prepared for me. At other times, we and sometimes, Harold would meet on a Saturday afternoon in the Acaster Tea Rooms after Sis had finished work at Palfreys Shoe and Haberdashery Shop. We always sat in the back room well away from the windows that overlooked the green and the High Street so that if Father walked past, he would not see us and we knew that he would never set foot in a tea shop unless he had to or it had suddenly started to serve beer. The passing weeks also meant that Sis would sometimes visit me at Mrs Smith's, although nobody was fooled as to the true purpose of her visits, namely to see Harold.

Sometimes, as Harold and I ate our lunch with our backs resting on a wall or in the shade of a tree, I would see my friend take an envelope from his pocket and with obvious pleasure read the letter that it contained. I could recognise my sister's neat and tidy writing anywhere and as I had now fully accepted what was happening, I enjoyed the pleasure such letters gave my friend.

One day as Harold returned one such letter to his pocket, he saw me looking at him with a smile on my face.

"Well? What's up with you?"

"Nothing, but I don't know why you're making such a big secret about it. A blind man could see those letters are from Sis."

Harold laughed breaking any hint of tension between us and I also laughing said, "For the life of me, I cannot fathom out what you see in my sister. As far as I am concerned, speaking as her brother, you understand she will always be a flat-chested, runny nosed pain – but, of course, I might be biased!"

"Give over, Jack. I am not sure what standards you are applying but if it's Dotty from the tea rooms, then you need your eyes testing. Sis is lovely and one day I plan to marry her."

The silence that followed signified that those last few words had surprised both of us. Harold was the first to feel the need to fill the silence. Without looking at me he asked,

"Well, what do you think then, Jack?"

"I think you need your head looking at, that's what I think but I suppose I could do worse for a brother-in-law. Does Sis know about your grand plan?"

"No. You're the first person I've asked."

"Well, I think you'll find that you are meant to ask Sis not her brother, you great lump!"

"What will your father say?"

"I don't know and I don't care. All you have to do is to wait until she no longer needs that bastard's consent. What about your mother – she can be just as scary when she wants to be?"

"Mum likes Sis – she always has done and I am pretty sure your mother likes me. But I will wait and not because of your father but because I want to be more set up for life first. I want to make something of myself. I don't want to be doing this for the rest of my life."

***

With each passing month, the threat of war with Germany became ever greater. Like many young men of our age, Harold and I discussed it, not in terms of the geo-politics involved but rather the opportunities for adventure and as a result, the chance to experience life outside of Acaster that it would present and how we were determined not to miss out.

Nobody was really surprised when on 4 August Great Britain declared war on Germany. The newspapers carried their reports of the statement made by the Foreign Office.

Owing to the summary rejection by the German government of the request made by His Majesty's government for assurances that the neutrality of Belgium would be respected, His Majesty's Ambassador in Berlin has received his passport and His Majesty's government has declared to the German government that a state of war exists between Great Britain and Germany as from 11 pm on 4 August.

The next day when I came down to my tea and toast, I happened to glance at Mrs Smith's copy of the Daily Mirror which was lying on the table and saw the headline *Declaration of war by Great Britain after unsatisfactory reply to yesterday's ultimatum.*

It was the news that Harold and I had been expecting and indeed hoping for and during that day over our bread and cheese, we made our decision to enlist at the earliest opportunity. As we both worked on the estate, we believed ourselves to be both fit and healthy and therefore we were both confident that we would easily pass the medical. The main obstacle to our enlistment was our age as neither of us was yet 19, the minimum age required.

We knew, however, that the legal and medical considerations would be as nothing compared to the emotional reaction we would face in telling our mothers and Sis about our plans. Over the next few days we discussed our options but we could not decide the best way to proceed. Should we tell them first and then attempt to stand firm against what we knew would be tearful pleadings to stop us or just do it and own up to it afterwards?

***

It wasn't just the young men who were discussing the threat of war as Lord Acaster had also been planning for its likely outbreak. Lord Acaster regularly met each week with Captain Roland Hargreaves, his estate manager, and so Hargreaves was not unduly surprised when Lord Acaster entered the estate office one morning. Hargreaves stood and then asked Lord Acaster if he would like a small nip of whiskey and when both men were seated with their drinks, Lord Acaster came to the point.

"Ah, Hargreaves, I wanted a word with you in confidence, you understand? In the event that we go to war with the bloody Germans, something that seems increasingly likely with each passing day, I want the estate to play its part by raising a company of men drawn from the estate and the surrounding area and I would like you to command it. I would like you to understand that I am too old, I've been told. What do you think?"

"Well, sir, I know the boys are keen – it's all they talk about – always on about it being over by Christmas and missing out. I am honoured that you would like me to command such a company."

The two men savoured their whiskey and eventually Lord Acaster spoke.

"Lord Kitchener knows that our army is nowhere near large enough to take on the Germans. The War Office has decided that a way to encourage enlistment is to offer men the opportunity to serve alongside their friends and colleagues. I am though very concerned that communities like this one, who provide a company of local men run a very real risk of being decimated because if these men fight together, then they can equally die together, should it all go wrong. If that happened, then Acaster would have its heart ripped out."

Captain Hargreaves agreed but then put a counter argument.

"I agree with your lordship but realistically, if the men don't serve with their pals, then they can quite easily enlist somewhere else and the effect could be just the same and therefore in my opinion, we will be making the best of a bad job. I know I would always prefer to serve and, yes, die if needed, alongside my mates."

Lord Acaster looked across at Hargreaves. "Thank you, Hargreaves – you are a good man. I want every man from the estate who enlists to be assured that their job will be there for them when they return and that I will do my utmost to support their families while they are away or if the worst happens."

***

A few days after the outbreak of war posters appeared around Acaster, on the noticeboards outside the church, the Church Hall and in shop windows with Lord Kitchener pointing his finger with the words *Britons: Lord Kitchener Wants You. Join Your Country's Army! God save the King.* It was a powerful poster and Jack remarked to Harold that wherever you stood, it looked like Kitchener was staring straight at you and following you with his eyes.

Harold and I were aware of the plans for a company to be raised from the estate and we were excited to see a notice go up calling for men over the age of 19 to go to the church hall at 7.30 pm on Friday, 28 August and we fully intended to be there. As agreed, neither of us spoke to our mothers or to Sis about our plans and they in turn never spoke to us as they, naively, believed that as the two of us were not yet 19, it was something that could be left to another day and perhaps the war would be over by then.

On the appointed day, we joined a group of men, gathered around the steps leading to the door to the Church Hall. We both knew many of the men there and both nods and handshakes were exchanged. Over the preceding days, we had taken the opportunity to talk to Harold's cousin, Herbert, who was older than us and worked on the railways and he had encouraged us to enlist. He said that he had heard that recruiting sergeants were by and large not too fussy about ages, particularly as they received a bounty for every man enlisted and therefore there was no need for us to take along our birth certificates.

"Stand straight. Look 'em in the eye and tell 'em you are 19 years and one month. You won't have a problem."

As we stood at the foot of the steps waiting to be called forward, we were nervous that someone would say something about our age as many of those present knew our true age but everyone there shared the common purpose of enlistment and, other than a smile or a sly wink, nobody said a word as all were prepared to collude in the deceit.

Harold and I felt our hearts nearly stop when the door opened and Father stepped out and stood surveying the men in front of him. Inevitably, he saw us and we could pretty much see the calculation going on in his head as he worked out whether it was better to call us forward and humiliate us in front of the other men for being under-age with some sarcastic remark about 'go home to your mothers' or doing nothing and thereby potentially solving a problem. After what seemed an eternity, he smiled at us before turning his back and re-entering the hall.

"What's he going to do?"

"No idea."

"You must have – he's your father."

I looked at Harold and shook my head. "Bill Brown will do whatever Bill Brown thinks is best for Bill Brown, no matter how hurtful to the rest of us."

***

We decided to hang back and take our chances at the end of the session in the hope that tiredness and boredom would make those inside less particular about who was enlisted. Eventually, we were called forward and entered the hall where we saw, through clouds of tobacco smoke, a recruiting sergeant standing beside a trestle table behind which sat an elderly officer. Behind the officer was the stage where the curtains, looking shabby in the absence of footlights, were closed to allow the medicals to take place with some degree of privacy behind them. Captain Hargreaves was also there and he gave us a nod and a conspiratorial wink when he saw us standing in the line. No man in that hall on that Friday evening would ever have thought of revealing that anyone seeking to enlist was under-age. Fathers, too old to serve themselves, felt pride that their sons were going to fight the enemy. In some cases, both father and son stood in line to enlist together. Although not physically present, some mothers, wives and girlfriends who, although naturally worried, also felt pride while those who did not by and large knew better than to make a scene.

The two of us joined a queue which under the circumstances proved to be quite entertaining. As anxious as two under-age boys were to enlist, there were others past the age where they could usefully serve who were equally keen to join up. Some had decided to knock a few years off their age. Others had tried to hide their grey hair by the liberal application of boot polish and this ruse was only revealed when they politely removed their hats or caps in front of the officer to reveal a black line around their head. One old soldier, Clem, had turned up in his full Boer War uniform including a kilt, requiring the officer to display some tact and diplomacy in explaining that his country would be better served if he stayed behind to keep an experienced eye on the town while the other men were away.

Eventually, Harold was called forward first and asked for his name, address and occupation but, as I was relieved to see, not his birth certificate by the officer.

"Are you willing to join His Majesty's army?"

"Yes, sir."

"How old are you?"

Without hesitating, Harold replied looking straight at the officer,

"I am 19 years and one month, sir."

"Another one, Sergeant! Very good then, sign here, please. Right, now move to the side over there and wait to be called to see the doctor."

I was then called forward and the process was repeated. As we stood waiting to see the doctor, I looked across to the other side of the hall and saw Father standing there with a smile playing around the corners of his mouth. When Father was sure that I was looking at him, he nodded and left the hall.

For two fit, young men the medical was a formality and we were not at all concerned when we were called behind the curtain to see the doctor who, after a cursory examination that involved answering a few questions, listening to our breathing through a stethoscope, an eyesight test, a check of our feet and the embarrassment of us coughing while he cupped our balls in his hand declared us fit for service.

The evening finished with us standing with those who had successfully enlisted for the duration of the war, taking the oath of allegiance to the Crown and the King's Shilling. The sergeant then stepped forward and told us to report to the hall at 09.00 hours the following Monday morning when we would start our journey to the training camp. Then having been dismissed, the two of us and the other men excitedly burst out of the hall, talking loudly, laughing and clapping each other on the back. Like all the men, our initial excitement was soon tempered by the realisation of the enormity of what we had done and the knowledge that we would now have to explain our actions to our families and loved ones.

***

I met my Mum and sis in the tea rooms on the Saturday afternoon, half-expecting that they would already know as I was sure that Father would have delighted in telling them the news. However, they did not know and their shock was followed by anger and tears.

"Why on earth have you done such a stupid thing? You are too young for a start – I am going to see Lord Acaster himself and put a stop to this nonsense!"

"Mum, please. It's what I want. I couldn't carry on working on the estate and meeting you in here, nice and cosy on a Saturday afternoon, knowing my mates are over there doing their bit and getting wounded or worse. I promise you that I will be careful and the great thing about going with your mates is that we can all look out for each other. Lord Acaster has said that we can have our jobs back when the war is over and it will be over by Christmas – you see."

It was painful to see my mum and sis so upset and Mum seemed physically unable to let go of my hand and Sis dabbed at her eyes as she asked me, "And what about Harold?"

"We joined up together."

"How could he do that without telling me after all his talk about our future?"

I really had no answer to that question. "Best talk to him, Sis."

"Oh, I will and right now!"

Sis left and as I could see where she was headed, I was grateful to remain in the teashop with Mum, who still seemed unable to let go of my hand.

"Mum, I know it's hard for you to understand but try to look pleased for me. Promise me you will be there on Monday when we march away. Please, Mum, it will mean a lot to me."

However, Mum, was in no mood to make it easy for me and refused to say that she would be there and so on. "I'll see" had to suffice.

***

Later, when Harold and I met up, all Harold would say was that his mother had threatened to kill him, which in the circumstances we both found quite funny and that Sis had been distraught. However, she had, after some pleading on his part, agreed to wait for him and had even promised to write to him every week. The rest of the weekend passed in a blur of bravado, quiet reflection on the implications of what we had done and our preparations for leaving. For some of the men and Harold and I were no different. This would be the first time that we had ever travelled outside the boundaries of Acaster.

***

Breakfast at the Smiths had been a silent affair that Monday morning. Mrs Smith was adamant as she bustled about to keep herself busy that she would not be coming to the Church Hall to watch us march off. As much as she loved Harold, she would not do it, recognising that it was the only way left to her of punishing him for his stupidity and furthermore, she was damned sure that she would not allow herself to be seen blubbing in public – she would do her crying right there at the kitchen table and in private.

When the time came for us to leave, Mrs Smith stood by the front door and looked me in the eye as she shook hands with me but then pulled my head towards her as if to kiss my cheek. With her mouth close to my ear, she whispered with some vehemence, "Look after him. Make sure he comes back in one piece, otherwise if the Germans haven't killed you, then I will."

Slightly shaken, I moved off down the front garden path to allow Harold and Mrs Smith a degree of privacy. Harold hugged his mother and when she kissed him, both had tears in their eyes and others mingling on their cheeks. By this time, I was standing outside the front gate fidgeting and with my back to the sad scene being played out at the front door. I then heard the front door shut before Harold had reached the gate. Without looking at me, Harold walked past me and quickly set off towards the Church Hall and neither of us spoke on that short walk.

***

When we arrived at the hall, we were directed to put our bags on the back of a cart where there were already many bags and cases of a variety of sizes, condition and description. Many of those who had enlisted were standing with their families saying their tearful goodbyes. Husbands hugged their wives while in some cases small children clasped the legs of their soon-to-depart fathers. Boyfriends coyly held the hands of their girlfriends and accepted small lucky tokens from them that were carefully secured in pockets.

Mum and Sis, much to my relief, were there and so we spent the precious minutes left before the order to form up was given, talking to them. Harold took Sis aside and the two talked and I saw Sis give my friend an envelope and a small handkerchief. Harold then, both shyly but purposefully, kissed Sis before we were ordered to form up in front of the hall's steps.

The recruiting sergeant, who we now knew as Sergeant Kennedy, was at the top of the steps and in his best parade ground voice ordered us to form up in four lines and stand to attention as Lord Acaster, Captain Hargreaves and Reverend

Stoddart appeared. Despite the sadness of the occasion, there were many there who could not stop themselves from laughing at the trials and tribulations of the men as they tried very hard to form up in straight lines and to stand at attention. While that was going on, I saw Father standing to the side of the steps ensuring that nothing untoward marred the proceedings. Lord Acaster then stepped forward to address the men.

"My brave men of Acaster, please, stand at ease! I want to personally and on behalf of the nation thank you for coming forward to join the fight against Germany and its allies. As I stand here, I feel immensely proud as do your families as we look at 'A' Company, to be known as the Acaster Company, of the 4th Battalion of the Sussex Rifles.

"I regret that I cannot serve with you and believe me I have tried to call in favours but to no avail. They say that I am too old. You will, however, be in the safe hands of Captain Hargreaves and your N.C.O.s who I have charged with bringing you all back safely.

"I have no doubt that you will make your families and Acaster proud and through your courage and that of thousands of men like you from up and down the country, this war will soon be over. I give every one of you my solemn promise that while you are away, I will look after your families and when you return, there will be a job for all of you.

"God Bless You!"

Captain Hargreaves then stepped forward and led the men and those gathered to see us off in three cheers for His Majesty followed by a further three cheers for Lord Acaster. Finally, Reverend Stoddart, prayer book in hand, led us in the Lord's Prayer followed by a blessing.

Sergeant Kennedy, having been told to carry on by Captain Hargreaves, then gave the order "Tenshun". There were as many physical variations of 'Attention' as there were men standing in front of him but the sergeant kept a straight face and made no comment – that could wait for the drill sergeants.

'Left turn' followed, although inevitably there was some confusion and laughter as a handful of men turned right and then had to sort themselves out. The sergeant waited for Captain Hargreaves to take up his position at the front of the column and then gave the order "Forward march" and we set off on the two miles to Acaster Junction.

Accompanied by Clem, again in his uniform and playing the bagpipes, we marched away to the shouts and waves of those left behind, the 'music' causing some of the men to do a little jig as they went down the road. I looked for Mum and Sis and saw both waving with one hand and wiping away tears with the other. Harold in turn was upset to see Sis crying and tried his best to lift her spirits with a cheery wave and a smile – not that he felt particularly cheery or smiley himself as he would have liked his mother to have been there. It was as they marched past the Stag, that I saw Father and as we passed, I was surprised to see him stand smartly to attention and salute.

***

It was early autumn and the weather was getting noticeably colder in the early mornings and at night, which was made worse for the men as due to a shortage of accommodation, the new recruits were living under canvas in one of the many dozens of tents on Surrey's Frensham Common. Spread about the camp, which was the size of a small town, were canteens where alcohol could be purchased at prices lower than those in any public house outside the camp, although we quickly learned the penalties for over-indulgence and shops selling groceries with maximum prices fixed by the War Office. In addition, there were also tea and barbers' tents together with a small theatre, where periodically variety shows were staged. The washrooms and latrines were very unpleasant as they were hot, smelly and infested with flies in the spring and summer and cold and still smelly in the autumn and winter.

We lived ten to a tent with our metal-framed beds spread around its edge and tables down the centre. The interior of the tent, replete with the heavy musk of ten men, tobacco smoke and damp clothing, was lit by a handful of lamps giving off a weak, oily, yellow light. As some men sat at the tables playing cards, others lounged on their beds while a few tended to their uniforms and equipment. After a long day in the kitchens, we sat on our beds and studied our rough red hands.

"Honestly, Harold, I never knew there were so many potatoes in the world. Two hours we were stood there peeling and scraping. I joined up to fight the Germans, not prepare boiled potatoes unless we are thinking of using them as weapons to throw at the bloody Germans. I never peeled potatoes at home if I could help it."

Harold laughed and told me to cheer up because tomorrow he had heard that we were to be promoted as we were moving on to peeling carrots.

"You have to admit that boiled potatoes and a few carrots will be an improvement on the diet of stale bread and cheese for breakfast, dinner and tea that we have been served up so far."

"No, seriously, Harold, at this rate we will still be here at Christmas and the war will be over. They were quick enough to enlist us and then what? There's nothing organised. Why the urgency to sign us up if they haven't got the guns and uniforms for us? We're still wearing our own clothes. On that route march yesterday, we had to carry broom handles instead of rifles and when it started raining, old Smillie even put his umbrella up as he marched along and not a word was said either by Hargreaves or the sergeant."

"I know. All we seem to have done is to march here and there for miles, dig trenches, stick bayonets in a few sandbags and peel sacks of potatoes. It felt more real all those years ago when we played at fighting the Boers. The one thing we haven't done is fire a sodding rifle!"

"I struggled not to laugh at those sandbags with the two eyes drawn on them and little, white crosses marking the heart and guts and the sergeants shouting out orders as to where to stick our bayonets. It did though make me think whether I could do that to another man – German or no German."

At that moment, the corporal entered the tent and handed out the post that had arrived that morning and which for most of us was usually the highlight of the day. I got a letter but yet again Harold was disappointed as there was no letter from Sis.

"What's going on, Jack? She wrote to me on the day we marched off and a couple of times after that to which I replied and now nothing. I write when I can but get nothing back. She promised me that she would write to me every week. Can you write to her, Jack? It's driving me mad not knowing. Is there anything in your letter?"

I recognised Mum's writing but knew even before I started to read it that its contents would be as bland as all her previous weekly letters had been. I scanned the two sides of spidery writing and looked across at Harold.

"Sorry. There's no mention of Sis. Don't worry. I'll put something in my next letter."

Unsurprisingly, Acaster seemed a different and a much quieter place for those left behind once we had marched off to war. As the weeks started to pass, their natural fears had to be suppressed in order for life to continue if only for the sake of the children.

From the moment that we had marched off, Mum and Sis had become regular letter writers. Mum, bless her, wrote regularly to me telling me briefly about life in Acaster but her letters, as a general rule, barely mentioned Father and this was usually nothing more than telling me that he was doing his bit to keep Acaster safe.

***

Early days, Sis wrote to me as well but not as regularly and when I did receive them, her letters were full of pleas for me to "look out for Harold" and it was almost an afterthought when she added, "And, please, look after yourself as well."

Father hated writing letters at the best of times and stated quite openly to whoever would listen that in his opinion, Kitchener was right and it was better for a serving man if he never received a letter from his family and loved ones because it would only disturb his peace of mind, adding that "it wasn't the coward's fear of death but the fear that death would prevent a good soldier from re-joining those he loved". That was the problem and would hamper the army's ability to fight.

He knew full well who Sis was writing to and once he saw letters coming back from Harold, he decided that he would put a stop to it.

All letters from the Brown household were routinely placed in a tray in Father's office and either he or Constable Tibbins, who had been posted to Acaster and now slept in my old room, made sure that they were put in the pillar box outside the Stag. This made it easy for Father to remove the letters from Sis to Harold and throw them onto the fire and quite quickly he did the same with any from her to me. As tempting as it might have been for Father to open and read the letters, he decided against doing so because he felt that he did not need to know what was in them as it was sufficient for his purposes just to destroy them. In any event he had been young once and so he felt reasonably sure of what would be in the letters.

It had also been easy for Father to put an end to the post from Harold arriving. One day he had very casually stopped their postman, Bob Froggatt, for a bit of friendly banter. Father stood with his hands behind his back as Bob leant against his bicycle glad for a rest. They had chatted and joked about inconsequential things for a few minutes before Father said, tapping the side of his nose,

"Oh, and by the way, Bob, when you deliver post to the Police House in future, you must now put all of it through the letter box on my office door. On no account must you give the post over to Alice, Sis or anyone else. Orders direct from Whitehall, no less."

With that, he smiled at Bob, wished him a good day and walked away confident that Bob would do as he was told. The day before his encounter with Bob, Father had removed the strip of wood blocking the back of the old letterbox on the door to his office and fitted a lockable post box to which only he had the key. Mum had asked him what he was doing but the single word 'Whitehall' and a tap to the side of his nose ensured that the conversation went no further. Consequently, each day Father would unlock the box and throw any letters from Harold straight onto the fire. He hadn't thought beyond the end of February when there would no longer be the same need for a fire to be kept burning because he hoped that by then, that Harold would be just another fatality on the Western Front.

As the weeks went by, Sis became more and more concerned at the lack of letters from Harold and what it might mean. Sis and Mum had kept to their Saturday afternoon ritual of tea at the Acaster Tea Rooms, still asking for a table as far away from the front window as possible. To the accompaniment of conversation from the tables around them, tinkling crockery and the squeak of the wheels on the cake trolley, they sat and talked but the lack of letters from Harold became a regular and urgent topic of conversation for Sis.

"Why hasn't he written to me? We promised each other that we would write every week and I have kept that promise – well, pretty much anyway – but there's been nothing from him other than a couple of letters at the beginning. Now even Mrs Smith is ignoring me in the street. Does Jack put anything about Harold in his letters?"

Mum leant across the table and patted Sis's hand.

"Jack's letters are very general and all he wants to do is to reassure me that he is alright and that he is getting bigger and stronger. Thanks to the training. He does mention Harold and he seems to be fine too. Perhaps, he is just busy – try not to worry. I'll ask Jack about it in my next letter."

***

Father could see that Sis was unhappy about the lack of letters from Harold and he teased her about it whenever the chance presented itself.

"Don't get upset about the likes of him. I was a soldier once, don't forget and so I know all about young men away from home. He'll be having the time of his life and won't be giving you a second thought. His eyes will be out on stalks. What with a bit of money in his pocket and as much beer and female company as he can want."

Inevitably, Sis would get upset at this and go to her room and Mum would inevitably hold her handkerchief to her mouth because, as Father well knew, his words equally applied to me and even himself when he was in the army and what mother liked to think of her son indulging in such behaviour – and what wife liked to think about what her husband may have been up to while he was away?

In her next letter to me, Mum wrote:

Sis is getting really upset because she has stopped getting any letters from Harold. They had promised each other that they would write every week and she, poor thing, has done her best to keep to that. She will be really upset if Harold wants to end things and if that is the case, then she needs to know. Please, Jack, see what you can do.

Mum's letter must have crossed with mine:

Harold wants to know why Sis has stopped writing to him as they had apparently promised each other that they would write every week. Harold has kept his promise pretty well, apart from a couple of days when he had hurt his hand and he is worried out of his mind that Sis has finished with him. Please, Mum, see what you can do and ask Sis why she has stopped writing to me too?

It didn't take Mum too long to work out what was happening. As upset as she was at what Sis had been put through, the fact of the matter was that she had never stood up to Father and she was not about to break that particular habit on this occasion and provoke his anger. However, Mum, who could not bear to see Sis so upset and was a lot more intelligent than her husband had ever given her credit for, reasoned the problem through and came up with the solution. In future, Sis's letters to Harold would be brief to enable them to be sent tucked inside her letters to me and she made me promise to hand them on unread. Harold's equally brief letters to Sis would be sent tucked inside my letters to Mum and she too solemnly agreed to pass them on unread.

The next time they were in the Tea Rooms, Mum told Sis that it was Father who was stopping the letters but that he was doing it from his belief, as misguided as it might be, that Harold did not need any distractions while away in the army. Mum also got Sis to agree that it would be best if she didn't say anything to her father and Sis accepted this and Mum was rewarded as a big smile lit up her daughter's face for the first time in ages. Mum made no attempt to fool me but equally she could not bring herself to tell me the whole truth and simply said that Father had forbidden Sis to write to Harold. She had briefly considered getting Harold's mother to send and receive letters but she was not inclined to involve her particularly as Harold had clearly written to her of his concerns and her failure to acknowledge her or Sis clearly showed what she thought of the matter.

Mum never said anything to Father but, unbeknown to Sis, letters addressed to Harold still kept appearing in the office tray and as Mum and Sis had similar handwriting, he never noticed as he continued to throw them on the fire. He was confident that his plan had worked although the one thing he could not fathom out was why Sis had started to look and act happier than she had done for a long while? He was not unduly troubled by this although he did wonder if she had met someone else.

I read Mum's letter and knew straight away what had been going on and I silently cursed Father for his never-ending ability to be cruel to those that he should have loved and cared for above all others. For me, the dilemma was simple – what to tell Harold?

As much as I wanted to lash out at Father, I was prepared to suppress that urge in favour of the medium to long term benefits. One day this war would end and I didn't want to bring about a situation where Sis had to choose between her family and Harold because I knew that there would only be one winner. But what should I tell Harold? I was reluctant to tell a lie because we had never lied to each other and in my experience lies only led to more lies and therefore truth was always the best policy.

***

We were all excited despite that day's long, hard route march because on our return to camp, we had been directed to the Quartermaster's Stores to be at long last issued with our khaki uniforms made up of a peaked cap, trousers, puttees, woollen socks, shirts, vests, regulation field boots, service tunic, great coat and equipment webbing. Our excitement was heightened by the news that tomorrow we would be going to the shooting range at Bisley, one platoon at a time, to be issued with a Short Magazine, Lee Enfield rifle.

There was the sound of laughter and good-natured complaints as we tried on the various components of our uniform only to discover in some cases that they were either too big or too small and various swops were swiftly arranged to sort the problems out. A typical comment was, "That corporal in the stores must have something wrong with his eyes. How did he expect me to get into that?"

Harold and I, like the rest of the company, were pleased that at long last we looked like soldiers, although neither of us relished the blisters that we knew we would get breaking in our boots.

Later that day, when we returned to our tent after tea which was always the last meal of the day, I told Harold what I believed was going on back in Acaster.

"It's the old man, Harold. He likes playing games with people's feelings and he's a cruel bastard. He isn't and never has been happy about you and Sis. So the reason you haven't been receiving letters from Sis is that he has, without her or Mum knowing, stopped them being sent."

Harold was a good-natured soul but even he struggled to remain calm in the face of this news. "Why? What have I and Sis ever done to deserve this?"

"If it wasn't you, it would be someone else, so don't go taking it too personally. Mum has come up with a way around this problem. She says that you must send your letters to Sis inside my letters to Mum."

Harold started to protest but I held my hand up to shut him up and continued in a voice full of false concern.

"Don't worry, neither Mum nor I will read your outpourings of love. Sis will send her letters to you inside Mum's letters to me. The old man won't know a thing – he's really not as clever as he thinks he is. Mum had thought of approaching your mother to help but she has started ignoring Mum and Sis, so she thought it best to leave well alone."

Harold groaned. "That's my fault, Jack. I wrote to Mum and mentioned how upset I was that Sis had stopped writing to me."

"You bloody idiot, Harold! Anyway, Mum has got it sorted. Come on, let's go to the canteen."

***

The next morning the Acaster Company was woken by reveille at 3.30 on what was a cold and frosty morning and with parade due at 4.15, there was a rush to put on our uniforms and down a breakfast mug of tea with a hunk of dry bread and cheese from the mess tent. We then stood to attention on the parade ground as the rollcall was made and those from the first Platoon stood with their kit bag and bed roll, weighing some 60 pounds on their backs, while their instructors walked up and down their lines pointing out infringements in their appearance.

For the next 30 minutes we were addressed by various officers on a variety of matters from our responsibility to look after our uniforms and equipment, the need to always be smart on parade and the need to take care of our feet which would be routinely examined by our officers. The army took foot care very seriously because care of a soldier's feet was a vital military duty and any man found with blisters or foot rot would be put on a charge. The responsibility for carrying out these inspections fell to the lucky platoon commanders. This caused some amusement amongst the men and Harold whispered to me, "All that education and stately homes and you end up with our feet in your hand."

We were all quiet as the first platoon marched out of camp towards Farnham Railway Station to begin the journey to the firing ranges that were some 15 miles away at Bisley, where they were to be based for the next week with the remaining platoons following at two-day intervals. Until it was your platoon's turn to leave for Bisley, your time was spent marching, preparing trenches, bayonet practice, drills and physical education.

Finally, it was time for fourth Platoon, our platoon, to leave camp and our journey was slow as the train was diverted into sidings on a number of occasions to allow troop trains making for Southampton to pass unimpeded, as it made its way towards Brookwood, where it then took a branch line that ran directly to the firing range, passing through its perimeter fencing and a guard post. Despite the journey, we all seemed in good spirits as we climbed down from the train and were told to form up in the square outside the small station. As we looked around at our new surroundings, we saw a large tent which was open at the front. Inside we could see trestle tables, behind which were stacked boxes of rifles, ammunition and bayonets, which were a frightening 17 inches in length and many of us went pale at the sight of them because they were longer than those we were used to back at Frensham Common.

When we collected our rifles, we had to sign for them in a register and the sergeant in charge made it very clear that we were now responsible for our rifle at all times and serious consequences would befall anyone who lost it.

Having queued up and signed for our rifle, bayonet and ammunition, we formed up and made our way to a number of tents to leave our kit and where you met one or two men from the other platoons, there was inevitably some banter before being quick marched to the ranges where we lay on groundsheets and fired our rifles for the first time.

We all displayed variable standards of shooting ability but the instructors were quick to spot the potential of Harold and I as we seemed to take to the discipline effortlessly considering we had hardly handled a rifle before. Shot after shot found the centre of our targets and gradually over the days we found ourselves firing at targets that were sited further and further away with equally impressive results.

During one session, a small group of officers, including Captain Hargreaves, came to watch proceedings through their binoculars and in particular the abilities of the two of us and later that day, we were both summoned to our company commander's tent.

"Well, Brown and Smith, it appears that we have two exceptional marksmen in the company. I have been asked to put you forward for specialist marksman training at the end of which, if you have passed, you will be awarded your badge and as a result, you will see your pay increased. You are fortunate that you will be held back for a course that is about to start. Do you have any questions? Yes, Brown?"

"Sir! Will this mean that we will have to leave the Acaster Company?"

"No. You will return to the company once your training has finished."

"Thank you, sir."

Once dismissed, we returned to our tent, pleased that our abilities had been recognised and very much looking forward to our specialist training and we didn't mind that we would be staying behind when the rest of the company returned to Frensham Common. After our tea and a visit to the canteen with the others, we both settled down to write our first letters since arriving at Bisley, using Mum's subterfuge.

Dearest Sis,

I am sorry about all this silliness over our letters and I am grateful that Mrs Brown has sorted something out for us. Your letters mean so much to me and I was really worried when I stopped getting them. Despite Jack saying I'm soft in the head, your photograph goes everywhere with me and I must look at it at least ten times a day.

Can you still remember our kisses on the morning when we marched off from Acaster and how we both cried at the thought of being apart? I can and always will. Those memories will have to do until we meet again and can create some new ones.

We are all fine and Jack and I have had the best week since we joined up. At long last we have been issued with our rifles and have now fired them. In fact, Jack and I have done so well that we are being held back for more training. If we do alright, we will be issued with a badge and will get a pay rise.

According to the other chaps, we will be getting 72 hours leave soon and I cannot wait to come back and see you.

Anyway, dearest, its lights out soon and so I will wish you goodnight.

Yours forever,
Harold

***

Both of us enjoyed our period of specialist marksman training and the challenge of being on the firing range with other soldiers drawn not just from our company but from other units and regiments too, who had displayed better than average skills with a rifle.

Each day we received instruction and fired at targets over variable distances of up to 400 yards always under the watchful eyes of the instructors and a group of officers. The officers stood behind us, observing the targets through their binoculars and then making notes on the clipboards they held.

After breakfast on Friday, which was to be the final day of training, we formed up in full kit and marched to the ranges where we came to attention before being addressed by an officer, who we had not seen before, who oozed arrogance and walked with a slight limp.

"At ease, men! I am Captain Pardew. Now, the simple fact of the matter is that there are 20 of you on this course and you have all done really well. However, I have now decided that only 18 of you can pass and be awarded your badge. Today is about finding out whether you can be one of those 18.

"You will shortly fire at targets that will be set up at 100, 200 and 400 yards. You will fire six rounds at each target together with a further six rounds at a target that will be set up at 600 yards. The overall scores will be added together and the top 18 will be presented with their badges. Good luck."

Two instructors, bright white bands on their right arms, made their way along the lines, with one instructor carrying a canvas bag containing numbered pegs while the other had a clipboard on which he noted, against each man's name, the number of the peg they had drawn. We were then dismissed and told to make our way to our firing positions which were set out along the top of a raised embankment, where we took our place according to our numbered peg. Harold and I, who seemed to be the youngest there, walked together and took up our positions with neither wanting to be one who would miss out on the badge and neither wanting our friend to miss out either.

The white paper targets appeared from out of a trench, which was sited the required distance away and stood out against a further tall embankment behind, on top of which numbers were displayed corresponding to those on the pegs in front of us. When we were all settled on the ground sheets, the order to commence firing at 100-yard targets was given. "Six shots rapid fire. Begin!" There was an unmistakable feeling of tension amongst the men that had not been there on previous days and as a result one or two shots missed their target.

After the last shot had been fired, the order to clear weapons was given and we all got to our feet and were allowed to relax for a few minutes, many of the men nervously taking the opportunity to have a smoke while others stretched their limbs and the instructors waited for the scores to be brought to them by a messenger on a motorbike. The two instructors then quietly entered the scores onto their clipboards before handing them to Captain Pardew.

Once again we were ordered to form up and move to the firing position for the 200-yard targets. Captain Pardew stood in front of us and read out our names and the peg number we were to fire from. It was Private Bright and Corporal Jones, who were told to go to positions 19 and 20 and both looked nervous fearing, correctly, that their position reflected their score from the previous round.

I was relieved to be allocated peg number five while Harold went to peg number seven. We all settled down and made any adjustments to our rifles that we felt were needed before the officer gave the order, "Six shots rapid fire. Begin." When the firing had been completed, we all responded to the order "Clear weapons" and stood up, once again stretching our limbs as we waited for the motorbike messenger to bring our scores to the instructors.

When the scores had been recorded, the order was given to "Form up! Tenshun! Left turn. Quick march!" We then marched to the next firing position and the process of allocating the firing positions for the 400-yard targets was repeated. Corporal Jones looked relieved as he found himself allocated peg 16 but Bright remained in the bottom two and was joined by Private Kenny. This time I found that I had been allocated peg number three while Harold was moved up to peg number five. Once again we went through the procedure of adjusting our rifle sights before being given the order, "Six shots rapid fire. Begin!"

It was a very nervous group of men who stood around waiting for the results of that round to be brought to the instructors. The men were trying hard to work out from the look of the others how they might have done.

"How do you think you've done, Harold? I think I've done alright."

Harold felt confident enough but he was a little superstitious and therefore he was not inclined to possibly jinx his chances by saying so and therefore to my amusement, merely shrugged while he looked down the range waiting to see the motorbike messenger appear.

The process of allocating shooting positions was repeated and this time Privates Bright and Kenny found their positions unchanged as did Harold and I. We were now to fire six rounds in our own time at our target, which turned out to be a papier mache head that was to appear periodically above the ground 600 yards away.

Even though it was a cold morning, I could feel sweat running down my forehead and into my eyes and down the back of my neck and my hands felt clammy. I thought about the key points made by the instructors namely that without a tripod, a stable rest for the rifle had to be created by the arms alone, the need for uniform shoulder pressure on the rifle and to press rather than pull the trigger having first taken up some of the trigger's slack.

As far as I could tell, Harold looked relaxed enough as he looked through the sights on his rifle. He too would have been thinking about what the instructors had told us about shooting with empty lungs by breathing in, exhaling and then

48

firing. I remember glancing at Harold as he looked through the rifle sights, waiting for the head to appear and suddenly there it was and Harold quickly brought the front sight to bear on the target, emptied his lungs and fired and was rewarded by the head shattering into a cloud of dust.

Eventually, it was all over and we formed up and stood to attention in front of Captain Pardew.

"At ease, men! That completes the final exercise. You will parade at 15.00 hours to receive your badges, train passes and letters for your company commanders. Please ensure that you have packed up all your equipment and belongings ready to leave."

We were then allowed to fall out and make our way back to the camp for our meal in the mess tent where there was a lot of excited chatter as the tension eased. Whether anyone wanted to or not, we all ended up talking about the morning's events with a mixture of bravado and nerves. As we were finishing our food, one of the instructors entered the tent and we all fell silent as he went over to Bright and Kenny and quietly asked them to go with him. Inevitably, the rest of us nudged each other and nodded in the direction of the departing men, relieved it wasn't us and it proved to be the last time that we, the remaining 18 men, were to see those particular comrades.

At the appointed time, we all formed up on the square and were given the order "Tenshun!" when Captain Pardew appeared.

"At ease, men. I congratulate you on having passed this Specialist Marksman course. You have all displayed remarkable ability to shoot a rifle accurately which will stand you and your comrades in good stead when you find yourself at the Front.

"I have chosen not to read out the individual scores as I don't believe that would serve any useful purpose and so I will read your names out in alphabetical order. However, the sealed letter that I am about to give you for your company commander does detail your scores and I will leave them to decide whether to give you those or not."

The parade was once more brought to attention while an instructor read out our names and each of us in turn came forward, saluted Captain Pardew, shook his hand and received our badge, letter and travel pass.

***

Later that afternoon, Harold and I were on the train making our way back to Frensham Common, enjoying our first experience of travelling with our rifles.

"We did it – we passed. Come on, let's get these badges sewn on before we get back."

"Where do they go then, Jack?"

"On our right lower sleeve. I checked with one of the instructors."

However, the last thing on our minds when we got back to the camp on Frensham Common was to show off our new badges after having reported to Captain Hargreaves and hearing the news from the other men.

"Good to see you back, men. Those badges look good on your sleeves. I am sure we will need men who can shoot well when we get to France. Yes, you heard correctly. We are off to France but first of all, you have got 72 hours pre-embarkation leave.

"Lord Acaster expects that the company will arrive in Acaster tomorrow lunchtime and he has kindly arranged a dance in the Church Hall tomorrow evening to which you and yours are invited.

"Your train back will leave tomorrow morning at eight precisely. Don't miss it or you will be spending your leave here scraping vegetables and doing sentry duty. You must be back in camp by 08.00 on Tuesday or make no mistake, you will face a charge."

***

The Acaster Company paraded early the next morning with everyone anxious to be dismissed and to start our journeys home or wherever we had decided to go. However, we were not to be dismissed until we had been addressed by Captain Hargreaves.

"Men, you have conducted yourselves very well so far and have impressed your instructors. You have earned this leave which I want you to enjoy but I must give you this word of warning. Even while on leave, you are still soldiers and Lord Kitchener has asked that all soldiers about to go on leave are given this same message – always be on your best behaviour and resist the temptation of liquor and women. Now off you go and make sure to be back here in 72 hours – in other words by 08.00 on Tuesday."

Harold and I, like most of the others, felt sure that Acaster was the destination of the whole company and there followed a fairly raucous train journey that involved changing at Brookwood to a mainline train which would take us to Acaster Junction. There was then some surprise and not a few ribald comments shouted out, when one or two men slipped away and got on a train heading in the opposite direction towards the bright lights of London. Once again there were a few delays in sidings to allow troop trains to pass but the journey passed quickly enough and at each station we saw boy scouts on the platforms ready and willing to fill any water bottles that needed replenishing.

"What's the first thing you're going to do when you get back, Jack?"

"I'm going to take the back doubles and go to the tea-rooms and wait for Mum and Sis and while I am waiting, I'm going to treat myself to whatever I fancy off the menu."

"Will that include a bit of Dotty on the side too?"

Harold expected and as a result was not disappointed when he received a single knuckle jab to his arm as we both laughed, exhilarated by the prospect of 72 hours leave.

"What about you then?"

"Straight to see Mum – she'll kill me if she found out that I had been somewhere else first. I want to straighten her out over the letter business. I don't want any bad feelings between her and Sis or her and your mother, come to that. Perhaps you could ask Sis to come over later – perhaps later we could all have some tea together?"

"I am sure that Sis would like that – she'll be dying to see you. Will your mum be alright with me staying with you while we're back?"

"I can't see that being a problem. What about your dad? Are you going to try and straighten things out with him? This could be the last time you see him and therefore your last chance to make your peace with him?"

"I'm sorry, Harold, but I've nothing to say to that man. I hope that I never do have to see him again as believe me it can only end badly."

***

The fact that the men were home on leave did not remain undiscovered for long once the first man in khaki was spotted. I had made my way to the Acaster Tea Rooms and took a table at the back of the room where Dotty was only too happy to dance attendance on me and flirt outrageously as she took my order.

Dotty had only just brought my plate of meat and two veg to my table when the door burst open and Mum and Sis stood there looking anxiously around the room. With my fork halfway to my mouth, I stood up and waved them over. I began to think that Mum was never going to let go of me as she hugged me more tightly than I would have believed possible while I still gripped my fork down which gravy was starting to dribble. I looked over Mum's shoulder and Sis gave me a sympathetic smile that did not hide the fact that she was wondering where Harold was.

"Sit down, Jack. Don't let your food get cold. No, don't wait for us – we'll order what we want, won't we, Sis?"

I savoured the first mouthful of my food and licked the shaft of my fork as Mum started to bombard me with questions.

"Why didn't you tell us that you were coming? How much leave have you got? How was your training? My, you've filled out."

There was much more in that vein that I answered while trying to enjoy my meal. Once my meal was finished, I decided to play the same trick on Mum and started to ask her questions while she was eating her toasted tea cake.

"And what about you, Mum? How are you?"

"Oh, you don't have to worry about me. I am fine and life goes on. Your father will be pleased you're home too. Now just let me enjoy this tea cake."

"Will he? Really?"

"Now don't be like that, Jack. He is your father after all. Put it all behind you for all our sakes – eh, Sis? Now hush while I finish this."

While Mum contentedly spread butter and jam, on the remaining half of her teacake, Sis looked at me but instead of answering Mum's question, asked one of her own. "How's Harold? Where is he?"

"He is fine, Sis. He went straight to see Mrs Smith to smooth over things with her. He would like you to go there later and we can all have a bite to eat. He has really missed you."

My comments brought a shy smile to Sis's face. "Yes, I would like that."

"Jack, you will stay at our house, won't you? You can't have your old room back but I'll make you up a comfortable bed downstairs."

"Sorry, Mum, but I will be staying at Harold's. It's for the best but don't worry – you'll see plenty of me."

Mum looked disappointed but accepted what I said because she knew that once I had made my mind up, then nothing on earth would change it, which was unfortunately a trait that I shared with my father.

"Is that your new badge on your sleeve?"

"Yes. It's a specialist marksman's badge. Harold's got one as well. We really enjoyed the course and we both seem to have a natural eye for it."

"Does it mean that you will be doing more dangerous things when you get to the Front? I suppose this leave means that you will be going there once you get back?"

"I shouldn't think so. Now don't start worrying about what might happen. Just enjoy the fact that I am here now, today. Tomorrow can take care of itself."

When the daylight started to fade, Sis and I made our excuses and left, with me relieved to get away and Sis enjoying the anticipation of seeing Harold. Mrs Smith greeted us warmly and hugged Sis and I but nevertheless there was a cloud in the room that needed to be dispersed and Mrs Smith quickly decided that she would be the one to do it.

"Now listen you two. Harold has told me about the misunderstanding over the letters. Now I'm not as green as I'm cabbage-looking but let's just say no more about it. Life's sadly too short."

***

Lord Acaster had made a good job of organising the dance and the hall was decorated with red, white and blue bunting, a small band played popular tunes on the same stage where a few short months before army medicals had been conducted and down one side there were trestle tables with sandwiches, cakes and bottles of beer and lemonade. I escorted Mrs Smith to the dance and enjoyed the sideways glances from some of the men while Harold walked with Sis, although admittedly they lagged some distance behind. Mum was also there, sitting on a table all by herself as Father was on duty and leave or no leave he would never attend such a dance. He was determined not to cut anyone any slack. It took me just a matter of moments to persuade Mum to sit with us and soon she and Mrs Smith were chatting away and at one point, spurning offers from some of the men present, they danced together.

Before the dancing really got under way, Lord Acaster appeared on the stage to formally welcome us all home and then once finished had left to applause and cheers from the men.

Given the unusual circumstances that all those there that night faced, the evening was a mixture of heady excitement and melancholy. Harold danced with Sis and despite the noise around them, they were soon chatting quite happily. Anyone who bothered to look at Harold and Sis would have seen two young people in love and enjoying each other's company.

Harold laughed as he said, "We could slip away somewhere."

"Your mum would kill us if she found out."

They were both engulfed in laughter as Harold shook his head and muttered ruefully, "What are we going to do about Mother?"

"Don't forget we would have to avoid my father as well. He's about somewhere."

"I have been well trained in manoeuvres – particularly night manoeuvres!"

I had found Dotty pouring herself some lemonade and although I was flattered by her attentions, it was more that I was really just happy to have someone to talk to and dance with on that one Saturday evening.

On the stroke of 11, the dance ended and some of those who remained stayed on to help clear everything away. With so many willing and in some cases slightly merry, the hall was soon getting straight and people started to drift away. Harold and I said that we would see Mum and Sis home while Mrs Smith told Harold that she would stay behind to finish up and he should come back for her in half an hour.

Mum and I arrived at the Police House some moments before the others and stood in the porch as I politely refused Mum's attempts to get me to enter the family home. Eventually, with arrangements made for the following day, Harold and I set off back to the hall happily chatting about the dance and our plans for the following day with our heads down in an attempt to gain some protection from the cold wind that had sprung up. It was a dark night and unsurprisingly neither of us noticed two shadowy figures standing in an opening between the last two shops before the church hall.

Harold was walking alongside the shop fronts while I had turned to walk backwards so that I could look at the police house as it grew smaller behind us when one of the figures stepped out. As Harold was unaware that someone was there, he had no chance of avoiding bumping into whoever it was.

"You need to watch where you're going, my lad." We both recognised the voice and immediately looked into the face of Father who did not seem at all upset and indeed he seemed quite pleased to see us. The other figure stepped forward and we could see it was Constable Tibbins.

"Well, Jack, got anything to say to me? Surely you were going to come and see your dear, old dad?"

"No, well, please yourself. Constable Tibbins, I think this man is drunk – what do you think?"

I watched as Constable Tibbins stood directly in front of Harold and made a show of sniffing around Harold's mouth.

"Come on, Father, there's no call for this."

"The law's the law, Jack, as you well know. Now Constable Tibbins, in your opinion is this man drunk?"

I turned to Tibbins. "Don't let yourself get like him. You can be better than that."

Tibbins looked at me but it was a look that said, "Yes, but what can I do?"

"Well, Constable Tibbins?"

"Judging by his breath, I'd say that this man has been drinking Sergeant."

"Constable Tibbins, did you see this man deliberately walk into me? He could have caused me a nasty injury – couldn't he, Constable Tibbins?"

Constable Tibbins was now in a place of his own making. He had lied once and so the second lie came more easily despite the glance he gave me.

"Yes, Sergeant."

"Father, what in God's name do you think you are doing?"

"Don't you dare blaspheme and take the Lord's name in vain. The law applies to all men – or at least it does in Acaster as long as I wear this uniform!"

Harold stood there listening and watching. I grabbed his arm and said, "Come on, Harold. He's had his bit of fun now, let's get to the hall and collect your mum."

"Constable Tibbins, I think these two young men are about to resist arrest so draw your truncheon as we may need to use some force to detain them."

We froze. I looked at Father but spoke to Harold. "Let's not give him the chance to enjoy himself any further."

I turned to Father and returned his stare. "What is it you want?"

"Much better, lads, manners don't cost anything now, do they? I want you back on the train to wherever you have come from. There is a train leaving the

Junction at 10.30 tomorrow morning and you had better be on it and then we won't have to say a word about this to anyone – understand?"

"Or what, Father?"

"Constable Tibbins and I can escort you to the Junction now and he can then stay with you until that train comes in the morning because in the circumstances and I am sure you will both agree. I don't think it would be in anyone's interest to take the pair of you to the Police House. Meanwhile, I will go home and write my report and contact the authorities. I am sure that you will be suitably met at your destination – I would think that returning without your kit must be a chargeable offence under military law. I will, of course, with much regret, have to inform Lord Acaster."

"But, our kit and rifles are at Mrs Smith's."

"If we need to take you to the station now, then I will personally collect your kit from your mother, Harold, and of course I will have to explain the circumstances to her. Of course, I could not be held responsible if those items got lost in transit what with everything that is going on.

"Alternatively, and you will have to give me your word. You will make sure that you and your kit will be on that train at 10.30 tomorrow morning. Constable Tibbins will be there to make sure that you are. You will tell nobody about this. When Mrs Smith is going off to church, you will make an excuse – tell her that you will follow her – and then you will walk in the opposite direction to the station. Have I made myself clear, lads?"

"You're a wicked old bastard!"

"I will pretend that I didn't hear that remark for now, Jack, otherwise I would have to do something about it now, wouldn't I? Well, what's it to be?"

I looked at Harold who nodded back. "We will leave in the morning."

"Make sure you do as Constable Tibbins will be there to see you off. And I repeat, don't try to see or contact Sis before you go – either of you not understand? Not a word to anyone, not even your mothers."

***

Sunday mornings revolved around the church and so Mrs Smith was up early preparing breakfast and then putting on her finery or Sunday best as she had always referred to it. Harold and I seemed subdued which she unquestioningly put down to a combination of over consumption the evening before and the fact that tomorrow we would be leaving Acaster.

Sis walked happily to the church with our parents in expectation of seeing Harold and spending time with him later in the day. I am sure that Father would have had a contented look on his face which none but Mum might have noticed.

Mrs Smith walked to church on her own having received assurances from us that we just needed a little while longer to clean our boots. We gave her enough time to be a fair way towards the church and then left the house and turned in the opposite direction and walked quickly towards Acaster Junction, which we accomplished without anyone seeing us.

By the time the service started, it was too late for Mrs Smith, Mum or Sis to turn concern for where we had got to into actively going to look for us. As Reverend Stoddart slowly climbed the steps to the pulpit to begin his sermon, our train was pulling out and Constable Tibbins had begun his walk back to the town.

1915

They had been difficult letters to write and Harold and I had agreed that the circumstances of our sudden departure were best left undisclosed. I wrote to Mum while Harold had to write to his mother and to Sis and neither of us could deny that the recipients of our letters would be anything other than upset.

Two days later, Mum received my letter and Sis hovered about her to see if there was a letter from Harold. Despite being cross with him, she would have been so pleased when Mum passed a letter to her that had been folded inside mine.

Dearest Sis,

By the time you get this letter, we will be in France. It is only 30 miles away but it will feel like the farthest corner of the world.

I cannot begin to explain Jack and I leaving so suddenly but it has nothing and yet everything to do with my feelings for you. Simply put, I took the coward's way out as by leaving as we did we avoided the upset and the memories of a sad goodbye on the Monday morning but instead, I hope we are left with such fond memories of our time together on the Saturday.

Please don't judge me too harshly and continue to write to me. I don't know when I will next see you again but your letters will keep me going until I do.

I have written to Mum to try and put matters right and I would very much appreciate you keeping an eye on her for me.

I have asked Mum and I would like to ask you as well, if you could from time to time send me a parcel. Some of the others say that the things to ask for are socks, scarves, candles, potted meat and rice but rest assured I will be grateful for anything.

Going off to France is both exciting and scary but at least I have Jack with me and we will look out for each other.

Anyway, Sis, I must finish now but I will write when I can.

Yours loving,
Harold

***

Sis would have read and re-read the letter by the light of a candle in her bedroom and knowing that Father was out patrolling the streets of Acaster, she would have settled down to pen her reply.

Dear Harold

Thank you for your letter. You must know that your sudden departures are very upsetting for those of us left in Acaster. I am pleased that you don't appear to be one of the soldiers who Clem told your mother he saw having words with my father and Constable Tibbins after the dance on the Saturday. Clem had drunk a fair bit so he wasn't seeing so clearly at the time but he swears they all seemed angry.

It is hard to accept that when you receive this letter, you will be at the Front. Please take care of yourself and keep an eye on Jack. I will write to you as often as I can but in the meantime, I have sent you another photograph of me that I had done professionally by Mr Rogers, the chemist.

I will do my best to send you parcels and please let me know what things you need. I will also look out for your mum, although she is probably the last person in Acaster to need it.

Come back soon and in one piece.

All my love
Sis

***

The training camp at Etaples, some 15 miles south of Boulogne, had proved to be an unpleasant surprise to the Acaster Company. We arrived at the base by train and were amazed at the sight that met our eyes as the hillside opposite the station was a mass of white tents. We thought the camp on Frensham Common was big but it was tiny in comparison with Etaples with its tents, marquees which were used as dining halls with the odd wooden buildings here and there. There were one or two hospitals on the edge of the camp with each ward having its own marquee. On arrival, we were left waiting for what seemed an eternity until a sergeant, who was known as a 'canary' thanks to the yellow band around his cap, arrived to direct us to our tents. The encampment was a sprawl of tents and home to up to 100,000 men and we took care to take notice of landmarks that would help us locate our tents over the coming days.

Tired after the travelling, our evening meal of bully beef stew slipped down a treat. Then, we went back to our tents collecting two blankets on the way. Captain Hargreaves gave us 30 minutes to settle in before we were required to parade on a patch of bare ground that was replicated at intervals across the encampment. It was at this parade that we were introduced to our platoon commanders.

Captain Hargreaves told us that we would be spending two weeks at the camp which was so close to England and all that we loved and yet at the same time close enough to the Front to hear the big guns from time to time.

Standing next to the captain were four young officers who shuffled their feet nervously as they surveyed the men. We soon learnt that our platoon commander was to be Lieutenant Hadley, a man who looked more like the academic than the fighter we needed and wanted him to be. It was therefore fortunate that in Sergeant Watson, however, we had a man who looked like an experienced platoon sergeant who had at least advanced into battle unlike the rest of us. Afterwards, an extremely arrogant young officer arrived to read out the camp regulations and then we were dismissed.

The rest of the day was our own and so Harold and I, with a few others, decided to explore a little bit. We discovered where the Church Hut was located and more importantly the Tipperary Hut and the Lady Angela Forbes Rest Hut as these were the places to go for some decent food – tea, bread and butter, eggs, custard and fruit – all at reasonable prices.

Harold at the earliest opportunity penned a letter to Sis, mindful of the fact that not only would Lieutenant Hadley read his letters but they would also be read at the giant military postal sorting office in Regents Park, London.

My Dearest Sis,

Well, we have arrived and Jack and I are both in good spirits.

I hope that you are well because the thought of anything being wrong with you would worry me to death. I am determined to do my bit to defeat the Germans but I dream of the day when the war will be over and that you and I can begin a life together, a life in which there will never be a place for bully beef, biscuits harder than house bricks (although come to think of it, I've not eaten anything that you have cooked me yet) or periods of such boredom. I can't say as we are likely to enjoy this training and it will be a relief to move on.

It is very cold and so I would be so grateful to receive a parcel from you and please do your best to send me socks, books, mittens, candles and rice.

Jack is writing a letter to his mother and so I will finish now so that he can tuck mine inside and they can begin their journey back to Acaster.

I treasure the photograph you sent with your last letter.

Write soon, my love.
Harold

***

Conditions at the camp were appalling and we were marched at the double two miles through the dunes to the training grounds known as the Bull Ring every day except Sunday to undertake training in gas warfare, formation and bayonet drills. By the time the intensive training sessions were completed and we marched again at the double back to camp, we were exhausted although, as hungry as we were, the thought of a meal that each day without fail consisted of bully beef, two biscuits and an onion was not overly enticing. We quickly grew tired of the old joke of 'what's worse than finding a maggot in your biscuit? Half a maggot!'

"Harold, what a shit-hole this is. The canaries are nothing more than bullies who apparently have never even served at the front. I heard old Hargreaves talking to Lieutenant Hadley and he said they were all blood and bayonet merchants.

"And what about that gas training. Did you see the instructors laughing as we had to pass through that chamber filled with gas and laughing as we came out retching our guts up and telling us that it was just to get us used to it! Bastards!"

"It's all right for the officers as they get to sleep in proper beds, have proper baths and decent food over the other side of the river in Le Touquet. It must be special the way they post guards on the bridge to stop men like us going over there. We have to make do with stalls set up by the locals to sell postcards, fruit, and chocolates at prices that make your eyes water."

"I was talking to a man over at the latrines and he said that some of the men who had been wounded and had been sent here to recover have founds things so bad that they are returning to the Front before their wounds have properly healed. That's bloody awful for the poor devils and says everything we need to know about this place. What do you make of Lieutenant Hadley?"

"He's all right. He looks as if he would be more at home in a school room than leading a platoon of soldiers out here. Watson seems to know what he's doing and I think he will see us and Hadley right."

There was one day of training that Harold and I enjoyed which was allotted to rifle shooting on a range just outside the camp. The range had been built in the sand hills complete with a trench as the firing point and targets some hundred yards away. We were sorted out into groups of a dozen men and each group fired a volley and the noise was deafening and not like anything we had experienced before. After ten rounds, we walked to the targets and brought them back to the range officer who recorded our scores. Those who met or exceeded the expected score were passed and allowed to return to the camp while the others had to fire another ten rounds until they were passed. Happily Harold and I passed first time and after taking our kit back to our tent we headed to one of the rest huts and rewarded ourselves with a nice mug of tea and a slice of pie.

Given our feelings about Etaples, it therefore came as a relief when the company was told to parade early the following morning in full kit ready to leave for the Front. Some days later, Sis received the following letter.

My Dearest Sis,

How are you, my dearest?

I don't want you to worry but tomorrow we are off to the Front. We are all looking forward to it if only to put an end to the days and weeks of training. The war might not have ended by last Christmas as we had all hoped and believed, so we have just got to make sure that it is over by Christmas this year – and what a wonderful present that would be!

Jack is fine, although like the rest of us, he is also nervous at the prospect of what is to come and perhaps that's a good thing as it will make us careful not to do anything silly.

Thank you for your parcel which came yesterday. It is now quite cold so the gloves, socks and balaclava will be very useful. The cake and biscuits that you sent me were very good and I have shared them with Jack. I look forward to the day when I can enjoy your cooking – and certainly without a fat rat lurking nearby ready to eat any crumbs that are dropped. Some of them are as big as a cat and seem to have no fear.

I think of you all the time and can't wait to see you again. I will write to you as soon as I can.

All my love
Harold

***

Through later conversations with Sis, I have been able to put together what was going on at home and it proved what a bastard my father was.

The air of concern, almost as pervading as a winter fog, hung over the town of Acaster and its surroundings as news spread that their men were going to the Front. Acaster did not exist in a bubble and news of the numbers of the dead and wounded from the Western Front were available in the newspapers so it all seemed very real to those in the town. There was also a regular reminder of what their men were facing because when the wind was blowing in the right direction it was possible to hear the sound of the guns from France.

While Mum and Ester Smith were concerned, they chose to mask their feelings by concentrating on what was in front of them and choosing to worry only about the matters they could do something about and Mum had decided that she had to be strong for Sis. At times this was easier said than done and they wept on many occasions when they were on their own. Sis, however, felt that she was on some sort of emotional rollercoaster and as a result had good and bad days.

This was one of those bad days and her face and eyes were puffy from crying which Father could not fail to see when he came home for his tea. Conversation had always been difficult since we had marched away and with Sis barely picking at her food and Mum looking pale and drawn, Father inevitably could not resist the opportunity to turn the emotional screw.

"I can't remember weather like we have had today – can you, Alice? Talk about four seasons in one day."

Mum agreed with a nod of her head as she fussed about bringing their evening meal to the table while Father went on.

"The men on the Front will be having a bad time of it what with the rain, the mud and the cold. I remember what that was like when I was fighting the Boers."

Mother looked pleadingly at Father. "Don't talk about it, Bill. Can't you see that Sis is already upset?"

"Why? I'm just saying that it will be hard for them. And then of course there's the shelling. I remember shelling and I don't mean peas. It's the not knowing where the shells will land and the damage they cause when they do. And, the shrapnel! That can slice a man's head clean off.

"You can train men til' the cows come home but they need to learn by experience very quickly. Stick your head up too far and bang a sniper will get you. Do you know the German snipers will even wait for a man to go into a latrine to do his business and shoot him while he is at it? While he's sitting there! A man likes to enjoy some peace and quiet in the toilet but not out there. Still, probably cures constipation."

Father laughed while tears were now trickling down Sis's face and Mum reached out and clasped her hand while he pretended not to have noticed and continued as he wiped a piece of bread around his plate.

"Did you see the length of those bayonets the men had? Horrible, horrible things they are. I can still remember the sound that a bayonet makes as it slides into a man, a kind of hiss, the look of shock on their faces and then the scream. It's easy enough to stick a bayonet in but funnily enough, not so easy to pull it out. I had to do that once by putting my foot on a Boer's chest and tugging hard to get it out.

"Now they've got machine guns that can cut men down like a row of corn. Cut a man in half. I thought I had it bad in the Boer War but the weapons being used in this war are far worse."

Father looked up and feigned surprise at the effects his words had on Mum and Sis, who was sitting upright, her face a picture of misery and Mum once more had her handkerchief up to her mouth.

"Come on, why the tears? I was only thinking out loud. Don't worry about them. Don't worry about Jack and Harold. They will have got themselves a comfy job with plenty of food and a soft bed, miles behind the lines. Soft, young buggers the pair of them. Well, I'm off to the Stag for a beer. Sleep tight, ladies."

Sis struggled to hold her emotions in check as she helped Mum to clear the table and wash-up and then she wished her goodnight and went up to her room but not before Mum told her that she would be writing a letter to me which she would put in the post tomorrow. Up in her room, Sis cried for a while and then spent some time composing herself before she settled down, pen in hand.

Dearest Harold,

It is so hard, my love, to think that by the time you get this letter, you will be at the Front. I really can't bear to think of you and Jack there and the dangers that you must face.

Acaster seems so quiet since you, Jack and the others left. People are getting on with their lives but it is as if they are waiting all the time for news.

I had tea with your mother earlier this week and she seems very well and is as strong as ever. When this war is over and you are safely home, I would like us to move away from Acaster and make a fresh start somewhere, anywhere.

I am thinking of becoming a nurse and helping to care for the many casualties that are being brought back to England. What do you think of that, Harold?

Your mother has sent you a parcel and I will put one in the post to you soon. You must take care, my love. Give my love to Jack.

All my love
Sis

***

The Acaster Company had made its way to the Front and no amount of training could have prepared us for what we saw as we moved forward. Hardly any of us had ever seen a dead body before, let alone parts of a dead body hanging from the branches of trees that we passed, but this was a sight we quickly grew used to along with the sight of men with a wide variety of wounds. The sights, sounds and smells of war could not have been anticipated and could not have been trained for but we had to learn and acclimatise quickly.

The Company was given a brief period of time in reserve before moving up to the support trench, making our way up the communication trench at night having been sternly warned by our guide to 'keep your bloody heads down'. The night sky was dark apart from the many flares that lit up the landscape. The traffic up and down the communications trench varied from supplies and food going forward to the wounded making their way back, some on stretchers, some assisted by a mate and others on their own but all needed the company to stop and press ourselves up against the trench wall to let them pass.

The night sky was clear and full of stars as Harold and I stood on the fire step in a small bay of the forward trench looking out over no-man's land after yet another largely uneventful day.

"Do you think that's the same sky as they are looking at back home, Jack?"

"Yes, but without the flares. It's so bloody cold that I can't stop myself shivering but at least it's quiet although, Potter, lanky devil, nearly copped one from that German sniper at stand-to this afternoon. He certainly needed his tot of rum after that I would imagine."

"And a change of underwear I should think. I can't stand this damp. It creeps up your whole body which is no surprise as we spend all day standing or lying down in mud almost up to our knees and then it pisses down with rain the rest of the time. When we signed up, I never thought it would be like this."

"Would you have volunteered if you had?"

"No!"

***

Acaster received news of its first casualty at the same time as Sis received her latest letter from Harold, which had been written and sent before the incident concerned. Details were non-existent apart from the news that the man had been killed in action. Those at the Front knew that Potter, who was a slow learner, and failed to keep his head down and so the sniper had got him early one morning as he ate his breakfast.

The Potter family lived in a small cottage in an outlying village but Acaster still viewed him as one of their own and Lord Acaster was one of many visitors who called to pass on their condolences and to leave small gifts.

Dearest Sis,

We have just completed five days in the front line. We are cold, wet and covered in mud but otherwise well as long as we keep our heads down.

It's been very quiet here to tell the truth and boredom is an issue. Jack and I laugh that the highlight of every day is Lieutenant Hadley checking our feet which makes us glad that we aren't officers.

The food isn't great so any rice, potted meat, oxo cubes or jam that you can send me would be lovely and I will share it with Jack. Thank you for the balaclava you sent me as it really keeps my ears warm. Mum also sent me one but I have given that to Jack.

I know I keep asking you to send me things and yet I have nothing to give you in return other than to tell you that I love you, my dearest, and can't wait to see you again.

All my love
Harold

***

It was about this time as well that two developments occurred back in Acaster. Firstly, with me out of the way, Father's physical abuse of Mum started again. Father was careful to ensure that Sis was out of the house at the time either at work or visiting Mrs Smith. He was also careful to ensure that he only ever hit Mum where the bruises would not show. Sometimes he attacked her when she failed to meet his exacting but ever-changing standards, however, there was also a more basic issue in the marriage.

Starting from the moment that I had left the house back in 1913, Mum told me that she had been increasingly cold towards Father, a man who had never hidden his appetites and he was feeling increasingly frustrated. He could and still did force himself upon her but it was a cold, passionless coupling which Mum endured and all the time kept her head turned towards the wall, tears trickling down her cheeks and gripping the sheets so tightly that her knuckles were white with the effort. Father wasn't worried about the pain that his penetration caused Mum, in fact he found the thought of that arousing in itself, along with the sense of power over another individual. The problem, as he had finally had to admit, was that penetration of an unwilling partner was painful, in fact too painful, even for him as well.

Consequently, and this was the second development, he decided that he had to find his relief elsewhere. With the vast majority of the Acaster men away with the army, there were a number of women who he felt ripe for his attentions. Father was a complex character who liked a challenge and disliked women who he saw as easy. He also had a liking for mischief and so one day, he strolled confidently up the path and knocked on the door of Ester Smith, a widow and the mother of Harold. Ester Smith opened her door and looked her visitor up and down.

"Sergeant Brown. How can I help you?"

"Good afternoon, Mrs Smith. There have been a couple of attempted break-ins around here together with a number of reports of prowlers in the area. If you will let me, I'd like to check your windows and doors. Can I come in?"

Ester Smith stepped aside and Father entered her small, neat home and casually brushed past her having made no attempt to wipe his feet on the doormat. He walked through to the scullery, glancing into the front room as he passed and turned to look at Ester with his best smile on his face.

"Is there any chance of a cup of tea then, Mrs Smith? Put the kettle on while I take a look around."

Ester Smith was a strong woman and now that her husband was dead, she would not normally have danced attendance on any man let alone Father but she was prepared to see where this might be leading. She was well aware of the gossip about him in the town together with the advice to take care if you were ever alone with him. As Ester put the kettle on, Father made a real show of checking the windows and doors and went out into the yard to check a small outbuilding. By the time he returned, again without wiping his feet, Ester had a teapot on the scullery table and two cups and the kettle boiling on the range.

"Do you take milk and sugar, Sergeant Brown?"

"Yes, please, and one sugar. Why don't you call me Bill?"

"Where's Constable Tibbins today?"

Father looked at her with a wolf-like smile on his face. "He's checking the houses and buildings on the other side of the High Street. I thought I would check this side and we will continue to carry out these checks from time to time so you will be seeing more of me."

Ester made no comment as she considered whether her visitor's last remark represented a threat or a promise and continued drinking her tea while looking at Father over the rim of her cup, as he sat there and looked around taking everything in.

"Nice place you've got here. How do you manage to keep it up? I'm quite good with my hands or at any rate I've never had any complaints, so I could come over and help you."

"Now why would you want to do that, Sergeant Brown?"

"Well, with Harold away, I feel obligated to look out for you."

Father looked up from his cup and found Ester looking back at him, more than happy to hold his gaze.

"There is no need to trouble yourself, Sergeant Brown. Lord Acaster is very kind and only too happy to send someone over if I have a problem."

"Well, even so…"

Ester, having decided that matters had gone far enough, stood up and looked down at Father.

"I think, Sergeant Brown, you should finish your tea and go as I am sure you have a lot to do."

He sat there determined that he would leave when he decided and not Ester Smith. Ester started to clear things away while he sat there and watched her. Eventually, he set his cup down, stood up, put on his helmet and in his own time moved to the front door which Ester was now holding open. The hallway was quite narrow and so he enjoyed slowly brushing against her as he made his way to the front door. Ester stood her ground and her face showed no reaction to what had happened. He turned towards her and said,

"Goodbye now, Mrs Smith, and thank you for the tea. I will call again to check that everything is fine. Don't forget if you want anything done, then I am happy to come over. With your Harold away, who knows when you may be thankful for a friend."

With that he set off down the path, nonchalantly whistling to himself because in Ester Smith, he recognised a challenge and Father never backed down from a challenge. As she closed the door, Ester was also smiling at what she saw as yet another man who could not have been any more obvious about what it was that he wanted.

***

Snipers were reviled by their enemies. Most casualties in a war are random caused by artillery fire or a machine gun firing at a line of advancing men, so in that respect it is impersonal. However, a sniper has a choice about whether or which enemy soldier to kill as he alone decides when to pull the trigger and that somehow feels different to those affected by it. A man classified as 'killed in action' could have been killed by a sniper when doing nothing more offensive than writing home or forgetting to duck or in some instances doing no more than going about their everyday business.

We were in the support trench sitting on the firing step and enjoying some morning sunshine after a bout of heavy shelling, when Sergeant Watson found us and said that we were to report, at the double, to Captain Hargreaves, who was up in the forward trench. As we made our way up the communications trench, with watery mud oozing over the duckboards and therefore over our boots, we had to stand to the side to let a stretcher party pass by. Whoever it was on that stretcher looked in a bad way and his head and face were covered by a bloody cloth so we were not able to tell whether it was anyone we knew. At the head of the communication trench we saw a board with a crudely painted skull and crossbones and the word 'sniper' beneath it. We found Captain Hargreaves in his dug-out looking angry and furiously sucking on his pipe.

"Stand easy. There's a bloody German sniper somewhere out there and he's just shot Private Jenkins. Apparently that's the 18th casualty he's inflicted on this part of the line. Now I seem to remember that you two are the company's specialist marksmen so I want you to get the bastard. Here, take my periscope and one of you can spot for the other. Just don't get yourselves shot. I don't want any more letters to write – understood? Now, any questions?"

"Sir! Do you have any idea whereabouts he might be?"

"It's thought he might be about 400 yards away in the remains of the old farm just behind their line."

We had found what we considered to be a reasonably secure point of the parapet where there was a gap between the sandbags on the top of the trench that was wide enough to enable a rifle to be used but seemed small enough not to be easily noticed by a sniper four hundred yards away.

"You do realise that if we see this Gerry sniper, then he will be pretty much the first German we've seen since we got here."

"Yes, I know. Here Harold, keep your bloody head down and give me your cap."

"Why?"

"Listen, you look carefully at that farm through the periscope while I hold your cap up on this stick, so it's just above the sandbags. If we are lucky, then Fritz over there will stick a bullet through it and that will help to confirm the direction he is shooting from. With any luck, you will see a glint of something or a muzzle flash that will show where he is."

"So, if this works, then I will spend the rest of the war with bullet holes in my cap. Bloody hell, life just gets better and better! Here, take it."

***

Later that day, we were once again standing in front of Captain Hargreaves who this time had a broad smile on his face.

"Well done. Hopefully, we will now get a little peace from Gerry's sniping. Make them think twice about it. I intend to mention your efforts in my report. Now you can return to the support trench and I will have a word with Hadley about a double rum ration for the pair of you."

The walk back to the communication trench seemed an anti-climax as we received only muted congratulations from our colleagues. What we didn't know at that point was that whilst the men were relieved that a particularly troublesome and therefore reviled sniper had been killed, they also knew that, apart from any other retribution, another would take his place before long.

Back in the support trench and having enjoyed our double tot of rum, Harold asked the obvious question, "What did it feel like to shoot him, Jack?"

"I didn't feel anything at the time other than a sense of relief that he would not kill anyone else. It's only now when I think about it that I feel that nothing will ever be quite the same again. I can't really explain it and perhaps it's something that every soldier feels differently about afterwards."

***

That evening, Harold couldn't find sleep and so he settled down to write a letter to the one person he was desperately missing.

Dear Sis,

Thank you for your last letter and parcel. The fruit cake was delicious.

I have had lots of time to think about you going into nursing and I am sure you will make a really good nurse. The men who are coming back deserve the best care. I would like to move as well but as we say what are we going to do about Mother? Still, if we did move away, I would like to try life in another country. If it didn't work out, we could always come back but just not to Acaster.

I probably should not tell you this but Jack and I finished off a Gerry sniper a few days back. Jack fired the rifle while I spotted for him. As a result, Captain Hargreaves has told us that we are both being taken out of the line for a bit. I can't tell you where or why but at least we will be away from the firing.

The hardest part of this war is being away from you, my dearest.

Please, don't worry as Jack and I are fine, although perhaps in need of a good bath.

All my love
Harold

***

Father stood deep in the shadows, carefully watching the house opposite. He had been standing there for some time but anyone passing by, and many had, would not have seen him. His police uniform was covered by a dark cape which hid his silver buttons and whistle chain and so to all intents and purposes he was invisible. He had often thought that being invisible would make policing so much easier as it would grant the ability to enter and leave premises unseen and to listen in on conversations. He had smiled at the thought that invisibility could be useful in other ways too.

A light was on in the front room and he could see a figure going about its business beyond the undrawn curtains. He had always enjoyed watching someone who was unaware that they were being watched. When he was certain that there was nobody else in the house or in the street. He left the shadows and made his way to the front gate which he opened quietly before making his way up the path to the front door.

A sharp, insistent rap soon caused the door to be opened and a weak light shone out onto the porch.

"Sergeant Brown?"

"Good evening, Mrs Smith. I was passing and noticed your light was on. Is everything all right?"

"Why shouldn't it be?"

"There has been some petty thieving around and about and so it pays to be careful. It's cold out here – any chance of a cup of tea?"

Ester Smith had the type of face that made her look as if she was amused by something that only she had heard or seen and she looked at Father for some seconds with a smile hovering around her lips before she answered,

"I was just about to put the kettle on, so why don't you come in?"

Father went to step into the house but Ester did not move.

"This time, Sergeant, you can wipe your feet before you come in."

Although he was momentarily taken aback, he did as he was told before removing his cape and helmet.

"You must be lonely, Mrs Smith, with your Harold away? Don't you have any friends?"

"I'm not lonely. If I need to talk to someone, then I am quite happy to talk to myself or indeed pass the time of day with Mrs Brown. By the way, I haven't seen her for a couple of days. Is she unwell?"

Father smiled. "She had a little fall in the scullery and banged her head on the table. She can be a little clumsy but she's not too bad, thank you."

Ester brought the crockery and spoons to the table and then poured the tea adding one sugar to her guest's tea. He put out his hand as if to take the proffered cup and saucer but instead allowed his fingers to gently stroke the side of her hand.

"A good-looking woman like you should not be living alone. It's not right. It's a waste."

"Last time I looked, Sergeant, there wasn't a law against it. Look, Sergeant Brown, do you think you're the first man to ever knock on my door with something other than my welfare on their mind. In fact, it's obvious from the way they fidget about that. It's not their head, that's the problem – it's what hangs a couple of feet lower they're concerned about. So, I'll tell you what I tell them, just so that there are no misunderstandings. My James was the first and will always be the only man for me. So you can take your intentions somewhere else. Now go."

Father liked a feisty woman and relished the fact that combat had been joined and smiled as he got to his feet. He took his time to put his helmet and cape back on and then leant down so that his face was almost touching Ester's and she could smell the stale smell of pipe tobacco on his breath.

"I hope you don't come to regret those words, Mrs Smith. I will repeat what I told you the last time I was here, that one day you may need me as a friend. Who of us ever knows what is around the corner? Good night to you, Mrs Smith."

Ester watched him saunter nonchalantly down her front path and into the night before she closed her front door. She stood with her back to it and realised that although she did not find Bill Brown in the least attractive and felt that she had the measure of him, she was more than happy to engage in some verbal jousting with him if he continued to knock on her door.

1916 (Part One)

The German Army had entered the war with men who had been trained and equipped to be snipers. It had taken the British Army a long time to learn from the evidence that was mounting up daily that, in terms of the number of men killed by snipers, it needed to listen to men like Major Hesketh-Pritchard and set up its own sniper training schools. The British Army had given the appearance of approaching the war as if it was a gentlemanly game of cricket and as a result had been slow to embrace the tactics Germany was quite happy to utilise because they were viewed as unsportsmanlike.

Harold and I had been put forward by Captain Hargreaves and accepted, on the strength of a number of notable successes against German snipers, in the first cohort of men to receive formal sniper training from the man we would come to know as the 'Major'.

Dearest Sis,

How are you, my love? Have you made any decision about taking up nursing? It would be almost worth getting a Blighty and waking up to see your beautiful face looking down.

Jack is well and we are both being sent for more specialist marksman training. We don't know where we are being sent but at least it will be away from the Front. Sadly, you will be aware that we have taken some casualties. It is hard for us to see people we have grown up with get killed and wounded. Just two days ago, Proctor was killed by a mortar as he was mending the wire in front of our trench. Now any casualties are being replaced by drafts of men from all over the country which takes a bit of getting used to. We've got one chap from Glasgow and another from Newcastle and we can barely understand them any more than we can understand the French.

I have left the exciting news until last! Jack has been made a corporal. I am so pleased for him.

Well, my darling, please write soon.

All my love
Harold

***

"Well, here we are again back at Etaples and it's still a shit-hole."

"Yes, nothing seems to have changed. According to Captain Hargreaves, we need to report to the camp adjutant's office, wherever that is, to receive our orders for joining the course. God, I hope we don't have to stay here."

It had seemed almost too good to be true when, having found the camp adjutant's office, we were given travel passes for Boulogne and then for a ship back to England. The joy of returning to England could not be diminished by the long and tortuous journey ahead of us by road, ship and train back to the ranges at Bisley where our training was to take place.

Once again we found ourselves in a cohort of 20 men and exchanged nods and greetings, as we entered the tent to which we had been allocated, with a couple of privates that we recognised from our time on the Specialist Marksman course. Men were coming and going but once we had dumped our kit on an available bed, we made our way to the mess tent for some food which, I remarked, was as bad as it was the last time we had been there.

"Maybe we've been brought here to save the army by shooting the cooks. We'll be sent up into the dunes to pick off the cooks one by one. They might even try to give us a medal for bravery when in truth the real bravery comes when you try to eat this food."

"We are going to be so close to Acaster, Jack. Do you think we will get a chance to visit home?"

"No."

***

Once we had reached Bisley, we assembled in a large tent that was set out like a schoolroom and all the banter and chatter ceased as we came to attention when an officer and some N.C.O.s entered the tent.

"Please, sit down, gentlemen. I am Major Hesketh-Pritchard and I am in command of this Sniping, Observation and Scouting School. The general staff have at long last accepted that men are being killed each day at a rate that can no longer be blamed on stray bullets. One battalion lost 18 men in a single day to German snipers. Those of you keen on mathematics will be able to work out from the number of battalions in the frontline at any one time the scale of those losses.

"I have therefore been instructed to set up this school, which I am more than happy to do. My aim is to turn out snipers who will help us win this war because I believe that a man who can shoot well not only strengthens a unit but also raises morale when that unit knows that it contains some good shots. Gentlemen, I believe that when you return to your units, your actions will save the lives of thousands of your comrades. You will not only hunt and kill enemy snipers but because you will be able to snipe machine gunners and artillery observers you will disrupt what the Germans try do each day.

"You will generally be loved by your comrades but hated by the Germans who will seek to hunt you down and kill you, just as we do their snipers. You must understand that where this war is concerned, there are only two outcomes for you – survival or death. Capture is never an option when you are a sniper so welcome to the Suicide Club.

"A moment ago, I said that you would generally be loved by your comrades. Why not universally loved? The answer is simple because the men who will be around you as you go about your business know that what you do will provoke retaliatory action from the Germans who will machine gun or shell the area of the line that you occupied. A soldier who keeps his head down, can deny a sniper a target but that soldier cannot deny a shell or flying shrapnel. So some soldiers will not be happy that you are operating in their part of the line because it is the sniper that reminds them that they are at war because without you, they and the Germans would be sitting on top of their trenches looking at each other with curiosity and that is not something the generals can agree to or allow. Despite that, never doubt that what you do is important and will make a difference.

"It is my belief that snipers should operate in pairs with one of you observing and the other firing – and these roles can of course be alternated. You will be introduced to those two activities in the coming days because this course is built around three component parts – Finding Your Mark, Defining Your Mark and Hitting Your Mark. I hope that by the time you leave here that you will be able to hit your mark at any distance up to 1200 yards."

This last remark brought a shaking of heads and some muted laughter from some of the men, which the Major did not seem to mind because he happily smiled as well, however, it was quelled instantly when he signalled to one of the N.C.O.s who turned to a box on the table behind him and lifted out a brand-new rifle that was fitted with a telescopic sight which he then held up for the men to see.

"Some of you may have seen one of these rifles but I doubt if any of you have used one. You are going to hand in your existing rifles when you leave this tent and then tomorrow you will be issued with one of these beauties, a .303 P.14 Enfield Sniper's Rifle and if you pass this course, then you will take that gun with you back to your unit.

"Now, gentlemen, I think you should spend what daylight is left familiarising yourself with the camp and its many delights. Get a good night's sleep, breakfast well and be here in this tent at seven o'clock tomorrow morning. Now line up to hand in your rifle."

***

Mum had been thrilled when she had learned of my promotion and relieved at the news that, at least for a while, I would be away from the Front. Father was neither amused nor delighted when Mum, speaking from excitement rather than premeditated thought, said that there were now two Corporal Browns in the family and so gained another bruise for her trouble before he went out to the Stag.

The Stag was Acaster's equivalent of a London gentlemen's club but without the polished brass, freshly cut flowers, flunkey's who went about their business quietly and discreetly, a magnificent dining room and a French chef. Instead, the Stag had wooden surfaces that were both chipped and stained, a landlord prone to shouting at his clientele in Anglo-Saxon terms and pies prepared by the landlady, Mrs Olive Fawcett, which could be eaten at the bar or at a table that might be infrequently wiped over by a heavily soiled cloth. The main attraction for the men of Acaster was the almost total lack of women who frequented the

78

pub which allowed for a level of banter and language that they only felt the need to tone down when Reverend Stoddart made an occasional appearance.

Father leaned nonchalantly on the bar with a pint of ale at his elbow and surveyed the room. The evening's conversation had inevitably started with the war and the growing casualty numbers and there was a growing discontent with the generals and their apparent disregard for the lives of those serving under them. Constable Tibbins entered the bar having made a circuit of the town and shook the rain off of his cape.

"Over here, Harry lad. Is it your usual? Another pint, if you, please, Tom, and have a half yourself."

Tom, the landlord, nodded and set about pulling the beer while Harry Tibbins joined the group and after a couple of mouthfuls of his beer felt emboldened to make his contribution to the conversation.

"I met a couple of men from the estate this morning and they said that Lord Acaster is like a bull with a sore head at the moment because it seems that a big push is on the cards soon. Apparently, we don't want to do it but the French are insisting."

"That'll be a bad do…"

The conversation continued for some time as the French were vilified for their lack of fighting spirit and to hear some of the men speak, it seemed that the French were more detested than the Germans. Tibbins finished his beer and then left saying that he would make another circuit of the centre of the town at which point the conversation became somewhat earthier. Nobody could later say who had started it but soon Father was listening intently to comments about Ester Smith.

"I would. It's a shame that she is on her own. She doesn't make the best of herself mind but believe me there's a hell of a good body under those drab clothes."

"Tommy there tried his luck once. All he got for his trouble was a slap around the face from her and then another from his missus."

"What a waste if she grows old and shrivelled?"

It could, in all honesty, never be claimed that the conversation reached a level that was higher than the men's belts and Father had learned nothing new about Ester. Eventually, the landlord called time and the men drank up and began to make their way home. The exception was Father, who decided to walk past Ester Smith's house and having seen that she was still up, had stood in the shadows opposite. He felt himself almost instantly aroused when he saw that she was dressed for bed with a shawl around her shoulders and with her hair down as she moved around oblivious to her watcher opposite.

He was sorely tempted to cross the road and knock on the door but he was worried that when Ester opened it, he would not be able to control himself, whilst at the same time having to admit to himself that the pressure would have to be released somehow before he went home to the coldness of his wife. He slid his hand inside his trousers and realised from the reaction to the touch of his fingers that he was fast reaching the point of no return. He unbuttoned his flies and his eyes never left Ester for an instant as he brought himself and felt the warmth spill over his fingers and then onto the ground below and he would later realise that it was the first time he had masturbated since leaving the army. It was only when Ester went up to her bed by the light of her lamp that he left the shadows and returned home where Mum was pretending to be asleep and she was careful not to stir as he climbed into bed. Mum lay there tense as she waited to see whether Father would start pawing her but he quickly settled down to sleep. As Mum relaxed, she became aware that around the edges of the beer fumes coming from Father, there was an unmistakable muskiness which she recognised at once.

***

There was now no way that Father would not return to his vantage point and watch Ester as she went about her business unaware of what was happening in the shadows opposite her small house. There was an illicit excitement that Father had not experienced since he was a young teenager caused by the thrill of the thought that he might be caught. It was always more exciting when he pleasured himself in those days while thinking that at any moment his mother might walk in and catch him.

He had found a way of enjoying Ester without her knowing and in a situation where he was totally in control. He could imagine various scenarios in his mind involving Ester without the need to be confronted with the reality of the woman and in that way, he could never be disappointed.

One night as he stood there in the shadows with his right hand thrust down his trousers, he was disturbed by the sound of footsteps approaching. He pushed himself as far back into the shadows as it was possible to go and watched the slight figure of a man walk up the front path opposite and knock on Ester's door.

It was a clear evening with a bright moon and as he waited, the figure turned and he was amazed to see that it was Lord Acaster who stood there. When Ester opened her door, she quickly greeted her visitor who then followed her into the house. Minutes later he saw a light appear in the room that he knew was Ester's bedroom.

He could hardly believe what he had seen but some part of his brain must have been anticipating what was happening in the house opposite because he suddenly let out a groan as he felt the hot spurt across his hand.

"You're crafty old bastard! Lost out to a lord have I – but I'm afraid she, and his Lordship, will learn that I am a bad loser and I can wait."

***

Sis had, like most of those left behind, developed the ability to not dwell on things and overthink matters but instead lived for the day. She therefore was just so happy that Harold was safely away from the Front as she wrote to him.

My Dearest Harold,

I have no idea when or if you will receive this letter but I am so happy that for at least a while you will be away from the Front.

Mum and I are so thrilled that Jack has been promoted and I hope that you will get your two stripes soon as well. We were all sad to hear of Willie Proctor's death and his name has been added to a book of remembrance in the church. Reverend Stoddart hopes that after the war, Acaster will have a permanent memorial for those who have been killed.

I had tea with your mother on Saturday and she was in very good spirits. Mum has been a bit off colour and has spent days in her bed in complete darkness, complaining of headaches. Dad said that she was best left alone but that is hard to do, so I have gone up to check on her when he has been out. She would have heard me coming up the stairs and by the time I got to their room, she had turned away from the door. Please, don't tell Jack as I don't want him to worry.

I have not yet done anything about nursing as it would be so hard to leave Mum at this time.

Wherever you are, I hope that your training goes well.

I will love you always
Sis

***

Father, in thrall to a bad mood, decided to confront Ester Smith and let her know that he knew her little secret. Ester was surprised when she opened her front door and saw him standing there.

"Good Lord, Sergeant Brown, what brings you to my front door? Are there more prowlers in the neighbourhood?"

"Can I come in, Mrs Smith?"

Ester was not someone who could ever be intimidated and least of all by Father and so she enjoyed staring her unwelcome visitor out until he looked away.

"I don't think so, Sergeant Brown – do you? As far as I am aware, I have no need of the police today. So, I will thank you for your time but I won't delay you any further as I am sure a man like you must be needed elsewhere."

This opening exchange had not gone at all the way that he had imagined when he had stood opposite Ester's house and this served only to make his temper worse. He leant closer to Ester, placing his boot so that she could not shut the door and she could once again smell the stale tobacco on his breath.

"You think you are so clever, don't you? Well, I know his and your dirty little secret. Now, don't try and deny it. I saw him here the other evening. I saw the light in your bedroom. No man likes to be made a fool of or see another man take what he wants. You'll be sorry for ever making an enemy of me. All that fine talk about James being the first and only man for you – that's a joke and no mistake. Don't say that you haven't been warned."

"I have no idea what you are talking about or what you think you saw…"

"Is he here now? Does he pay you? I've got money as well."

"Who? How dare you!"

"You really want me to spell it out? You are providing, how shall I put this, favours to Lord Acaster. Won't that set tongues wagging if the facts get out? Imagine walking down the street and realising they are all talking about you."

"Go away or…"

"Or what? As a police officer I have noted that you have not denied what I know to be true. So, just remember what I've told you."

"You are an evil, spiteful man. Now go!"

He gave her a last look and turned and made his way for Ester at an aggravatingly slow pace, down the path and out of the gate and he heard the door shut behind him leaving Ester standing in her hallway feeling both fearful and angry.

***

"I want your training to be both instructive and enjoyable and so today, gentlemen, now that you have got your shiny, new rifles, you are going to learn how to master the two biggest problems that you will face as snipers – range and wind.

"In the field you will have an observer with you who will tell you the distances involved but you won't have an observer here. By the end of tomorrow, to pass this element of the course, you will have to judge and record correctly, using your eyes only, the distances of eight out of ten markers that have been set up along the range.

"To be the accurate snipers that the army requires, you must also learn about the telescopic sight. In my experience, using the sight is not a particular problem although the men who use it are. The problem occurs when the sight becomes dislodged or needs to be removed to be cleaned and you don't know how to put it back correctly in the exact same position that you took it off.

"I have seen rifles that have been some thirty inches out over a hundred yards and twenty-five feet out over a thousand yards. It is my belief that eighty percent of rifles fitted with telescopic sights are useless simply because of the ignorance of the men using them. Don't be one of those men.

"One last thing, gentlemen, from now on, you may only smoke in the evenings. You may not be aware of it but the smell of tobacco smoke on you and your clothes may help your enemy, the walker to locate you. You will hear more about the walker as the course progresses."

***

Father could hear someone moving about in the kitchen when he opened the front door. Attracted by the enticing odours coming from the scullery, he first off all hung up his helmet and jacket in his office before going to investigate.

"You're up then?"

Mum didn't turn from the range, where saucepans were bubbling away, to face him when she replied.

"Yes, Bill. I needed to make your tea."

"It's good to see you up. Where's Sis?"

"She's having her tea at Mrs Smith's, who is quite poorly at the moment."

"Nothing serious I hope. Let's have a look at you then. Come on, turn around."

"I'm in the middle of cooking, Bill. I'm fine."

He took a step towards her and his voice was cold as he spoke slowly. "Turn around, I said."

Mum stopped stirring the pan and turned to look at him. The bruises down the side of her face were a kaleidoscope of greens and yellows. He studied her intently for a brief moment before taking his place at the table.

"Best to keep in doors for a few more days and there's no need to worry Sis by letting her see you like that."

After he had eaten his meal, he sat in his armchair by the fireplace and watched Mum clearing away with a sad look on his face.

"You've only yourself to blame, you know. You make me so angry the way you go on. To top it all, you've not been a proper wife to me these last few years. I don't think you have been a proper wife to me since we had Jack and Sis. Yes, you make my meals, do my washing and look after the house but if that was all I wanted, I could get myself a housekeeper. I've got needs, you know, Alice, that need attending to and you want nothing to do with me. It's not right and no good will come of it."

Mum stood there, a stained apron around her waist and her handkerchief pressed to her mouth, watching while tears ran down his face and his pain and upset provided all the evidence that she needed to show what she had thought all along namely that this was all her fault. Slowly she walked across to him and put her hand briefly on his shoulder but had already moved away before he could respond.

***

"Good morning, gentlemen. I trust you slept well and are suitably bright eyed today. Why? Well, we are moving onto the subject of Observation because you cannot shoot what you cannot see.

"You will, this morning, undergo a medical – nothing to worry about but I do believe that you need to be amongst the fittest of soldiers for this work. You will therefore stay in this tent until you are required for your medical when you will be escorted to and from the medical tent to ensure that you do not communicate with another member of this cohort. You must understand that attempting to communicate will result in you leaving the course.

"The rest of the time is your own until you get escorted to the range where a number of military objects – and I will not list them for you or indeed give their number – have been concealed at anywhere from five yards to 300 yards. Your task is simple – using either binoculars or a spotting scope, locate those objects and record their placement on a sketch that you will make of the terrain. The sketch must also give the distances to the objects concerned. You will have 30 minutes to complete this task. The winner of this particular task will be allowed to make one five-minute telephone call from the orderly room. In the event of scores from the range being even, then my decision will be final and will be based on the clarity of the sketched diagram that you will have handed in.

"Once the task is over, you will be escorted back to the canteen where you will remain until the whole cohort has completed this task. While you are in the canteen, you may read, talk, play cards, smoke and sup from the mugs of tea that will periodically be supplied. If you need to leave the canteen, then you will be escorted at all times to stop you talking to those who have yet to do the task."

We all came and went from the tent under the watchful eyes of the instructors and having successfully undergone our medicals, we sat around in the tent waiting for our turn on the range. Eventually my name was called and escorted by an instructor. I was marched at the double to the range where I was handed a sketch pad before settling myself down on a ground sheet where I found the promised pair of binoculars, however, it was the spotting scope on its small tripod which I decided to use. I scanned the ground that stretched out ahead of me and quickly spotted, just ten yards from where I was lying, a muddy water bottle lying behind a small mound and noted its position on my sketch pad. I had a keen eye and started to enjoy myself as the task progressed.

Harold was naturally less confident than me and so he would have been nervous about the task but also, when it was over, confident that he had successfully spotted all the items. He later told me that he had quite quickly seen the papier mache heads of Fritz and Hans, looking out of two holes in the bank some 300 yards away and had noted these down on his pad before peering through the binoculars to ensure he hadn't missed anything, which was when he saw something glint to the right of those heads. He lowered the binoculars and then looked through them again and then he was certain. What he had seen glinting was a metal loophole that a sniper might use and scanning the bank he then found another one.

"How did you get on?"

"It was interesting. When you stare through a scope or the binos for too long, your eyes start playing tricks on you. Did you see the two metal loopholes up on the far bank?"

I looked at Harold in mock dismay.

"Yes, I did but they were well-hidden. I should think a few of the cohort will miss those. Once you've spotted the heads, it's so easy to think, that's it. Crafty sods!"

As we all started gathering in the canteen, there was a fair amount of banter and many a deliberate red herring was introduced that caused a slight moment of doubt even in those who were very confident about their performance in the task.

**

Saturday morning and Palfreys Shoe and Haberdashery Shop had not long been open when the telephone rang. These days, the shop was run by Miss Palfrey, a spinster in her late 40s with her increasingly grey hair pulled back into a severe bun through which she always pushed her pencil to ensure one was always to hand. Occasionally, old Mrs Palfrey would sit behind the counter offering advice and observing the comings and goings and particularly how that day's takings were going. With a deep sigh, Miss Palfrey stopped tidying the counter and answered the telephone,

"Acaster 741. Palfreys Shoe and Haberdashery Shop. How may I help you? Oh, I see."

Miss Palfrey looked over the top of her glasses, across the shop to where Sis was straightening up the shop's, many rolls of material ready for the day ahead.

"Miss Brown. There is a telephone call for you. The gentleman says it is urgent. Be quick – there's work to do."

Sis was not used to receiving telephone calls and wasn't at all sure how she should respond. She had only the way she had observed her father and Miss Palfrey deal with telephone calls to guide her and therefore did not realise the inappropriateness of her response.

"Who is it?"

"Miss Brown. I neither know nor care. Now come along as there's work to do."

It was therefore a very flustered Sis who took the telephone from Miss Palfrey, who stood there without looking at Sis, holding the telephone with her arm outstretched while with her other hand she continued with what she had been doing before she had been interrupted.

"Hello. Can I help you?"

"Yes, you can, Sis. It's me, Harold. How are you? I can't believe that I am talking to you. It's so lovely to hear your voice. How's Mum – she hasn't written for a while?"

"Harold, is that really you? I am very well, thank you. Harold, I have been visiting your mum a lot lately because she hasn't been well. I'm sure it's nothing to worry about. My mum is not well at the moment either – seems to be spending a lot of time in her bedroom."

The bell on the shop door tinkled as the day's first customer came in and Miss Palfrey glared pointedly across at Sis who dropped her voice to a whisper.

"Harold, I have to go. Take care and don't worry. Give my love to Jack. Love you."

"Love you too."

Sis put the telephone back on its cradle and came out from behind the counter with a warm smile on her face that all who saw it believed was solely for the customer but Sis knew better.

"Good morning, Mrs Carter. Isn't it a lovely morning? Now, how can I help you?"

As irritated as Miss Palfrey had been a few moments earlier, the frown disappeared from her face as she listened to the caring and friendly way that Sis had with people, knowing that her approach was a big asset to the shop.

***

Concerned about the news of his mother's health, Harold came looking for me and found me in the canteen sitting there with two steaming mugs of tea and two currant buns.

"Here you are? So how was the magic of the telephone? Did you speak to her?"

"It was wonderful. Her voice sounded so clear, just as if she was here in the camp and not miles away. She's fine and sends you her love. Apparently, your mum is poorly and is keeping to her bedroom and my mum is also ill, although Sis didn't say what's wrong."

"I am sure she will be fine, Harold. Now drink your tea and eat that bun because apparently we will be on the move soon."

"Where?"

"Absolutely no idea."

I was troubled by the news that my mother was unwell because I couldn't remember a day when my mother had taken to her bed because she was ill. I knew that a troubled mind was going to be of no use to me as I faced up to the challenges of this course and yet, try as I might, I could not stop the thought that perhaps she was not ill but had been hurt in some way instead and the suspicion grew that Father had something to do with it.

***

The instructors gathered around the two trestle tables that had been pushed together while the Major passed around the bottles of beers for the regular review meeting that he liked to hold in the early evening. In the company of his instructors, the Major was not concerned about rank and therefore everyone, in what was a relaxed environment, felt able to contribute freely as they reviewed the progress of the men on the course.

Major Hesketh – Pritchard was a tall, loose-limbed man with a lop-sided, toothy grin and a fervent belief in the importance of what he was doing. He had absolute certainty that effective sniping meant more lives saved and he was equally certain that it meant more than pointing a rifle and firing it. He was a man who valued character and attitude and had seen many a man who, although an excellent shot, had lacked the common sense and application needed to be a sniper. The meeting was therefore about weeding out the temperamentally unsuitable because they would not last long enough to justify any investment in them and would be a liability for the men around them.

"How are Privates Ward and Delaney doing? Ward seemed to struggle with the last task. He…"

In this way the abilities of each member of the cohort were discussed in turn and the talk ranged across all of the tasks and skills covered by the course up to that point. Although the meeting was relaxed, it was very focused and objective and no little tic or trait in any man escaped their scrutiny.

"What about Smith and Brown?"

"They seem very competent. My concern is that they seem to be joined at the hip. If you find one of them, then the other one is never far away. In that respect they are unlike any of the others in the cohort."

"I would like to see them working with a different partner."

The Major listened intently to the discussion and then summarised giving his perspective.

"I have been very impressed with this pair. I do understand your concern, however, I think we should allow them to continue as a pair. They are and probably have been for a large part of their lives, friends and consequently they understand each other and as a result they can predict what the other one is thinking and is about to do. Two men introduced today would take years to develop that rapport and might never do so."

The instructors and the Major continued to discuss the advantages and disadvantages which the Major encouraged because he saw the process as constructive and fostered a team approach amongst the instructors. There was very little doubt that if the instructors were called upon to follow the Major over the top, then they would do so without a moment's hesitation.

***

Sis had decided to visit Mrs Smith after work to see how she was feeling and had bought a small bunch of flowers from the shop, next door to Palfreys, that was selling them off at the end of the day. Sis knocked on Mrs Smith's door and was becoming concerned that there was no answer when she heard someone shuffling towards the front door. Mrs Smith opened the door and nodded a greeting as she stood aside to let her pass. Sis could see that Mrs Smith looked paler and frailer than the last time that she had visited her, which had only been two days ago. They moved through to the scullery and Mrs Smith, who was hunched over, sat down in front of the range which was struggling to give off some heat.

"How are you? Here, I got these for you to cheer you up. Shall I put them in some water for you?"

"Thank you, Sis. You shouldn't have spent your hard-earned money on buying me flowers. You're a sweet girl. You'll find a vase on top of the cupboard over there."

Mrs Smith said no more as she was wracked with a distressing cough and she held her handkerchief up to her mouth. It was the kind of cough that although bad enough in itself also caused sharp, vicious pains to shoot through the top of a person's head. Eventually, thanks to the glass of water that Sis had quickly poured for her. She was able to speak and watched as Sis busied herself making a pot of tea.

"Mary from next door came around this morning and insisted that Dr Jackson should come and see me. I didn't want to trouble him but she insisted and he called in early this afternoon. Thank you, this cup of tea is just what I wanted."

"Well, what did the doctor say?"

Ester waved her hand dismissively. "Oh, it's nothing to get worried about. He thinks I've probably got a chest infection that has managed to get a real grip of me. Just to be on the safe side, he wants me to go into hospital and have some tests but I don't know. I suppose I must be grateful that Lord Acaster has agreed to have me driven to and from the hospital and will pay for my hospital stay but it's a long way to go and I won't know anyone and who is going to keep an eye on you?"

They both laughed, although the effort soon brought on another bout of coughing for Mrs Smith.

"I think you should go, just to put our minds at rest. Mum and I will come and visit you."

"That's very kind of you. I'm going to have a little think about it. How is your mum?"

Having heard that Mum appeared to be no better, she then asked Sis whether she had any news from Harold and Jack.

***

The news from Acaster had unsettled both of us. I had always had an ability to compartmentalise issues and did so again with the news of Mum being unwell in some way. Harold, however, could not get the thought of his mother being ill out of his mind.

"Jack, when this course is finished, we will be sent straight back to France and the big push that everyone seems to be talking about. I can't bear the thought of going back knowing that Mum is not well. I have this idea in my head that I just can't shift, that I will survive this war but when I get back to Acaster, Mum won't be there. I can't live with the thought that I might already have seen her for the last time."

"Come on, mate, I am sure not knowing is difficult but I think you are reading more into it than is necessary. Your mum is as tough as they come. Being on this course has made it impossible for us to get any letters, so for all, we know she may be all right now."

"I know what you are saying but I can't help it. I just need to see her before I go back to France. Do you think they will grant me some leave? Your mum's not well so perhaps they will give you leave as well."

"Harold, with everything that is going on, I don't see any chance of us getting leave. You need to get your head right. We've come this far so let's make sure we pass."

***

It had been a long and tedious journey by train down to Newton Abbot and then a march, led by the Major, of some ten miles to our base at Holne Park, which was situated on the edge of Dartmoor. We crossed a small bridge over a river we soon came to know as the River Dart and went up a long drive that was bordered by oak trees on either side that led to a three-storey country house which had been requisitioned by the army in 1914.

It had been cold at Bisley and it was certainly cold and damp on Dartmoor, however, so far there had been very few night frosts, ice or snow that winter but even so we were pleased to learn that we would not be sleeping under canvas. Once we had been shown the two rooms that would act as our dormitories where we would sleep in bunk beds, we had quickly left our kit on our bunks and headed down to the mess for a hot meal before assembling in what had been the games room for a briefing. In the middle of the room, draped in a heavy cloth was a snooker table unlike any that any of us had ever seen in our working men's clubs or the backroom of the Stag. Those who lifted up the cloth saw a green baize that was well-looked after and free from the scuff and burn marks that we were all used to.

"Welcome to Holne Park, gentlemen. This will be your home for the next few days as you will embark on a number of training exercises and assessments on Dartmoor. For those of you who have never been to Devon before, let me tell you that Dartmoor can be a seductively beautiful mistress but like any woman, her mood can change very quickly, so beware and take no liberties with her. I want you to spend the rest of the time available to you before lights out, squaring away your kit and familiarising yourselves with the house and grounds. I am sure it will not take you long to discover the bar in the basement where you can obtain beer – however, there is a limit of one pint a night which will be strictly enforced.

"Now I will hand over to Sergeant Wilson, who will explain to you all you need to know about Holne Park."

A giant of a man, who had been standing behind the Major, came forward and studied us as we sat in front of him.

"I would also like to welcome you to Holne Park. The rules are very simple here. The most important rule is that unless you are on a training exercise, you may only leave the grounds with a signed pass from Major Hesketh-Pritchard. You wouldn't be the first men to think that you could slip away to the village of Ashburton to sample the pleasures of the local pub. I can tell you now, don't bother. Why? My wife is the landlady of that pub and my daughter is the barmaid and your accents will mark you out as outsiders. And I have a wife and daughter who tell me everything.

"You are of course free to wander the grounds to your heart's content.

"Now, breakfast will be at 06.30 in the morning. Here at Holne Park, we believe that cleanliness is next to godliness and so you will parade outside the front door of the house at 05.45 dressed in your vest, shorts and a pair of daps only. You will find a supply of daps in a box in the hall. Your evening…"

The Major had seen the confused look on our faces at the term 'daps' and with a smile on his face stepped forward.

"Please, excuse me for a moment, Sergeant Wilson. Gentlemen, 'daps' are what you will wear on your feet – plimsolls. Please, continue, Sergeant."

"Thank you, sir. Your evening meal will be served in the dining room at seven o'clock unless the Major has instructed otherwise. As well as the bar, there is also a games room in the basement where you can play darts, cards and dominoes. And before you ask, this snooker table is strictly out of bounds. Lights out will be 21.30."

The Major came forward again and gently touched the sergeant's arm.

"Thank you, Sergeant. We will, I am sure, try very hard to be your perfect guests. In the unlikely event that any of you fancy trying your luck in the village and you are caught, then you will automatically be returned to your units. Now, good night, gentlemen, and I will see you outside at 05.45 tomorrow morning. After breakfast, we will begin to look at the issue of concealment."

***

Although tired from our journey, many of us had struggled to sleep due to the silence, even though it was interspersed by snores, grunts, moans, farts, scratching and fidgeting and the almost tangible darkness of a rural Devon night and consequently many of us were bleary-eyed as we gathered on the drive outside the main door of the house dressed in shorts, vest and daps while fingers of mist swirled around us.

"It's bloody freezing" was a fair summation of how we all felt as we stood there shivering and unsure how we would ever get warm again. At 05.45 the door opened and Sergeant Wilson appeared with the Major and all of us, despite our surprise to see that they were also wearing shorts, vest and daps, snapped to attention.

"Right then, men. We are going to run from the house down to the River Dart. Once there, we will line up on the bank and at my command we will all jump in and submerge ourselves fully under the water. The Major will be watching and if any man fails to jump in or submerge his self then we will all get out and do it again. Understood? Now follow me."

The run to the river took no more than five minutes and we were soon standing on its bank shivering as we looked down at the dark waters flowing past us, surrounded by a cloud of water vapour that rose from our cold bodies.

"Now, on my command. Wait for it. Jump!"

We were a slightly ragged line of men that jumped in. The surprise was that every man did jump and fully immerse themselves in the water because the cohort contained men who could not swim and many who were almost strangers to water even when it came to personal cleanliness. Each man would talk later of the shock of the cold water as it enclosed their bodies. I have never experienced water so cold and the shock took my breath away but it was, I have to admit, also exhilarating.

We all climbed back up onto the bank and stood there shivering with our teeth chattering but a loud cheer went up when the Major threw himself into the river and ducked his head and shoulders under the surface. He climbed the bank with a big grin on his face and signalled for us to return to the house but not before Sergeant Wilson informed us, with a smile that whilst at Holne Park our mornings would all start that way. Back in our rooms, we all vigorously towelled ourselves down and discussed our unusual start to the day while getting dressed ready for what would now be an even more welcome breakfast. Harold looked as white as a sheet as he pulled on his trousers.

"I have never been so cold in my life. I can't stop shivering. I shan't know whether to drink my mug of tea or just hold it to get some warmth, Jack."

"I know. I am frozen too. The major's a sport for doing it – how many other officers would do that?"

"Not many, I shouldn't think and certainly not in front of the other ranks. Come on, this breakfast will never have tasted so good."

***

The cooked breakfast had tasted every bit as good as we had both hoped for and expected and so it was a contented group who gathered in the games room to hear what concealment would involve.

"Good morning, gentlemen. I trust you slept well and enjoyed your early morning dip. Today we move on to the topic of concealment. Concealment means getting yourself into a position where you can observe the enemy without being seen yourself. It's about being inventive, making use of the natural terrain and whatever is to hand."

We then moved outside and there followed instruction with demonstrations on building a hide, wearing ghillie suits and customising it to fit in with the surroundings and movement without attracting attention. The following morning we were again addressed by the major.

"Gentlemen, Dartmoor provides many opportunities for concealment and today you will be assessed on your ability to get to within 200 yards of two trained observers. You will maintain your position, hopefully unobserved, for 20 minutes and then fire a single blank round at the observers. To pass, you must remain undetected for those 20 minutes. Now, any questions? Good, then let's make a start."

***

The cohort had enjoyed various levels of success that day, although some had been spotted quite quickly. None of the men would argue against the need to keep their heads down but some found it difficult to lie in a prone position and keep their hips tight to the ground and consequently the observers would be confronted with a mound that did not fit in with its surroundings as the man lay amongst the bracken with his backside in the air.

I thought that I had performed well and lay there without the observers discovering my position, although I later told Harold that I had never known 20 minutes to pass so slowly.

Harold had moved into position quite easily and remembered that when crawling through grass or bracken that this had to be done in a zigzag manner rather than a straight line, otherwise those observing would see a trail of flattened grass. He had almost remained undiscovered for the required 20 minutes when a grouse that had inadvertently wandered towards him suddenly realised that he was there and exploded out of the bracken thereby disclosing his position.

"I couldn't believe it. Why did that bloody bird have to choose that moment to wander across to where I was lying up and then make as much noise as possible to get away from me. The observers were sympathetic once they had stopped laughing."

***

That evening, the Major and the instructors gathered in the games room to discuss the events of the day. On the whole, the cohort had performed quite well and as each name was mentioned in turn, there were no dissenting voices to their progressing to the next task.

"Private Smith seems to be a little out of sorts, a little preoccupied. I had a word with Corporal Brown while Smith was out on the moor and it seems the problem is his mother who is ill. I suggest we keep an eye on him."

"It's good to have you home, Mrs Smith."

"Now look. I think it's about time that you called me Ester."

Ester had been driven home in one of Lord Acaster's cars earlier that afternoon. She apparently had made a bit of a fuss when the chauffeur opened the rear door of the car but had eventually and reluctantly agreed to sit in the back feeling in her words like "Lady Muck". She was now sitting in a chair with a blanket around her shoulders while Sis bustled about making hot drinks and making sure the small coal fire was well-established. Sis had always wondered at the reasonable supply of coal in Ester's bunker and now knew why as one of the estate workers had just finished filling it.

Ester had spent the time between arriving home and Sis visiting, replaying her consultation with Dr Lowlands, a loud, rotund man, who considered rightly or wrongly that he was a friend to everybody. While Ester sat on her bed tense and stiff-backed, Dr Lowlands had sat on its edge and held her hand.

"It's not good news, I'm afraid, Mrs Smith. I am sorry to have to tell you that you have a mass in your right lung. Unfortunately, I must also tell you that there is no cure. We cannot operate on you because we fear that the mass is too close to your heart, however, we can give you some medicine to help you and so sadly, I think you need to go home and make sure you put all your affairs in order."

Ester stared uncomprehendingly at the doctor.

"Are you telling me that I am going to die? When? How long have I got?"

"I have no way of knowing with certainty, Mrs Smith, but it will hopefully be a little while yet. Now I'll leave you with Nurse Pulley."

As the tears started to roll down Ester's cheeks, the doctor stood up and patted her hand and left her to be comforted by the nurse as she got dressed and packed her small bag.

Sis sat in the chair opposite Ester and looked at the person who she dearly hoped would one day be her future mother-in-law once this ghastly war was over. Ester looked both older and greyer than before she had gone to hospital just a few days before.

"How are you, Ester? What did they say?"

Ester didn't look at Sis as she replied.

"It's nothing to worry about. It's just a nasty chest infection. It will soon go."

"That's good. You had me worried there for a while."

"Well, there's no need. I will soon be up and about. Have you heard from Jack and Harold?"

"No. I think they are still on their course. I miss their letters. It will be good to hear from them again."

***

"Well, good morning, gentlemen. Today you begin your instruction in the art of stalking. Where concealment is about waiting for the enemy to come to you, stalking is about going out and finding your target. It requires skill, patience and mastery of your telescopic scope.

"Your telescopic scope will enable you to take advantage of what I refer to as the sniper's light. Sniper's light occurs around dusk and dawn and your scope will enable you, much to your enemy's discomfort, to make use of poor light levels when your enemy may be a little bit careless as he assumes that you will not be able to see him. That will hopefully be the last mistake he makes!

"Now let me hand over to…"

What followed over the course of that day and the day after were intensive sessions on using the telescopic sights, taking account of any wind, choosing the firing position and extraction.

***

On the third morning we gathered in the games room and the Major walked in with a large mug of steaming tea which he carefully placed on the ornate mantelpiece.

"Gentlemen, today you will renew your acquaintanceship with Dartmoor. You will be given a map reference for a red and white pole that you will find out on the moors. On top of this pole you will find the head of our old friend Hans. Now, Hans will be looking in the direction of the two-man observation post that you then have to find. Without being observed, you will approach to within 150–300 yards of this OP and then fire two blank rounds whilst remaining undetected. The OP will then try to establish where you are and find you and you must remain undetected for a full 20 minutes. You must then extract yourself from your position undetected by the OP.

"Are there any questions, gentlemen? No, well, enjoy the task and Private Smith, please keep an eye out for the wildlife."

The major's quip produced some laughter and we left the room in good spirits, although Harold found himself subjected to some good-natured banter from some of the cohort including, obviously, me.

At the start of the day, if we had been asked about wind, there would have been the obvious barrack room comments but by the end of the day we had a reasonable grasp of the differences between the six basic wind patterns namely gentle, moderate, fresh, strong, very strong and gale force. Following an impressive practical demonstration by one of the instructors, we also learnt how to make the necessary adjustments to our rifle to account for wind speed so that if stalks of grass could be seen gently nodding in the wind, then this would indicate a light breeze of between one and two miles per hour. Suddenly we began to understand that there was so much more involved than just pointing and firing our rifles.

***

Dearest Harold,

I hope that this letter finds you well. In fact, I hope this letter finds you as I have no idea where you are and whether you are getting your post.

I am missing you more than ever and long for the day that this war is over and we can be together.

I have thought a lot about whether I should write this letter to you because I really don't want to worry you and I promised your mum that I wouldn't. You see your mum is really quite poorly. As you would expect, she is putting a brave face on things and is not willing to talk about it but she did recently go into hospital for some tests and she hasn't been the same since she came home.

Please, try not to worry and do your best. I will look after your mum. I have moved in with her so that I can be there for her – she was set against it but I didn't give her a choice and so, for now, I am sleeping in your room.

Give my love to Jack and tell him that Mum is not up and about again yet.

All my love
Sis

If we had some spare time, Harold and I had taken to walking in the grounds of Holne Park which reminded us of more peaceful times when we had worked on the Acaster Estate. As the days had passed, Harold had become more and more agitated about his mother's health and the lack of letters from Sis.

"Harold, you know full well that Sis will be writing to you but the army postal service will be struggling to get her letters from the sorting office in London out to the Front and they will either be keeping them there or trying to send them back through the system to catch up with you at Bisley – except we have now moved down to Devon."

Harold stopped and looked at me and the pain was etched across his face.

"I'm not sure that I can return to the Front without going to see Mum. We are so close to home that it would be an opportunity missed."

"Don't be so bloody stupid. If you ask for leave, then they will just laugh at you given what is happening over there at the moment."

"Who said anything about asking them?"

Harold turned and started to walk off but I grabbed him by the arm and pulled him around and Harold then saw the anger and concern in my face.

"You do talk bollocks at times, Harold Smith – do you know that? Do you ever listen to yourself speak? Do you even think before you speak? You are talking about desertion. You know what happens to deserters, don't you? We've seen what happens to deserters."

"I wouldn't be deserting. I would be just a couple of days, later then I should be getting back to the company. Old Hargreaves would understand."

"That won't be how the army will see it. If they let you get away with that then everyone will be doing the same."

Jack groaned as he saw the look on Harold's face. "Don't tell me you've got some sort of plan – you have, haven't you?"

"I have – I've really thought about this, Jack. It couldn't be simpler – we just get off the train and make our way to Acaster. By the time the army realises that we are missing, we will be on our way back."

"What do you mean we?"

Harold smiled. "We've always stuck together and it will give you a chance to see Sis and your mum. Am I wrong?"

"No!"

Ester Smith had protested at first when Sis told her that she was going to move in, just for a little while to look after her but she was secretly pleased as she knew she needed help. Sis still went to work at Palfreys but not before she had helped Ester down the stairs in the morning and set out her breakfast of toast with a mug of tea.

It seemed a very long day to Ester before she heard Sis, who she had grown to love almost as a daughter over the weeks, entering the house with a cheery shout.

"Oh. Hello, Sis. Have you had a busy day?"

Ester liked listening to her tales, although Sis was always careful not to overstate the comedy that she sometimes witnessed for fear of laughter causing Ester to have a painful bout of coughing. Sis would busy herself sorting out the fire and preparing their evening meal and while that was cooking, she sat down and shared a pot of tea with Ester.

"How have you been today? Have you managed to get a breath of air out in the yard?"

"It's been such a lovely day that I walked to the Junction and back – or at least I did in my head. Just don't seem to have much energy at the moment."

Sis never heard Ester complain or be self-pitying in any way but there were many nights after she had helped her up to her bedroom when she had lay awake in her bed and heard Ester crying herself to sleep.

***

"Well, gentlemen, this is the moment that counts. Today you will be tested on your shooting ability, which after all is the end product of everything you have done on this course. You may have the ability to lay hidden for days, stealthily stalk your target for days but if you are not an accurate shot, then what has it all been for?

"To pass this course, you will be required to fire at one of our old friends, Fritz or Hans. The catch, however, is that you must do your business with your first and only shot. You will need to determine the distance to your target and the wind speed.

"Gentlemen, you will be attempting the classic sniper's shot. You will therefore aim at your target's mouth. Why? Firstly, the teeth are brittle and will not deflect a bullet. Secondly, a shot through the mouth will exit through your target's neck and severe the man's spinal cord. Thirdly, if you aim at the mouth and you are slightly out then it will still, almost certainly be a death shot. You will have to use your telescopic sight because for this task you will not have the services of an observer."

***

We had been placed in a workmen's hut a short distance from a quarry where the range had been established and one at a time we would be taken under escort to the range. Once a man had fired his shot, he was to be escorted to an overseer's hut to ensure that he was unable to pass information to the others in the cohort. We were not under any time pressure as this task was about accuracy and patience and making sure our single shot counted.

There was a tense atmosphere in the workmen's hut as we all thought about the importance of the next few hours and tried to recall everything we had been taught and had learned on the course.

When I reached the quarry, I found the Major sitting on his shooting stick with a pair of binoculars around his neck and a clipboard in his hand.

"Take your time, Brown, and make yourself comfortable. You can use either the binoculars or the spotting scope. There is no rush as I have all day. Just make your shot count."

I settled down and decided that I would first of all use the binoculars to examine the quarry. The first problem I had to solve was the distance to the target and, as I looked down the quarry, I was quietly confident about my judgement. I could see at the end of the quarry that a wall of stones, some six feet in height had been thrown up, topped by sandbags. As I looked carefully at the sandbags, I could see gaps every now and again between them. Methodically. I moved the binoculars from left to right, confident that the target was at 300 yards, when I caught a movement in one of the gaps and there looking back down the quarry at me was the head of Fritz.

***

I was worried that with everything that was going on in his head, Harold would not be as mentally focused as he needed to be when he took up his position in the quarry. When he looked through the binoculars, he would have seen everything that I had seen. There was very little vegetation in the quarry and the strength of the wind where Harold lay was in all probability likely to be different to where the target was located.

Harold saw a head appear between the sandbags but he could not tell whether it was Fritz or Hans, although he was surprised and amused to see that whoever it was smoked. This effect was achieved by the simple use of a piece of tubing which was attached to the inside of the head's mouth. Whoever was operating, the head would then draw on their cigarette and blow a mouthful of smoke up the tube. When the smoke left the head's mouth, the wind moved the smoke gently away to the right which indicated a gentle wind and so he made the necessary adjustments.

***

Through the rifle's telescopic sight, I saw the head appear in the same gap again. I settled myself into position and took aim. The shot when it came echoed around the quarry and I could see that the head had disappeared. As I got to my feet, I looked around and could see the Major looking through his binoculars and then letting them drop down onto his chest as he wrote something on his clipboard but he never spoke to me as I was escorted away to the overseer's hut.

***

Sometime later, Harold walked through the door and looked at me before shaking his head.

"I think I may have missed."

"Why? You're a good shot."

"My head was full of Mum and what we are going to do. I just didn't feel right today."

"Look, let's wait and see, shall we?"

***

That evening we all gathered in the games room and were confronted with multiple heads of Fritz and Hans. Hanging around each head was a pair of cardboard dog tags bearing the name of the man who had fired at it.

I stood in front of my target and saw that the bullet had entered between the nose and the top lip. This was definitely a death shot and I felt justifiably pleased with myself. I walked over to where Harold was standing and saw that his shot had entered the right eye of his target and was therefore another death shot. I patted him on the back and Harold wrapped his arms around me in a giant bear hug.

"Gentlemen! You have all done exceptionally well. I am confident that when you return to your units that you will make a real difference and as a result you will save many lives.

"Now before Sergeant Wilson arrives with some pitchers of beer, I would like to present you with your Sniper's Badge. As you can see, it once again has two crossed rifles topped by a capital 'S'. I will leave you decide over the coming days, weeks and months whether that stands for 'Sniper' or the 'Suicide Club'.

"Ah, here is Sergeant Wilson. Enjoy your evening, gentlemen, as you have more than earned it. As for tomorrow, you will be pleased to know that there will be a final dip in the river followed by breakfast – I am sure that those who need it will discover that it is a splendid way to clear any muzzy headedness. After that, report to the office where you will sign for your travel warrants and then we will all march down to the station.

"Good night, gentlemen."

We were in high spirits after toasting the Major and the instructors, with the beer from the pitchers provided and then continued our celebrations in the bar down in the basement where we happily toasted each other again. Our spirits were such that there were no complaints about tomorrow's early morning dip.

***

The Major and the instructors stayed behind in the games room to complete the final reports on the men and a review of the course which the Army Office required before it would commit to any further cohorts although, had he been asked, the Major would have said that the success or otherwise of the course would only become apparent once the men were back in the field. Armed with glasses of beer, the Major led the instructors through a discussion on each participant.

"How has Private Smith performed on this course, gentlemen?"

The consensus was that Harold had coped well given the distractions on the home front caused by his mother's reported illness and all agreed that he was a quiet, likeable young man.

"Now, what about his friend, Corporal Brown? We've spoken before about him and Smith being joined at the hip and we all agreed that they make a strong pair."

"Brown has proved himself capable of operating on his own and in my opinion he is the best marksman on this course, sir."

The Major listened to the instructors pore over my performance and as my final report showed, it was agreed that I had shown exceptional ability across all aspects of the course.

"I could have stood right next to him out on the moor and I would never have seen him," was one of the comments made. The Major nodded and brought the discussion to an end.

"I have to say that I agree with you. If he can stay alive, then Corporal Brown will be a valuable asset in and around the Front and will inflict a great deal of damage on the Germans. I personally hope that he will be allowed to continue to work with Smith because they do form a very good team."

***

We had endured a long tedious day as we had marched to the station at Newton Abbot only to discover that our train was delayed and nobody was able to tell us when it would arrive. We saw plenty of trains and these did not stop as they passed through the station carrying troops and equipment to and from the coast. To start with, we cheered and waved at the men on the passing troop trains but as the day wore on, we barely registered the later ones that passed. The facilities at the station were limited and we were not allowed to leave the precincts of the station as we were under the ever-watchful eye of Sergeant Wilson. Consequently, as the day progressed, more and more men could be found sprawled out on the platform or in the tiny waiting room. Thankfully, the Major had arranged for food and hot drinks to be brought down from Holne Park as morning turned into afternoon and then into early evening.

When our small train finally arrived, greeted by some ironic cheers, it was a tired and irritable group of men who boarded the train. The journey was slow as the train was frequently diverted into sidings to enable the troop trains to pass.

1916 (Part Two)

Harold and I had not talked in any detail about how or when we were going to slip away to Acaster. When we had found a compartment on the train, Harold had insisted that we sat either side of the door to the corridor. I had quickly fallen asleep, wrapped in my great coat, soon after the train had left Newton Abbot and it took Harold some persistence to rouse me and when I finally awoke, it was to find my friend's hand over my mouth and the other hand indicating that I should be quiet. We were sharing our compartment with two others and they were deeply asleep if their snoring was anything to go by.

"Be quiet, get your kit and follow me."

"What…"

Harold put a finger to his lips as he stood and gently unlatched the compartment's door and slid it open before stepping out into the narrow corridor. The train was in darkness but there was enough of a moon to have some light for us to see by. Still half asleep, I lifted my bag down from the luggage rack and followed Harold who by this time was gently opening the carriage door. Harold dropped his bag onto the ground and after a slight hesitation followed it. When I reached the door, I could see Harold signalling to me to hurry up and jump. Harold then climbed back up and quietly closed the carriage door as a door swinging open when the train finally moved off would look suspicious.

"Where the hell are we?"

"I'm not really sure but it seemed too good an opportunity to miss."

"Oh, for God's sake, Harold! Is this what you call a plan? It would help if we had a plan to get out of this siding."

"Look, when the train stopped, I stuck my head out of the window to have a look around. There's a signal box up ahead. If we head that way, the signal box might tell us where we are and there's got to be a road or path from it that we can take."

There was a faint light visible inside the signal box so we moved quietly so as not to disturb whoever was inside. The signal box turned out to be an anti-climax as neither of us recognised the name of the junction that was displayed on its front wall. We carefully made our way up the narrow road that led off into the darkness and once at the top I came to a halt.

"Now, which way?"

"Left will take us back the way we've just come, so let's go right."

The first signs of dawn brought some mutual backslapping as it confirmed that we were heading in the right direction and a little later a road sign showed that we were ten miles from Salisbury.

"Come on, Harold, I think we should find somewhere to lay up for the day. It will raise a few eyebrows if two soldiers are seen wandering about and we can't risk that."

***

Sis was becoming more and more worried about Ester. There were some days when Ester never left her bed and it was as much as Sis could do to get her to have anything to eat or drink. If it was a working day, then Sis always felt torn between her job at Palfreys and the need to nurse Ester but as she could not afford to lose her job, she made sure on those days that she went back and checked on her during her lunch break. Miss Palfrey knew what was going on and despite her fierce demeanour, she chose to ignore those occasions when Sis returned a few minutes late.

Ester had not been at all happy when she found out that Sis had asked Dr Jackson to call one Sunday morning when she had again stayed in bed. Dr Jackson had spent some time with Ester while Sis had busied herself downstairs. When the doctor made his way downstairs, Sis could see by the look on his face that the news was not good.

"How is she, Doctor?"

The doctor smiled weakly and took Sis's hand.

"She is not at all well. I have given her something to make her more comfortable and she will sleep for a little while now. She is very lucky to have you to care for her."

After Dr Jackson had left, a sudden realisation that Ester was not going to get better left Sis feeling crushed and she sat in the chair staring into the middle distance thinking of Ester and poor Harold while tears rolled down her cheeks. It was the persistent knocking on the front door that caused her to finally stir and she was surprised when she found Lord Acaster at the door while his chauffeured car waited for him out on the High Street. The sight of Sis wiping her eyes brought a look of concern to his Lordship's face.

"It's Miss Brown, isn't it? May I come in?"

Sis was tongue tied and wiped her eyes as she stood aside to let his Lordship in. Lord Acaster seemed to know where he was going as he headed towards the scullery and seemed surprised that Ester wasn't there. He stood there looking disconsolately around as Sis pulled herself together.

"I called in to see whether Mrs Smith was feeling a little better today. How is she?"

"Would your Lordship like to sit down? Can I make you a cup of tea?"

"No, thank you. I don't want to put you to any trouble."

"Mrs Smith is not too well today and she is still in bed. Dr Jackson was here not too long ago and he has given her something to help her sleep. To be honest, I am very worried about her."

Lord Acaster nodded at this news and briefly looked away from Sis as if to regain his own composure.

"I see. Thank you, Miss Brown, and thank you for looking after Mrs Smith. Please, tell her that I called by and if there is anything I can do to help then please get a message to me. I have told Dr Jackson to send any medical bills straight to me so there is no need to worry about them."

Lord Acaster nodded to Sis again and then hurried out of the house and into his car.

***

The old barn did not have the look of a building that was used much with its doors hanging loose and a hole in the roof but nevertheless, we quickly built ourselves a hide at the back close to a smaller door that we quickly found was not locked and therefore gave us an escape route. We each had our water bottles and some bread and cheese which we were confident would keep us going until dusk when we would be able to move on.

"I think we should hide up during the day and only move at night. We can't risk being stopped and questioned."

As far as I was concerned, that was the obvious strategy but I was very uncomfortable with what we were doing and the implications if when we were caught, which was something that I saw as inevitable.

"I'm not happy about all this."

"Jack, go back to the train then – I won't stop you. If that one's gone, then just get on the next one. I'm sure trains are stopping there regularly. Tell them that you got off the train for a crap in order to spare your travelling companions!"

"Ha-ha, very funny! Look, we've always done everything together and this is no different, although I am worried about what will happen. I know you say we are just going to be a couple of days late reporting back but it's now going to take us a couple of days to even get to Acaster. If we had got off the bloody train at Acaster Junction, we would be there by now sitting in front of the range in your mum's scullery."

The two of us lapsed into silence. It was a dark night and in the silence we could hear rustling and the occasional cries of an owl close by.

"You do understand, Harold, don't you that if we are treated as deserters, then they will shoot us."

"It's like I told you, we're not deserting. Deserting is where you run away with no intention of going back. We do intend to go back. We're not shirking. We're not cowards. I am sure they will understand. It will be AWOL at worst – although you might lose your stripe."

The last few words were delivered with a chuckle and a nudge.

"Stop worrying and get some sleep."

***

Father was in his usual position at the bar and the conversation around him had ranged from the war to the state of the Church Hall roof that had developed a couple of leaks over the last few weeks and he dipped in and out of the chatter as the mood took him. He became very attentive when the conversation turned to Ester Smith.

"It's not good news about Ester Smith. Poor cow is really ill by all accounts. Not supposed to have much longer. Has your Sis said anything about it, Bill?"

Father had known that Ester Smith was ill but he had heard nothing to make him think that anything was serious and, of course, not that he would admit it. Sis had not told him what was going on. He had decided following his last visit that he would not embarrass himself by calling on Ester again and he had to admit to being somewhat wary knowing that Lord Acaster was involved.

"Sis did mention something about it but she swore me to secrecy."

Bill tapped his finger on the side of his nose and ordered another beer.

"Well, it's not good news apparently. You must be really proud of your sis moving in and looking after Ester. Apparently, Doc Jackson pops in pretty regularly. I wonder who is paying him for his trouble?"

As the chatter continued around him, Father believed he knew exactly who was paying the doctor and he was equally certain that if the boot had been on the other foot then he would not have done the same. He finished his beer and made his goodbyes and headed off into the night. In a few minutes he found himself standing in the shadows opposite Ester Smith's house. He could see a light on in the upstairs bedroom and then a movement in the front room caught his eye and he could see Sis standing at the window and apparently looking straight at him. He was confident that he was sufficiently hidden but the sense of being caught was undeniably exciting and it was of no matter to him whether it was Ester or Sis who stood there gazing out into the darkness. There was a sense of unfinished business where both were concerned and as his fingers crept down past the waistband of his trousers, he knew that he would be standing vigil on many a night from then on. Well, as he thought to himself, any port in a storm.

***

The walk to Acaster had been, much to our surprise, largely uneventful. There had been a couple of occasions when we had been forced to quickly take cover when we heard voices or the sound of a vehicle approaching. We had replenished our water bottles at every opportunity from the many brooks and streams we passed and scavenged successfully for food. Harold had waved away my concerns that such water might be contaminated and in any event neither of us fancied the risk of lighting a fire to boil it. On one occasion as I took a drink from my water bottle, Harold said with a smile on his face, "Best not to think of that dead sheep lying upstream!"

It was late on a Saturday evening when Sis, who with Ester, was sitting in front of the small fire in the front room, heard a sharp tapping on the back door. Ester had heard it too and, in a whisper, told Sis to take the poker with her as "you couldn't be too careful". Sis eased the bolt back on the door with one hand while holding the poker firmly in the other and opened it a fraction and peered out into the darkness of the backyard. Ester had made her way to the scullery by the time Sis dropped the poker and with a gasp flung the door open and lunged towards whoever was out there. When Sis reappeared, Ester was amazed to see her holding someone's hand and even more surprised to see that the hand belonged to Harold who sheepishly followed her into the room with me trailing behind.

"Hello, Mum."

***

Harold saw the grey pallor of his mother's face but initially put it down to the lighting in the room. However, when he took her in his arms to give her a hug, he could feel the sharp edges of her bones and she felt as fragile as a bird. He stepped back, unable to mask the concern on his face to look at her again and this time more intently.

"There's no need to look at me like that, Harold, because I'm fine. It's nothing. I'm just a bit chesty, that's all. Now what on earth are you doing here? How much leave have you got? Let's go and sit in the front room. It's more comfortable and perhaps if you ask nicely, Sis will put the kettle on?"

I said that I would help Sis but only after insisting that we could only use the front room once its curtains had been drawn and my insistence surprised both Ester and Sis.

"No need for that, Jack. I never pull my curtains. Anyone can see what I'm doing and what I've got. I've nothing to hide."

"Look, Mum, let's just pull the curtains, eh? Sis, could you go and do it for us, please?"

Sis looked questioningly at us and went into the front room and pulled the curtains and then with my help set about sorting out a cup of tea for everyone while Harold helped his mum into her chair and then lit the small fire that had been laid in the grate.

***

Father was surprised and disappointed when he saw Sis drawing the curtains because this was something he had never seen before on the many occasions when he had stood opposite the house. His policeman's instinct, honed over many years, had always made him question sudden changes of behaviour.

He had seen Sis and Ester turn to each other and Sis move towards the back of the house holding something in her hand, which he couldn't see clearly, slowly followed by Ester. He knew something out of the ordinary was going on, although he had no idea what but although it had got him interested, he decided against going straight over given the state of play between him and Ester. He was though interested and as a result he was determined to get to the bottom of this little mystery, although he could have no idea of the chain of events that would follow.

***

Behind those drawn curtains, there was a palpable tension in Ester's front room that night. Harold and I sat uncomfortably on the edge of our chairs looking from face to face. Sis, although happy to see us both, was becoming increasingly aware that this was not a straightforward visit. Whatever was going on had seemed to energise Ester who stared questioningly at us both. A mother's instinct that used to warn her that Harold had been up to something now told her that once again we were up to something.

"You remember that day that I caught you both bunking off school? Well, that's how you look now. So, what's this all about? I hope you've not done something stupid."

"Mum, we're just here for a quick visit. As we were passing, we thought it was a good idea to come and see you."

Ester shook her head and looked at Harold with a mixture of sadness and anger.

"Don't lie to me now – you've never lied to me, Harold, so don't start now. Look at you both. You're covered in muck and dirt, your boots are filthy and I doubt that either of you have seen soap and water for a few days or a razor, come to that. Does the army let you go about looking like a couple of old tramps?"

Harold looked at me and then turned back to Ester.

"I have never been able to lie to you, Mum, or rarely successfully, so the truth is we're not here on leave. We slipped away from the train down near Salisbury and made our way here. It's taken us a couple of days but I'm sure nobody will find us missing yet. By the time they do, we will already be on our way back."

Ester looked at me and said quietly, "What have you got to say about matters? It looks very much to me as if the two of you are deserting."

"We're not deserting, Mrs Smith. Deserting is where you run away with no intention of going back. We do intend to go back. We're not shirking and we're not cowards. I am sure the army will understand. It will be absent without leave at worst."

"I don't care what you call it because the two of you are going back tomorrow. Do you understand?"

Harold got up from his chair and went across to Ester. At first she shrugged away his attempt at a hug but then relented and he crouched down beside her and wrapped her in his arms.

"Mum, don't be cross with Jack. This was all my idea. When I heard from Sis that you were ill, I knew that I couldn't go back to France without seeing you. And, yes, I wanted to see Sis as well. Jack tried to talk to me out of it but I wouldn't listen and so here we are. How could I go back to France not knowing if I would ever see you again?"

Ester looked across at Sis. "Why on earth did you tell him? Look at the trouble you've caused."

"Ester…"

Before Sis could finish speaking, Harold got up and went over to her and put his arm around her shoulders.

"Mum, Sis did the right thing in telling me. I am so proud of the way that she has clearly been caring for you because I can see you are ill and I am sure that you're not the easiest of patients. I have no other family beside you, Mum."

"It cuts both ways, Harold. I have no other family beside you yet it didn't stop you running off to the army to play soldiers with Jack again."

"Mum, there's a war on…"

"And that's why, you young fool, that this is serious. Have you ever asked yourself how I would feel if I was to be told that you have been killed by the Germans? Now multiply that a hundred or a thousand times if I was to hear that, you have been shot by our own side. Now, clean yourselves up and get some sleep because you are going back tomorrow."

I looked across at Sis. "Is there a chance that I could see Mum before we go back?"

I am sure that Ester's head was telling her that knowledge of the two of us being there should not go outside her front room but her heart was touched by my request and so she softened a little.

"You will have to keep your heads down tomorrow and then slip away after dark. I am sure that Sis will do her best to come up with a good reason to get your mother here before you leave. Now let's get to bed. You two will have to bed down in here as best you can."

***

From his vantage point, Father saw a light appear in the upstairs bedroom. He had watched the house enough times to know that Sis always went to bed at the same time as Ester and wondered therefore why there was still a light on in the front room.

***

Nobody slept particularly well that night in Ester's house. Ester lay awake as she went over and over again in her mind the implications of what the two of us, now downstairs, had done. Although pleased to see us, Sis was worried that the punishment for our misdemeanour had the potential to be out of all proportion to an act that as far as she was concerned, had been carried out for the best of intentions. Harold tossed and turned as sleep refused to blank out his concerns about his mother's health. I was just worried about what would happen when we went back tomorrow.

The events of the previous evening and the lack of sleep conspired to ensure that Harold would not go back the next day because Ester was unable to leave her bed. Harold had climbed the stairs to Ester's bedroom with a mug of tea only to find her lying in her bed bathed in sweat. He helped her to sit up and gently placed a shawl around her shoulders. The effort brought on a bout of coughing and Harold was horrified to see that when Ester took her handkerchief away from her mouth that there was blood on it. Ester was horrified that he had seen it and quickly tried to hide it under the bedclothes.

Struggling a little for breath and unable to speak at that moment, Ester patted the bed for Harold to sit down, his face clearly showing the pain that he was feeling. Eventually, Ester's coughing subsided and she was able to take a few sips of her tea.

"Thanks, Son. I am pleased to see you, Harold, although I think you've been stupid. I didn't ever want you to know that I am ill but now you do and you're here. Look at you now, I think the army must suit you. You have filled out and I can see that you have become a man and so I will be honest with you. The doctors have told me that there is nothing they can do for me. I'm dying, Harold…"

Harold squeezed his mother's hand and leant forward and kissed her to stop the words from coming.

"Don't say that, Mum. There must be hope – doctors aren't right all the time."

Ester looked at her son and try as she might she could not stem the tears.

"You go downstairs now and I'll have a little nap and then maybe I will be able to get up later. And, Harold, thank you for my tea. Now, give your old Mum a kiss."

Harold helped her settle back on her pillows and pulled the covers up around her before giving her a kiss and hurrying downstairs.

One look at his face told Sis and I, who had been chatting quietly about our mother and her health, that something was wrong.

"She's not good. I saw her cough up some blood just now. On your way to work, Sis, could you go and fetch Doctor Jackson, please? Mum's just told me that she's dying or that's what she says the doctors have told her. So I want to hear what Doctor Jackson has to say for myself. Please, Sis."

Sis kissed Harold and hurried from the house, putting her coat on as she left and with tears misting her eyes she did not see the figure of our father walking towards her on the other side of the street.

***

Father looked at the hurrying figure of Sis and then at Ester Smith's house and from the look of his daughter he could tell that something had happened. He decided to watch Ester's house for a time and he was interested to see that the front room curtains had not been drawn. He knew that light was important in these houses and that the first thing anybody did when they went downstairs in the morning was to open the curtains, so why hadn't that happened today?

***

Sis was grateful to find Doctor Jackson at home that morning. He had had a busy night delivering a baby, attending the last hours of a dying man and dealing with an ulcerated leg. It was a wonder to others that he could face breakfast after such a night but it was never a problem for him because he believed, as had his father, that breakfast was the most important meal of the day.

Mrs Jackson had shown Sis into the surgery and had then gone to tell her husband that he had a visitor. Sis did not know whether she should sit or stand while she waited but such was her agitation that she had remained standing which had enabled her to move quickly towards the doctor, much to his surprise, before he had barely entered the room.

"I'm sorry to disturb you, Doctor, but I would be very grateful if you could visit Mrs Smith. You see she has stayed in bed this morning and she has coughed up some blood."

Doctor Jackson pulled his watch from his waistcoat pocket and looked at it intently.

"I just have something I really must attend to, Miss Brown, and then I will go and see Mrs Smith. I am sure something can be done to make her more comfortable."

***

Sis had thanked the doctor and it was only as she was closing the front gate that she decided to call at the Police House on her way to Palfreys and as she walked along, she put together an excuse that would cause her mother to visit Ester Smith. With so much going on, Sis never gave a thought as to who would have to open Ester's front door if she wasn't there.

***

It was a habit of Doctor Jackson's to always tell people that he had something that he simply had to attend to first even if on most occasions it was a lie. It was his unnecessary way of making himself seem more important and although he knew he did it, he couldn't stop himself and so as a result he compensated by always hurrying to where he needed to be. Consequently, he arrived at Ester Smith's house before Sis had arrived at work.

Father watched as Doctor Jackson knocked on the front door and with Sis still out, he fully expected to see Ester herself open the door. Therefore, the last person he thought he would see open the door was Harold but there he was quickly ushering the doctor into the hall and closing the door behind him. Father had not seen any other soldiers around the town for a while and the apparent furtiveness of what was happening at Ester Smith's served to fuel his suspicion.

***

Mum had not been at home when Sis had got there. Or rather she had been at home but had chosen not to let Sis see another round of bruises on her face as Father was becoming increasingly careless about where his blows fell. Sis, aware of the time and the need to get to work, had called out to Mum but not receiving a response and still not feeling able after all this time to go up to her parent's bedroom, had left the Police House having decided she would call back later in the day. As it was, she missed the return of Father to the Police House by a couple of minutes.

***

"Can I speak to Lord Acaster, please?"

"I will just see if His Lordship is in. Who shall I say is calling?"

"It's Sergeant Brown from the Police House."

"Thank you, Sergeant Brown. I will not keep you a moment."

Bill was not kept waiting long before he heard the familiar voice of Lord Acaster.

"Sergeant Brown. This is a pleasant surprise – how may I help you?"

"I am sorry to trouble your Lordship but we have received news that there has been an increase in break-ins at other estates in the county. I would ask your Lordship to be extra vigilant and let me know at once if you see or hear anything suspicious."

"Thank you, sergeant, for your concern which is much appreciated. Is there anything else that I can do for you?"

"No, thank you, your Lordship." Father paused for a second and then continued,

"Oh, there is one small thing. Do you know when any of our lads will be getting some leave?"

"I am very much afraid that leave is out of the question for the time being with everything that is going on over in France. Let's hope this war can be over soon."

"Thank you, your Lordship."

Bill sat slowly back in his chair and began to put the pieces of this particular jigsaw together. If the men of the Acaster Company were not on leave, then what was Harold Smith doing opening his mother's front door to Doctor Jackson? And if Harold was there, then it was a good bet that I wouldn't be far away either. He took a file from his desk drawer and looked through its list of contact details and having found the one he wanted he lifted his telephone once more and asked the exchange to connect him.

"Is that the Adjutant's office?"

"Yes. This is Captain Baldwin speaking. Who am I speaking to and how can I help you?"

"This is Sergeant Brown speaking from Acaster Police House. I believe I have discovered a deserter and there may be another one, here in Acaster as well. I would like some advice as to how to proceed."

"Thank you, Sergeant Brown. Do you have any details for this deserter or deserters?"

"Yes. I believe the man concerned is a Private Harold Smith of the Acaster Company, Wessex Rifles and if I am right, then the other man will be Corporal Jack Brown."

"We don't have any notification that these two men are absent from their regiment, so I wonder if there is an innocent explanation? Could they be on leave?"

"No. I have spoken to Lord Acaster himself and he assures me that no man from the Acaster Company would be home on leave at this time."

"Right, I would be grateful if you could keep them under observation. By the way where are they?"

"I believe they are in Private Smith's mother's house. This is the address."

Father gave Ester's address to the captain and repeated his request for guidance as to how to proceed.

"I will round up some of my redcaps and a lorry and we should be with you in no more than two hours. Can you keep this house under observation until we get there?"

At that moment, Constable Tibbins walked in and was about to make himself scarce as Father was on the telephone but he waved him to a chair.

"Yes, I think my constable and I can do that. What do we do if they try to leave the house before you get here?"

"You will have to do what you can to stop them. Now I must get on. I will be with you soon, sergeant."

Father put the telephone down and turned his chair around so that he was facing Constable Tibbins.

"We've got a bit of a situation, Harry. I need you to come with me to Ester Smith's house. I have reason to believe that her son, Harold, is there when he has no right to be. The army are coming to arrest him. Our job is to keep the house under surveillance and ensure that young Harold doesn't escape."

"Are you saying, sergeant, that he is a deserter? There is probably an innocent explanation. Why don't we just knock on the door and ask him?"

"I hope there is an innocent explanation but it's out of our hands I'm afraid, lad. This is a matter for the army.

"Now when we get to the Smith's, I want you to get yourself around the back where you can keep an eye on the rear of the house and I'll watch the front. Don't let anyone in the house see you. If Harold tries to leave the property, then give me a blast on your whistle and arrest him. I will be with you quicker than you can click your fingers."

"But what about your sis?"

"What about my sis? This has nothing to do with her? And it certainly has nothing to do with you!"

"But she and Harold…"

"There is no she and Harold. We have to do our duty whoever it might be. You have to learn that if you are going to stay in the police and be anything more than a constable. Now, come on."

**

Mum had heard the front door close and had moved quietly to the bedroom window in time to see Sis hurrying away. She would have loved to have sat down with Sis for a few minutes over a cup of tea and catch up with all her news but she was only too aware of the bruising to her cheek and her cut lip.

As she stood there watching the figure of Sis receding down the High Street, she became aware of her husband coming from the other direction. He looked red-faced and agitated but also determined and Mum stepped quickly away from the curtains in case he should see her.

***

"Harold. I must say I am surprised to see you here and you too, Jack."

I was standing with my back to the window with its curtains still closed while Harold stood in front of the fireplace and its fire that was badly in need of attention.

"Please, Doctor Jackson, sit down. Thank you for coming so quickly. How is Mum? She was telling me some nonsense about her dying."

Harold tried to make that last sentence sound like a joke but the look in his eyes and his obvious state of stress told a different story.

"I have given your mother something to help her sleep. Harold, I am afraid your mother was telling you the truth. She has an inoperable mass in one or perhaps both of her lungs and there is nothing we can do other than to keep her comfortable. I know your next question will be about how long she has left but sadly, I cannot give you an answer other than to say that I don't think it will be long. I'm very sorry. I will of course call back later."

Harold had been hoping that his mother had been confused or was being dramatic but hearing what the doctor had to say hit him hard and he fell rather than lowered himself into a chair. Tears began to roll down Harold's cheeks as he lowered his head into his hands. It was left to me to thank the doctor who said he would see himself out and that I should look after my friend.

I, somewhat awkwardly, went to my friend unsure of how to comfort Harold, who sat there with his head in his hands and his body wracked with sobs and so I made do with patting his shoulder. When his initial grief had subsided Harold looked up at me and shook his head.

"That's it. I am not leaving her now. How can I go off to the front and leave her? If she is going to die, then I am going to be there holding her hand and telling her that I love her."

I started to speak but Harold wasn't prepared to listen.

"I am not interested. I know what you think but it's my mother. Look, Jack, I don't want you to suffer because of me, so go. You will probably lose your stripes but it won't take you long to get them back. I'm happy to take my chances. Now I'm going up to sit with Mum."

***

The curtains were still drawn at Ester Smith's house as Father settled into a vantage point that gave him an unobstructed view of the front door from where Doctor Jackson emerged. He smiled at the prospect of having a ringside seat as Harold and possibly me, were arrested by the army and taken away. He told himself that he was only doing his duty although he recognised that on this occasion his duty also coincided with his personal feelings.

The back of Ester Smith's house looked out on the town's allotments and at this time of the year, there was nobody working on their patch of land which made it easy for Constable Tibbins to find a deserted shed that he could use as his vantage point and where he could settle down and wait without drawing attention to himself.

***

Father heard the lorry before he saw it pulling up just short of the start of the High Street in the direction of Acaster Junction. He saw six redcaps and an officer, who he took to be Captain Baldwin, climb out and make their way towards Ester's house. Captain Baldwin, short, middle-aged and with a thick moustache, left enough time for the two men that he had sent around the back of the house to get into position before he raised his officer's cane and rapped on the door.

I was sitting on my own in the front room and deep in thought when I heard the rapping on the front door. As far as I was concerned, it could only be my mother or Doctor Jackson and either would be welcome.

I had only opened the door a couple of inches when I found myself, painfully, flung back against the wall as the door was pushed violently open. It all happened so quickly and I found that my right side was trapped between the door and the wall while a cane was placed across my throat. The cane belonged to an army officer who spoke quietly but firmly to me.

"I'm Captain Baldwin. Those two stripes on your arm mean that you are definitely not Private Harold Smith, so who are you?"

My mind was still trying to deal with what had happened but I was beginning to realise that my worst fear about our situation had just become a reality.

"Corporal Brown, sir!"

Captain Baldwin's face was inches from mine when he snarled, the spittle hitting my face. "Well, Brown, where is your friend Private Smith? I know he is here somewhere."

***

Harold was sitting on his mother's bed and stroking her hand while he spoke gently to her. He had heard someone at the front door and then some voices but he was too wrapped up in what he was doing to worry about whoever might be downstairs. He was therefore totally unprepared when the bedroom door banged open and two redcaps burst into the room and grabbed him by the arms.

Ester, despite her weakness, screamed at the two intruders and tried to hang onto Harold's hand but he was soon manhandled out the door and down the stairs where he was met by an officer he soon came to know as Captain Baldwin and the sight of me with my own arms held behind my back by two further redcaps.

"Right, you must be Private Smith. I am Captain Baldwin of the Adjutant's Office at Aldershot and I am arresting you both on suspicion of desertion and you will both come with me now. Do you understand?"

By the time we were taken out through the front door with each arm held tightly by a redcap, the lorry had moved and was parked outside the house facing the way that it had come. We were unceremoniously bundled into the back of the lorry with our escorts while Captain Baldwin climbed into its cab next to the driver. The episode had lasted just a matter of minutes but had felt like an eternity.

***

Ester had quickly recovered from her shock and had somehow found the energy to leave her bed to look out of her bedroom window in time to see Harold and I pushed into the back of the lorry.

Ester stood there with tears streaming down her face and the palms of her hands pressed against the window as the lorry moved away but not before she had seen Father emerge from the alleyway opposite. She also saw the army officer touch the brim of his hat with his cane before he had climbed up into the lorry, in acknowledgement of Father, who then stood and watched as it had driven off in the direction of Acaster Junction. It was as he turned that she saw the smile on his face which beamed when he looked up and saw her watching him. He brought his finger up to the brim of his helmet in a mock salute and turned and began to walk in the direction of the Police House and he was quickly joined by Constable Tibbins who had left his hiding place in the allotments.

Without any hope of being heard, Ester shouted after them, "You bastard! How could you? How could you do that to them, to your wife and daughter and to me? How?"

***

Father and Constable Tibbins never spoke as they walked back to the Police House where they quickly entered the office.

"Close that door, Harry lad, and sit down."

Harry Tibbins was not sure that he really believed what had just happened. If anyone had told him that a father could do that to his own son knowing the possible outcome, he would have told them to get lost. He looked across at Father and saw him looking back as if he was reading his mind.

"Harry, police work can be hard but the law is the law. It doesn't pay to dwell on these things. Now, listen to me and listen well, you must never speak of what's happened today to anyone because you might well be called as a witness. Do you understand?"

"I had no idea that my son, Jack, would be there and even if I had, it would have made no difference. How could I deal with people in Acaster if they thought for one minute that I had made an exception because it was my son? I would have lost their respect. Now take the rest of the day off, forget all about it and I will see you tomorrow."

***

Constable Harry Tibbins went to his room and sat deep in thought on his bed and he had much to think about but eventually, with his decision made, he set about packing his few things into his suitcase. He left the house without either Mum or Father realising that he was gone but before he left, he had written a letter, which he had placed on his pillow, addressed to Mum to apologise for leaving so abruptly and to explain what had happened. Harry Tibbins as he then was, because he wanted nothing more to do with the police, headed straight to the station and took a train to London. He left the station at Waterloo and entered the first recruiting office he came to. A little more than an hour later he was a soldier and at his own request was told to go straight to the Woolwich Barracks.

***

Ester had not left her house for a while but she had somehow found the strength to get dressed and get down the stairs as she was determined to confront Father if it was the last thing that she ever did on this earth. The few people that she passed on the way to the Police House barely recognised the frail bundle of skin and bones with her unkempt hair and she made no attempt to acknowledge their greetings as all her concentration was focused on putting one foot in front of the other.

She entered the Police House just as someone left Father's office and, without any apology to the one person waiting to see Father, she went in and closed the door firmly behind her.

If Father was surprised to see her, then it didn't show as he got up from his chair and came towards Ester with concern for her written across his face given that her hair was wild and un-brushed and her clothes were not those she ordinarily would have been prepared to be seen out in.

"Ester…"

"Get away from me, you bastard! And it's Mrs Smith to you."

"I must ask you to keep your voice down."

Ester was determined to remain standing despite the effort it was clearly taking.

"Why? Don't you want people to know what you have done?"

"Ester…Mrs Smith, please, sit down. I have no idea what you are talking about."

It's hard to know what surprised Father more, the fact that she hit him or the force of the blow but either way he was shocked and sat back down in his chair.

"Does Alice know that you've been sniffing around me? Does she know that you threatened me because I wouldn't let you touch me? That's what this is about isn't it? You think this is your revenge and it will teach me some sort of lesson.

"What have those two boys ever done to you to deserve a firing squad, eh? Jack is a good lad but let me see, he stood up to you, didn't he? What has Harold done? Oh, yes. He fell in love with your daughter and you're jealous, aren't you? I can put two and two together, so I also know that you slap Alice about. You are an evil bastard, Bill Brown. I know that I am dying but that is made more bearable by the thought that where I'm going, there is no chance of bumping into you at some point in the future because when you go, it will be Hell for you."

The effort proved too much for Ester and she had to sit down as her body was wracked by a bout of coughing the force of which Father for one had never seen the like of before. Eventually, it passed and Ester, with a speck of blood in the corner of her mouth, got up from the chair and faced him. They looked at each other for a moment before Ester spat in his face and as the thick globule of spittle and blood trickled down his cheek, she turned to go but not before saying, as she held the door handle. "I will make sure that Lord Acaster knows what an evil bastard this town has for its police sergeant. I am sure he knows the chief constable and then you will be out on your ear. You're not the only person who can think about revenge."

As Ester left the office, she found Mum in the hallway looking horrified as she stood there with her handkerchief held as usual close to her mouth.

"Ester, what are you doing here? What's all the shouting?"

Ester pointed at the office door. "Go and ask that bastard, your husband, in there what he's been up to. Ask him what he's done. Ask him to tell you about the nights he knocked on my door looking for a shag. I feel sorry for you, Alice, living with a man like him. Don't deny it. I might be dying but there's nothing wrong with my eyes because I can see those bruises as well as anyone can."

The effort of confronting Father had taken its toll on Ester and she was not able to manage the walk home. She staggered along as best she could, her halting progress drawing attention but collapsed a little way from her front gate. Fortunately, her neighbours saw her fall and had to carry her inside and put her to bed, having summoned Doctor Jackson. Ester was never able to tell Sis or Lord Acaster what had happened as she was almost certainly dead before Jack and Harold found themselves in the guard room at Aldershot. Sadly, she was dead before Sis returned from work.

***

The man waiting to see Father had been thoroughly entertained by the excitement and shouting and as Ester left, he stood up and made his way to the office door only to be beaten to it by Mum, who apologised and went in closing the door behind her.

"Why is Ester so upset? What have you done? I don't think I've ever seen Ester like that."

Father was half expecting, when the door opened, that it would be Ester coming back to add an afterthought and he was determined to appear nonchalant as he took out his handkerchief to wipe her spit off of his face. He was not expecting it to be Mum who came into the office.

"Sit down, Alice. You really shouldn't be down here. I have no idea why Ester Smith is so upset. She was ranting like a mad woman."

"Something must have got her into that state. She looked so poorly. And what did she mean about you sniffing around her?"

Father finished wiping his face and returned to his chair which he turned to face Mum.

"I had heard that she was quite ill and I just think the illness has affected her mind. I couldn't make head nor tail of anything she was saying and such hatred too – she even spat in my face. If it had been anyone else, then I would have had no choice but to lock her up for her own safety and that of others. And Doctor Jackson would have had to arrange to have her taken away.

"Seeing her like that, I can't imagine how Sis has coped. Now don't worry and leave things to me. I'll call on Ester later and check that she is all right. How about sorting out some tea? Harry's around somewhere."

***

Tea somehow got lost in the events that followed that early evening. Sis was understandably very upset when she returned to the Police House later that day bearing the sad news that Ester Smith had passed away and that Harold and Jack had been taken away by the army.

126

Mum had been busy at the range preparing some tea while Father sat in his favourite chair reading his paper and smoking his pipe and while Mum had been quick to go to her daughter and give her a hug, Father's face had gone ashen and he had remained silent.

"What are you talking about? Are you telling me that Jack and Harold have been here in Acaster? How? Why? Why have they been taken away?"

Mum looked across at Father, who said nothing but through her gulps and sobs, Sis told them everything that she knew and that Harold and I had not been deserting but just taking a detour on their way back to the Front so that Harold could see his mother.

"It was such a shock when I went back to Ester's after work. When I left for work this morning, I had no idea that anything like this would happen. The neighbours apparently found her collapsed in the street which I cannot understand because she hadn't been out of the house for ages. And Harold and Jack weren't there because someone said some soldiers had been to the house and…So Ester died alone with nobody she loved around her. She was just lying in her bed and not long after I got there, the undertakers arrived. It was so sad. I just don't know what has been going on. I am so scared now about what might happen to Jack and Harold."

Mum could make no sense of what Sis was telling them and to distract herself, she went back to sorting out the assorted pans that were boiling and bubbling on the range. When the tea was ready, Mum set the plates on the table.

While Mum had gone upstairs to fetch Harry, who had not responded when she had shouted up the stairs, Sis and Father sat opposite each other at the table but neither spoke as both were deep in thought and each for different reasons. Eventually, Sis looked at Father and asked, "Do you know what's going on? Someone said…" Father never looked up from examining his nails as he cut her off with a curt.

"No."

Neither Father nor Sis had been aware that Mum had entered the room where she heard what had been said and they were startled when they heard her say quietly but forcefully, "I know."

Both looked around to see an ashen-faced Mum standing in the doorway holding a small sheet of paper. Mum's voice cracked with pain and anger as she pointed at Father.

"I know, Bill. I know what you did and why Ester was so upset when she was here earlier."

Sis looked from one to the other of her parents. "Mum?"

"Are you going to tell her or shall I?"

Father knew he was cornered but he had no idea how and his natural instinct had always been to go on the front foot in such situations as this had always worked in the past and he hoped would serve him well again. Sis was struggling to recognise the woman standing in the doorway as Mum, showing a force of personality that she had never before given signs of possessing. Father tried to laugh off whatever was going on.

"Alice, have you been at the sherry? Sis, pass me the sherry bottle, will you? Let's see how much she's had. I have no idea what you are talking about. Now, behave yourself."

"Or what, Bill? Will you hit me again but this time in front of Sis? You see Harry Tibbins couldn't take anymore of you. He's gone. Left his uniform on the bed and taken his things. He's gone off to join up. And he's left a letter. Let me read it to you."

Father realised the game was up and he was desperate that Sis should not hear what he suspected Harry's letter contained.

"Sis, go to your room, now!"

"Stay where you are, Sis. You should hear this as well."

Father rose from his chair and started to come towards Mum as if intent on snatching the letter from her hand. On this occasion, however, even he could see a different look in her eyes and instead he said that he was having no part of this nonsense and was going to the Stag. It was the look blazing from her eyes that stopped him from even doing that because he could see that she was not to be cowed anymore. He returned to his chair and sat there with a look that said he was resigned as to what was to follow and yet his mind was already starting to weigh up what excuse he could make that would reduce the impact of what he feared was coming.

"Harry has such neat handwriting, don't you think, Bill?"

I am sorry to have left without saying goodbye but I am afraid that I cannot take anymore. What happened this morning at Mrs Smith's house has made me feel both shocked and ashamed for the part that I played in it.

If being a policeman means turning in members of your own family knowing that they may pay with their lives, then I want no part of it. Seeing Jack and Harold taken away by the redcaps for desertion, hearing Ester Smith's shouts and cries and then being told to deny any involvement by Sergeant Brown has been too much for me. To think that I might have played a part, albeit a small one, in getting the two of them shot is going to stay with me for the rest of my life.

I'll take my chances as a soldier which just now I see as being more honourable than being a policeman. I hope this matter gets sorted out quickly and that someone somewhere will see sense and let them go back to the Acaster Company.

Yours
Harry Tibbins

"Well?"

Sis was now standing, holding on to the table for support as she looked at Father.

"Is it true? Is that what you did? Harold only came back for a couple of days to see his mother because I told him that she was very ill."

Father looked defiantly at his wife and daughter.

"Yes. Look, you must understand that I had no alternative. I am a police officer and I had to do my duty. How could I uphold the law here if I'd turned a blind eye? People would have laughed at me. I knew Harold was there but I had no idea that Jack was there as well."

For Sis it was as if the scales had fallen from her eyes and she was seeing Father for the first time. Here was the man she had looked up to as her father who she could now see for what he was – spiteful and uncaring – that she had lived up to that moment as only a daughter can love a father.

"How could you do that?"

"Look, I told you enough times – soldiers on active service should not get letters from home. It's not good for them. It distracts them and it never ends well..."

This was too much for Mum who could see the effect his words were having on Sis.

"Don't you dare make Sis feel guilty for what you've done here today. I am so angry with you but I'm even angrier with myself. You are a bully who I should, for the children's sake, have stood up to years ago. God knows why but you have never liked Jack. He is your son who has grown into a fine young man. You should have felt proud of him and yet you have always been cruel and resentful towards him. What has Harold ever done to you except fall in love with your daughter? And it would appear that what Ester said earlier was right and as she rejected you, she had to be punished too and now she is dead, thanks to you. I've been a fool for so many years."

Mum's words seemed to deflate Father in front of their eyes and while he started to sob, he made no attempt to protect himself when Mum launched an attack on him with her fists.

"What else could I do? I did it for you. I did it for us. I could have been dismissed from the police. We would have lost this house and my pension. We would have been the laughingstock of the town. If you had acted as a proper wife, then I would never have looked at Ester Smith. You understand, don't you, Sis?"

Sis made no attempt to hide her hatred. Mum had finished her assault and Father had moved towards Sis as if for comfort only to be met by a stinging slap across his face that made his ears ring and his nose bleed.

"Don't you dare come near me. I hate you. I'm sorry, Mum, but I can't live here anymore. I am going to live with Aunt Bessie in London. She's always said I can go there if I wanted. I'll get the Palfreys to send my wages on. I'll write to you, Mum, whenever I can."

With a last contemptuous look at Father, Sis picked up the bag that she had brought from Ester Smith's together with her hat and coat and left the Police House and Acaster, although none of them could know that she would never return.

As soon as the front door had closed behind Sis, Father looked pleadingly at Mum. "Please Alice. Don't you leave me as well."

"Oh, I'm not going to leave you. You may not think it but my leaving you would be too easy for you, so I'm going to stay and every time you see me, you will be reminded of today. And you had better hope that nothing happens to Jack and Harold because if it does or you ever hit me again, then you will have to sleep with one eye open because I will kill you but only after I have told Lord Acaster the whole story and given him Harry's letter."

The food on the range had long since passed the point where anything could be salvaged, much like their marriage, and so their tea was never eaten that night.

***

Over the subsequent days, Father's cunning started to return and he was damned if he was going to be bested by anyone, let alone his wife. He was confident that despite everything Sis would never speak out about what had happened and by way of preparation, he planted the seed that she, silly girl, had run off with Harry Tibbins. People were amazed and often said, "What your, Sis?" And then shrugged as if nothing could surprise them anymore. Father wasn't worried about Harry Tibbins turning up as he was prepared to gamble that the war would take care of him. Father therefore concentrated on the twin problems of Harry's letter and Mum. The more he thought about it, the more he believed that given time he would be able to find the letter.

He also came to the conclusion that he had lost all feelings for Mum years ago and the more he thought about it, the angrier he became because that woman had consumed his life. Whatever he did, Father had to be confident of carrying it off in such a way that he emerged unscathed.

***

One evening a few days later, Father emerged from my old room where he was now sleeping just as Mum reached the top of the stairs. Mum was a creature of habit and always went to bed at the same time each evening and so this was not an accidental meeting as he had been sitting on his bed waiting for her and as soon as he had heard her climbing the stairs, he quickly blocked her way. Mum, standing on the top step, could not bring herself to look at Father's face and so she did not see the smile playing around his lips.

"How are you, Alice?"

"Please, let me get by Bill. I want to go to bed. I'm very tired."

Father didn't move as he looked down into her tired and troubled eyes.

"You look pasty-faced. Have you been out recently, Alice?"

Mum shook her head. "You know I haven't, Bill. How could I look like this?"

"So, people still think you are poorly then."

And then Father's voice hardened. "You think you have me where you want me, don't you, Alice? Well, I am afraid you don't. You never have."

They were the last words that Mum ever heard as Dad gave her a gentle push in the chest that was enough to send her tumbling down the steep flight of stairs. Mum's body was contorted as it lay motionless at the foot of the stairs and he could tell by the unnatural angle of her head that she was dead.

Father made no attempt to go to her and with one last look he returned to my room and calmly dressed in his uniform before descending the stairs and stepping over Mum's body, taking care not to step in the growing pool of blood where her head had struck a corner on the way down. With a smile of satisfaction, Father left the house via the back door and made his way up the garden and out of the back gate onto a little used and therefore slightly overgrown path that took him eventually up to the rear of the Church Hall, a route that he had scouted earlier and when he emerged onto the High Street he knew he was safe in the knowledge that his progress would not have been witnessed. He made sure that he patrolled up towards the Stag and was more than happy to engage a couple of locals in a bit of banter.

After a while he returned home and of course 'discovered' Mum's body and with a sob in his voice called Doctor Jackson who found him sitting on the stairs apparently bereft and the doctor confirmed that Mum was dead.

"She has some old bruises on her face, Bill. What caused those do you think?"

"Alice was not a strong woman. She had bouts of depression that had slowly got worse. I tried to get her to come and see you but she wouldn't – ashamed I think because she had started to drink. She was a clumsy woman at the best of times, always falling over or bumping into things. My poor darling."

As far as Doctor Jackson was concerned, there were no suspicious circumstances although it was not possible to determine whether Mum had tripped or thrown herself down the stairs and the undertakers were called to take her away. There was no inquest due to the prevailing circumstances of the time and so Mum and Mrs Smith were coincidentally buried on the same day a week later in the churchyard and Father attended both and received the commiserations of those present who, of course, had no reason to suspect him of being directly responsible for one and indirectly for the other death.

And of course, at that time I didn't know either.

***

1917

Dear Sis.

I am sure that London must seem like a different world after Acaster. We are still in Aldershot waiting to find out whether we are to be sent back to France...

Aldershot was so close to home; however, it might as well have been a thousand miles away. Harold and I were kept in separate cells in the guardhouse which were cold, damp and bleak. The army went to great lengths to keep us apart and for much of the time, there was nothing else to do but sit on my bunk and hear the persistent drip of water from somewhere close by. If we were lucky, we were allowed 30 minutes of exercise a day in a small, enclosed compound under the watchful, if bored, gaze of a guard. 30 minutes of walking in a small circle but at least it was enough to feel the air on our faces. We were treated as criminals because as far as the army was concerned that was exactly what we were. As a consequence, because there was nothing to be gained from doing otherwise, I decided early on to keep my head down and to do everything I was told so as not to make matters worse. Harold though kept protesting that we weren't deserters, we were always going to return to the Front and that this was all his fault but he eventually stopped bothering thank God.

***

Aunt Bessie was Mum's sister and we had seen little or nothing of her as we grew up because as I later found out she hated Father, although she had always sent us cards and presents at Christmas and on our birthdays. It was her cards with their consistent invitation to visit her that had led Sis to leave home and get on a train from Acaster Junction to London with Aunt Bessie's address written out on a small piece of paper.

Sis was very tired by the time she stood on an almost unnaturally clean front step straining her ears to detect a movement on the other side of the front door. Eventually, to her relief, the door opened and there stood Aunt Bessie who was a few years older than Mum. Much to her dismay, Sis found herself standing in front of a very severe looking woman dressed in black with her grey hair pulled back into a tight bun, and small, round glasses perched on her nose and a look that threatened to freeze the blood of anyone in the vicinity.

"Yes?"

"Aunt Bessie? It's me, Sis. I've come to visit you."

Aunt Bessie looked from Sis to the bag at her side and back again. "That bag tells me that this is more than a visit. Come inside, girl, and tell me why you look so dreadfully upset."

Aunt Bessie led Sis through to the back of the house and into a small sitting room where she told Sis to make herself comfortable while she fetched some tea. Sis settled into one of two armchairs in front of the fireplace and looked around the room which was more richly furnished than anything she had seen in Acaster. A photograph of a handsome man in military uniform was prominently displayed on a side table and Sis got up in order to examine it more closely, which she was doing when Aunt Bessie returned.

"I see you have met Stephen. Handsome devil, isn't he?"

Sis looked questioningly at her aunt who ushered her back to her chair while she placed a large tray on a table nearby. When Sis had been provided with a cup of tea and a slice of cake, Aunt Bessie settled herself in the other armchair.

"I can see that this part of the family was rarely talked about in your house. Your father was and is a difficult man, who for some reason, took against me right from the beginning and consequently never made me feel particularly welcome. I have always put it down to his fear of strong women who he could not control as he has never shared my views on a range of matters. Stephen was my husband, sadly we never had children and he was the love of my life. He was a successful actor and theatre director and made a lot of money but he was in search of one last adventure which sadly this damned war provided for him. He couldn't wait to join up and would not listen to me. Infuriatingly, he was just another intelligent man convinced that it would all be over by Christmas and he simply could not be expected to miss it. He had played the part of a soldier on stage many times and could not be persuaded that the reality would be so different.

"I remember standing by this fireplace as he kissed me and told me not to worry before rushing out of the house. It was September 1914 and I like to think of him as one of the first who gave his life in defence of those poor Belgians."

Aunt Bessie picked up her cup and took a satisfying sip whilst looking at Sis over its rim. Sis looked back at her aunt with a look of great concern and dismay on her face. "What happened?"

"Stephen rushed out of that front door that you have just come through and promptly collapsed and died of a heart attack on the pavement outside."

"What? But…the photograph?"

"I know…but I like to think that he died a happy man. He saw himself as a soldier and a fighter and therefore it seems appropriate to have that photograph on display which was taken for one of the many West End productions he was in. It perfectly captures how he saw himself at the end.

"Now, enough of Stephen and tell me about your troubles."

Aunt Bessie listened while Sis gave her an edited version of events in Acaster.

"With Harold and Jack taken away, I couldn't face staying in Acaster and so I remembered your frequent invitations to come and stay with you and hope they were truly meant."

"I am pleased that you have come to me as I could do with some company and you could do with some help it seems."

From that moment Aunt Bessie decided to make it her business to turn Sis from the nervous, naïve girl who had appeared at her front door into a confident young woman, whilst at the same time helping her deal with the issue of Jack and Harold.

***

I was sitting on my bed looking up at the few inches of sky that I could see through the small, barred window high up on the cell wall when I heard the sound of footsteps approaching. I heard the key turning in the lock of my cell door and a barked "Tenshun! Officer in the room" as it swung open.

The guard stepped back to allow a lanky, young lieutenant to enter my cell and then he took up position with his back against the wall opposite my cell door which had been left open. The lieutenant motioned for me to sit down and then looked around forlornly for somewhere for him to sit before reluctantly lowering himself on to the opposite end of my bed.

"I am Lieutenant Jones and I have been appointed to defend you. There has been an initial hearing of this matter to determine jurisdiction and I am afraid it has been decided that you should be taken to France under guard to face a Field General Courts Martial. You must be in no doubt that if found guilty of the charge of desertion that you are likely to face the death penalty.

"It would be in your interests to ensure that you do not admit to having deserted because that would be the end of the matter and no mitigating circumstances…"

"Excuse me, sir, what are 'mitigating circumstances'?"

"They are excuses, reasons for your action that the court could take into account in determining sentence."

I remember looking across at this young officer, who was not much older than me and feeling sorry for him. He looked a real fish out of water sitting uncomfortably on the edge of the bed in that cell. Clearly this is not what he had joined the army for.

"Sir, are you a lawyer?"

To be fair to him, Lieutenant Jones was honest enough to admit that he was not legally trained and he had never acted as a defence lawyer before.

"When are we to be taken to France?"

"Just as soon as the paperwork is complete, you will be taken to Etaples. I am not sure what will happen after that. We won't meet again so I will wish you all the best."

"Sir, do you believe that deserters should be shot?"

"I have enjoyed absolute certainty since taking up my commission that a man who falls asleep at his post throws his weapon away or absents himself from the battlefield lets down his comrades and endangers their lives and must be punished as a deterrent to others. I must admit though that your case has given me pause for thought.

"You were not at the Front, you had not fallen asleep at your post or thrown away your weapons but you had absented yourself from your regiment for reasons that I can understand. And, if you are to be believed, you had every intention of returning to your regiment. It is for that reason and that reason alone that I wish you all the best."

"Thank you, sir."

With that Lieutenant Jones picked up his file and, with me standing to attention following the guard's barked command, left my cell at which point the guard slammed my cell door shut and locked it. I then listened to their footsteps as they walked back down the corridor.

***

Aunt Bessie's education of Sis started with a Sunday morning trip to Hyde Park, where they headed towards Speakers' Corner. Through a slight mist, they saw people out riding, families making their way along the paths and above the trees a number of tethered barrage balloons.

Speakers' Corner was a combination of variety show and outdoor debating chamber and the weather on that Sunday morning had done nothing to dampen the enthusiasm of those attending for this weekly event. Situated where the park and Oxford Street converged, the audience was made up of all shades of society. Some came to indulge their love of heckling, some came to enjoy the farce and others came to listen and to think about what the speakers were saying, comparing it to the official news spread by the newspapers and considering what any variation between them might signify.

As always there was a strong contingent of religious speakers and Aunt Bessie and Sis stopped to listen to the entertaining exchanges.

"God is your support…"

The rather tall and austere figure dressed in black with a musical, Welsh accent was halted mid-speech by some hecklers in the crowd around him and by one in particular, who seemed blessed with a particularly loud voice. This man had a face that was heavily scarred down one side and he stood supported under his right arm by a crutch that compensated for his missing leg.

"Where was your God when we went over the top on the Somme? Where was he when I was lying in a crater with my leg blown off? There is no God and even if there is, he's not interested in the likes of us. So God will support me eh? Well let's see!"

With that the man threw aside his crutch and promptly toppled over to a mix of groans, shouts and laughter. "No, he's not here then," he shouted as someone passed him his crutch and helped him up.

The man received loud support from many in the crowd while any who harboured an opposite view felt inhibited in the presence of a number of ex-servicemen with their disabilities.

As they moved on, Aunt Bessie asked Sis if she had ever thought about God and war. When Sis said "no". Aunt Bessie said that over the coming days she should think about the illogicality of all sides in a war believing that God was on their side.

They next stopped to listen to a speaker from the Socialist Party, who was eloquently making the point that successive governments had done nothing to prepare the country for a war of this length.

"Citizens, the government through its iniquitous Defence of the Realm Act has given itself unlimited powers to control and regulate your lives – and yet you do nothing! Unless you act now, it will be too late!

"They have made strikes illegal and have put our taxes up by twenty percent whilst lowering our wages! You gallantly agreed to voluntarily see milk, tea and meat rationed – how long before that is made compulsory?

"You saw bread rationing introduced last month, so not only do you struggle to eat a crust, but you will also soon be deprived of the means of making a cup of tea to go with it! Last month this government introduced its Food Rationing Order – you can be criminalised for putting your food aside for a later date! When will this government accept that we are tired of this war and tired of them?"

It was a popular argument to make and there were few if any dissenters. Sis moved on and listened as Aunt Bessie pointed out that within 200 yards of where they were standing were houses with occupants, who if they had heard of food rationing would be horrified to think that it applied to them.

They next joined a crowd listening to a well-dressed man who was delivering, what was obviously popular, anti-German rhetoric.

"How can any German in our midst be trusted? From top to bottom they need to be removed from their positions, whatever and wherever that may be and sent packing. We must boycott all German businesses…"

A man somewhere in the middle of the crowd was heard to shout out, "What about the King? He's German. How can we win this war with a German in the Palace?"

Someone else shouted out about the Tsar and his German wife coming to Britain making it clear that they were not welcome. Sis had never thought about it before but standing there she now found herself agreeing with the very strong, anti-German sentiment. She did, however, see herself as one of those who supported the Royal Family but like many of the others, there she felt, even if she had been so inclined, too intimidated to speak up.

Sis was horrified, therefore, when Aunt Bessie applauded a man who bellowed, "Let's do what the Russians have done and get rid of them. Here's to a Red flag flying over Buckingham Palace! Here's to the spirit of Petrograd taking hold in the streets of London!"

They moved on and forced their way to the front of a small crowd that was gathered in front of a young woman with a yellow complexion that had been caused, Aunt Bessie explained, by exposure to TNT that identified her as a munitions worker. The yellow complexion led to such women being commonly referred to as 'canaries'.

The young woman was holding forth on the unfairness of women not having the vote. Standing silently and somewhat nervously, behind her was a small group of women who felt it was their duty to support her including one or two other factory workers, a nurse, three women wearing the suffragettes' sash and a smattering of others drawn from all parts of London life.

"Women are good enough to work in factories producing shells for our gallant troops – work that is both difficult and dangerous – and yet we cannot vote! Can you have forgotten the Silver town explosion already – 73 killed and over 400 injured – and all mostly women and yet we cannot vote?

"Why are you men so scared of us women? I'll tell you why because you are worried about what we women will want in the future – you worry about what will happen to your wages once this war is won. Your trade unions worry about maintaining their rules and power over you, the workers, when the war is won. Politicians, as usual, are only worrying about votes once this war is won. Well, let me tell you something. If we don't win this war, then you really will have something to worry about – what will happen then to your wages? What will happen to the trade unions and the politicians? You should be ashamed – shouting abuse at me because without me and the women filling the gaps left by the men who have gone away to fight, then this country would have been beaten by now. Make no mistake though, win or lose, everyone's life will change – there can be no going back!"

Sis was moved by the young woman's words and admired her bravery in standing there and facing men who if they had heard her were certainly not listening and she was an easy target. Sis admired her resilience and the force of her argument in the face of heckling, abuse, spitting and even the odd stone. Aunt Bessie had seen a man close to them pick up a stone, ready to throw and with Sis in her wake headed towards him and ensured that she stepped down firmly with her left foot on his right foot whilst placing her left elbow sharply in his midriff. Sis was amused that at the same time Aunt Bessie managed to apologise profusely for her clumsiness before the man knew what had happened.

Eventually, they started to walk back and Aunt Bessie asked Sis what she had thought of what she had just witnessed?

"On one hand, it was very amusing and entertaining but I can't stop thinking about the young woman and what she had said about the unfairness of women being expected to shoulder the burden of the war effort on the domestic front and yet being denied the vote. How can anyone think that is acceptable?"

As they moved on Aunt Bessie told Sis that "…the young woman had spoken the most sense and she was right that whatever happened when the war ended, life would never go back to how it was before. We women must not let it!"

**

Aunt Bessie had helped Sis to compose a letter to Lord Acaster. Sis knew that he had had a soft spot for Ester Smith and was their best chance of help, although Aunt Bessie was concerned that you should never underestimate the power of the Establishment of which he was undoubtedly a part to look after their own interests before all others.

Miss S. Brown
c/o Mrs B. Hand
3 Atheldene Road
Victoria

London

Dear Lord Acaster,
I am writing to you in the hope that you will be able to help my brother, Corporal Jack Brown and his friend, Private Harold Smith, who have been arrested as deserters. Both Jack and Harold volunteered for the Acaster

Company in 1914 and both have seen action and now successfully passed their Specialist Marksman and Sniper training.

Your Lordship, they are both proud to serve their country and would never dream of deserting. As you will know Your Lordship, Ester Smith was very seriously ill and I told Harold. Consequently, on the way from their sniper's course in Devon back to the Front, they decided to make a detour to Acaster so that Harold could see his mother as he feared it could be for the last time. They were not deserting as they had every intention of returning to their regiment although perhaps a few days later than planned.

Your Lordship, this is a sad business and it is all my fault. If I had not told Harold about his mother, then none of this would have happened. Please, Your Lordship, I beg you to do whatever you can to sort this matter out so that Jack and Harold can return to their regiment in France. They are both excellent shots and I am sure that they would be able to make a difference.

Yours Sincerely,
Miss S. Brown

***

Aunt Bessie busied herself with the help of Sis, moving chairs around in her sitting room and preparing some light refreshments. Sis counted eight chairs and gradually over the course of the early evening they were occupied by a variety of women who sat happily gossiping until Aunt Bessie called the meeting to order and introduced Sis.

"Welcome, everyone. Let me introduce my niece, Miss Sis Brown, who would like to help us achieve our objective of votes for all women."

There followed a murmuring of greetings and the sharing of warm smiles.

"Miss Hawking, I would be grateful if perhaps you could summarise the situation for my niece's benefit?"

Miss Hawking, Sis subsequently learnt, was a schoolteacher, who spoke very quietly and earnestly.

"The government is proposing, thanks to its Electoral Reform Bill, to give the vote to women. Specifically those women over the age of 30, those over the age of 21, who own their own homes or those married to householders."

Miss Hawking paused and looked around the circle and Sis could see the unmistakable passion burning in her eyes.

"I wonder whether Emily Davison, who had already been arrested nine times and force fed 49 times, would think that worth the personal and ultimate sacrifice she made in throwing herself in front of the King's horse at the Derby in 1913. Although it represents some progress, our fight cannot be over until all women have the same voting rights as men."

"Thank you, Miss Hawking. My niece and I witnessed a young woman being foully abused at Speaker's Corner. It is no longer enough to have these cosy meetings in our homes and to take part in marches from time to time. I propose that we should go to Speaker's Corner this coming Sunday and lend our support and face down these bullies. All those in favour, please raise your hand."

The majority of those present had no hesitation in raising their hands while the remaining one or two, under a cold stare from Miss Hawking, slowly followed suit.

***

Lord Acaster sat in his study nursing a morning tot of whiskey, as was his habit, as he and his secretary worked their way through the small pile of correspondence on his desk. It was his Lordship's practice to savour his whiskey while he looked out of the study window at the Acaster Estate as his secretary, Akers, who had served as his adjutant in their army days, read any correspondence out aloud.

"…so that Jack and Harold can return to their regiment in France. They are both excellent shots and I am sure that they would be able to make a difference.

Yours Sincerely,
Miss S. Brown"

Without turning his gaze from the window, Lord Acaster said, "I know those young men. They both worked on the estate and there was never a hint of a problem with them. I remember the day they signed up – I seem to remember they were both nervous as they were underage.

"I am really not sure what I can do. There are a couple from my time at Sandhurst that I can speak to but I am not sure it would do any good. The army seems wedded to its practice of shooting deserters.

"I will, however, write to Captain Hargreaves and see if he can suggest anything as I am sure that he, like me, would not want them stood against a wall and shot."

***

It also turned out, much to Sis' surprise, that Aunt Bessie was a sister in a Voluntary Aid Detachment based at the Springfield War Hospital in Battersea. Aunt Bessie was delighted when Sis told her that she wanted to take up nursing. Aunt Bessie was a no-nonsense woman and she decided that the sooner Sis confronted the horrors that men routinely inflicted on their fellow man, the better because it would help her young niece to decide whether or not she was cut out for nursing.

Consequently, one evening soon after, Sis found herself standing next to Aunt Bessie at Victoria Station watching a hospital train arrive and its sorry cargo of wounded soldiers being unloaded. She did not have to stand there long before she had stopped thinking of Victoria as a station and instead saw it as a theatre of pain. Priests of all denominations were present and it was as much as Sis could do to stop herself from shouting out, "Where is your God now when the trains pull into Victoria Station every night bringing back the wounded from the Front?"

Those first off the train were the walking wounded each with a haunted look in their eyes and their uniforms still covered in mud and dried blood. Some of these once strong and vital young men were able to make their way to the waiting transport unaided although many needed the use of a stick or a crutch to make this possible. Some had to be helped by nurses or orderlies to make their slow and painful way along the platform. The crowds cheered and threw cigarettes and chocolate to the men, however, pain and tiredness meant that very few had the energy or inclination to respond.

The next to appear were the stretchers with the more seriously wounded. Some unconscious from wounds had their heads wrapped in bloodied bandages. Others had suffered amputations and many groaned at the movement of the stretchers. Lastly, when the bulk of the crowds had disappeared, came the stretchers of those who had died during the journey and whose faces where now covered by a rough, brown blanket. Aunt Bessie remarked that if a soldier was to die, then at least those who died on this last leg of their journey would get to be buried nearer to their loved ones.

There were members of the public there too. Some waiting for loved ones, who might never return and others had been drawn to the scene for a wide variety of reasons.

With the parade of pain passing them for some considerable time, Aunt Bessie observed Sis and was pleased to see that apart from an occasional look of horror or pity, her niece remained composed throughout.

***

The journey to Etaples was unpleasant and I thought that there was surely little that the army could have done to make it worse. We travelled in irons and under an armed guard and we were forbidden to speak unless spoken to although I hoped, by my small hand gestures that I had made,Harold would understand that he must keep his mouth shut. The guardroom at Etaples was even more Spartan than its counterpart in Aldershot and if anything, the guards were even less friendly. We were once again allowed 30 minutes solitary exercise a day in a small yard at the back of the guardhouse that was surrounded by high walls built from lengths of timber.

One morning after the usual breakfast of stale bread, jam and a mug of tea, my cell door opened and after I had been ordered to stand to attention, a young officer strode in with a buff folder under his arm. Once again the door was left open and a guard stood out in the corridor.

"Sit down, Brown. I am Lieutenant Crowe and I have been assigned to defend you at the courts martial that will soon be convened to hear the case against you. The court will ask you whether you are guilty or not guilty – how do you intend to plead?"

Crowe didn't seem to lack confidence and his body language and briskness told me that he considered this to be a tiresome assignment, far beneath his abilities and expectations, and one that he intended to complete as soon as was decently possible.

"Sir, have you done this sort of thing before?"

"No and hopefully, I won't have to do it again. Now how will you plead?"

"Not guilty, sir!"

With more than a hint of disappointment and irritation in his voice, Crowe asked, "Please explain."

"Can I stand, sir?"

Crowe waved his hand as if it was of no consequence to him but I felt better able to gather my thoughts if I could walk up and down all eight feet of my cell.

"Sir, we had just successfully completed our sniper's course and we were returning to our regiment from Devon. Harold – Private Smith – had found out from my sister that his mother was ill and he was worried. We knew that the train would take us fairly close to Acaster and Harold was determined to see his mother before continuing the journey back to the regiment. Before joining up, I had lodged with Harold and Mrs Smith and so, as his best friend, I decided to go with him.

"The plan was to see his mother and then to continue our journey the next day, however, his mother was worse than we had expected and Harold would not leave her. Sir, we were not deserting as we had every intention of returning to our regiment. At worse we were absent without leave."

Crowe signalled for me to sit down again.

"You see, Brown, the army cannot have men deciding to take off when the fancy takes them whatever their circumstances. My advice to you is that when the court asks you, plead guilty…"

"But, sir, I was told that if we did that, then there was nothing more that could be said."

Crowe looked at me with an expression that combined weariness and hurt.

"Who told you that?"

"Lieutenant Jones back at Aldershot, sir."

"Who is Lieutenant Jones?"

"He was assigned to defend us."

"Where is Lieutenant Jones now?"

"Back at Aldershot, sir."

"Exactly and now I am here to defend you. Now, think about what I have said and we will speak again. I will now go and speak to Private Smith."

As soon as Crowe moved towards the door, the guard ordered me to stand to attention and I watched as the door clanged shut and heard the key turn in the lock. Only then could I sit down on my bed and I was, to say the least, confused by the conflicting advice that I had received.

"Well, that was exciting," said Aunt Bessie.

Aunt Bessie and Sis were standing in the small laundry room at the back of the house, sponging and brushing mud and other assorted muck on their coats. Sis smiled not so much at what her aunt had said but the fact that she had forgotten to take her hat off and was standing there with it at quite a rakish angle.

"Those brutes need to be taught some manners."

They had just returned from Speaker's Corner where they and the rest of Aunt Bessie's group had stood in a show of solidarity behind a young woman who had repeated the unfairness of how women were being treated and that things would have to change. The group, with the exception of Aunt Bessie, had stood there nervously with just their umbrellas and small cardboard placards to protect them, fidgeting from foot to foot.

The men who had gathered resembled, as Miss Hawking whispered, a pack of wild animals circling around and which could smell the fear on their prey. At first it was only insults that were thrown but the men soon tired of that and started throwing clods of earth and the odd stone. Some approached close enough to spit at them with surprising accuracy. The policemen who were there just stood and watched with their feet spread apart and their hands behind their backs. It was clear that they were in no hurry to intervene and seemed in fact to be enjoying the spectacle.

"Stand firm, ladies. These brutes must be faced down. We must not weaken."

Despite these words, Aunt Bessie could see that the others were not convinced so she stepped forward and gently touched the sleeve of the young woman and could feel her arm shaking on what was not a particularly cool morning. The young woman had tried to hide the fact that she was shaking with fear by wearing a coat that was heavier than was justified by the weather that morning.

"You should be ashamed of yourselves. Is this how you have been brought up?"

A partially eaten apple arced through the air and bounced off Aunt Bessie's hat.

"Who threw that? Come on, own up or are you a coward?"

Aunt Bessie had taken a step forward and Sis was amused to see the men instinctively take a step back.

"I repeat who threw that? I thought not. You are just a bunch of bullies. You know nothing about the young lady who is speaking to you or about my friends who have come to support her.

"When we leave here, some of us will begin work at the hospitals and on the trains tending to the wounded – and those men are brave. Others will go to work to produce artillery shells that are needed at the Front – work that is dangerous for all sorts of reasons. Some will be teaching your children tomorrow. Others will be driving buses and lorries around the city. And what will you be doing? The men at the Front would be horrified to see you here fighting what? A group of women! They would say if you are so brave and really want to fight then join up."

Sis and the others came forward and stood alongside Aunt Bessie encouraged by her words as much as the men seemed cowed. It was at this point that the policemen stepped in to disperse what remained of the group of men, many of whom had already melted away in the face of Aunt Bessie's verbal onslaught. Aunt Bessie looked sternly at the young woman.

"Now, my dear, finish what you have to say and then we can all go for a well-deserved cup of tea and a slice of cake."

Now having returned to Aunt Bessie's and standing there cleaning their coats, Sis felt that the morning had been worthwhile.

"Will we go again, Aunt Bessie? You were so strong when you faced down those brutes."

"Thank you, my dear, but I have always believed that you must not give in to bullies. Do it once and you will find yourself doing it every single time. I felt sorry for them because deep down, they know that their world will change whatever and there is nothing they can do about it and therefore they attack like animals. It has always been the way of the world. So in answer to your question, I think we will be going again."

***

It was not Lieutenant Crowe facing the prospect of standing in front of a firing squad and so he seemed very relaxed as he strode into my cell and motioned me to sit down.

"The courts martial will take place tomorrow at 08.00. I really hope you have taken on board my advice…"

I was still dealing with the news of the courts martial and therefore had not even registered the fresh footsteps approaching down the corridor.

"What advice would that be then, Lieutenant?"

I recognised the voice at once and was amazed to see the figure of Major Hesketh – Pritchard standing in the doorway although I think Lieutenant Crowe was even more amazed as he stood quickly to attention. The Major had a smile playing on his lips but his eyes blazed as he repeated the question.

"What advice would that be then, Lieutenant?"

"Sir! My advice would be that Brown here should plead guilty and hope that the court shows mercy."

"Lieutenant, your considered advice, as I suspect you are only too well aware, will, if followed by Brown, leave the court with no alternative but to recommend the death penalty. Well, thank you for your advice but you can now go. I will be taking over the defence of Brown and Smith."

"But…"

"Lieutenant, you look a little ridiculous standing there with your lips flapping now go and do something useful."

Crowe had little stomach for arguing with the major, particularly as he never wanted the assignment in the first place and quickly picked up his file and left without any further comment. The Major motioned me to sit down while he turned to the guard and told him to close my cell door. The guard was not about to argue and so once the door had been closed, he too sat on my bed and took off his hat.

"Sir, I don't understand."

"Of course, you don't. Now don't look so worried…"

"Excuse me, sir, but why are you here?"

The Major smiled as he pulled a file out of his briefcase.

"It's a long story, Brown. The short version is that Lord Acaster received a letter from your sister. He then wrote to your company commander, Captain Hargreaves, as well as one or two of his contemporaries from his Sandhurst days and a lot of good that did him. Captain Hargreaves, who seems a really sound man, wrote to me to tell me of your little problem and to ask for my help.

"Now, Brown, you should know that I have no great love for deserters as they put the lives of their comrades at risk. However, I am not convinced that shooting them is the answer. I certainly don't think it discourages others from deserting. I also believe that if the penalty for desertion is death, then all deserters must be shot but again it seems to depend on other factors which I won't bore you with now except to say it is applied in an unfair way.

"If a man has certain skills that when deployed will lead to the enemy being disrupted and discomforted and which will therefore save lives, then why in Heaven's name should the army stand that man up against a wall and shoot him?

"Since the first occasion when I saw you and Smith on the range, I knew that you had a special talent so why should one decision, for good or bad, lead to the waste of my time and my instructors' time and deprive the army of two bloody good snipers.

"At worst, you were absent without leave."

I was struggling to take this all in and so I would imagine it was now the turn of my lips to flap as the Major continued, "However, I will be asking the court to dismiss the charges against you and Smith on the grounds that…"

***

Sis had begun work at the Springfield War Hospital in Aunt Bessie's Voluntary Aid Detachment and fortunately by the time she started, there was a better relationship between the regular nurses and the volunteers that had taken a long time to achieve.

Each day Aunt Bessie and Sis would make their way to the hospital and Sis never lost her excitement and pride to be wearing her uniform of a light blue dress, white apron and a white starched cap. Sis was enjoying her work at the Springfield and Aunt Bessie always ensured that they worked the same shifts so that she could keep an eye on her. Aunt Bessie also enjoyed the time they spent walking to and from the hospital together as it gave them time to chat about a wide variety of topics.

"We have come a long way as volunteers. When I started the nurses and doctors referred to us using our initials VAD as 'Very Active Danger' but they have come to realise our value and we are more likely now to be seen as 'Valiant and Determined'. The wounded soldiers at the hospital even called us 'Very Active Dusters' or 'Victim Always Dies' but now we get 'Very Adorable Darling' more times than not – even me! Well, sometimes. Still it could be worse because as we are part of the First Aid Nursing Yeomanry we are sometimes referred to as FANNIES."

Aunt Bessie roared with laughter and Sis laughed too reflecting on her own limited experience of what would be termed banter by men.

"My feet have got used to the hours spent standing and running errands. When I started, my feet would be so swollen at the end of the day."

"Do you enjoy what you do?"

"Yes, more than I thought I would. I was shocked and upset early on by the sights and the suffering that I see but now I feel that I can control those feelings. I feel very sorry for these men as their lives will never be the same again. I just want to do the best I can for them."

***

The room for the courts martial reminded me of my old classroom back in Acaster with a small stage at one end of the room on which was set out a table behind which stood three chairs. In front of the stage were two more tables with two chairs each and to the side of the stage was a further table behind which sat a bored looking army clerk.

At precisely 07.58, I had been marched into the room to take my place next to the Major behind one table. Across from us, behind the other table, was the prosecuting counsel, a Captain Wallace from the Adjutant General's office, a small, humourless looking man. At precisely 08.00, a door behind the clerk's table opened and we were told by the clerk to stand as three officers walked through to take up their positions on the stage.

The officer in the middle, who was the president of the court, introduced himself as Captain Jessop and gave the names of the other two officers, however, given the circumstances, these were names which I promptly forgot. The Major immediately rose to his feet to address the court,

"I am Major Hesketh-Pritchard and I am defence counsel for Corporal Brown who is charged with a single offence of desertion…"

Captain Jessop had been scanning the file in front of him and the Major had clearly taken him by surprise, however, he quickly recovered and acted to assert his authority.

"Major Hesketh-Pritchard, this is most unusual as protocol dictates that the court should first hear from the prosecuting counsel…"

The Major was having none of it.

"With respect to the court and its protocol, I believe that time will be saved if I am allowed to continue. Thank you."

Captain Jessop was not about to fall prey to the charms of the charismatic Major and in doing so lose control of his court room.

"Please, sit down, Major. You will have the opportunity to make your submission to this court at the appropriate time. Now, Captain Wallace, we would be grateful to hear the case for the prosecution."

Captain Wallace stood and picked up some papers from his file.

"Thank you. This is a straightforward case in the Adjutant-General's view of desertion. Corporal Brown had been attending a sniper's course in Devon. At the completion of that course, he was given clear orders to return to his regiment which was based close to Ypres. Corporal Brown never arrived and thanks to information supplied by the Acaster police he was arrested at a house in Acaster. It is my contention that Corporal Brown had no intention of returning to his regiment and was wilfully absenting himself."

I could not believe what I had just heard. The information could only have come from one person, my father, and he would have been in no doubt about the possible consequences of his actions.

***

I am not sure if Captain Wallace said anything else, such was the mental turmoil and anger that I was feeling but then it was the turn of the Major who spoke confidently and quickly.

"The simple fact is that Corporal Brown did not, as Captain Wallace contends, desert. This is nothing more than a case of the necessary paperwork not arriving at its rightful destination at the right time. Corporal Brown, along with Private Smith, the next case on your list, had attended my sniper's course on Dartmoor. It is true to say that they are both first class shots, the best I have come across, destined to wreak havoc on this country's enemies as snipers on the Western Front. These men have the skills, courage and cunning to cause significant casualties on the German side and to disrupt their plans so my question to you is can the British Army afford to put them in front of a firing squad?

"I had been made aware that Private Smith's mother was very ill and to reward Brown and Smith for their performance on the course, I granted them two days leave before they were to return to the Front. Here is my notebook in which I have written this out but sadly because of orders that I had received to put on a subsequent course at very short notice, my note was never transcribed as a variation to their movement order. Consequently, this was never received by the men's company commander, Captain Hargreaves. In their excitement to go on leave, neither they nor my office thought to make sure that they had a signed note from me varying their orders. I, therefore, apologise to the court for causing this waste of valuable time."

The Major held the notebook out and the clerk came and carried it across to Captain Jessop who read it and showed it to his two colleagues before asking for it to be shown to the prosecuting counsel.

"Thank you, Major Hesketh-Pritchard. Any questions, Captain Wallace?"

There were no questions from a bemused looking Captain Wallace and so the Major continued, "Therefore, at the time that Brown and Smith were unfortunately arrested, they were, as far as they and I were concerned, legitimately on leave. I have here a letter from Dr Jackson, Mrs Ester Smith's doctor, that confirms the seriousness of her illness and that she sadly died later on the day, her son and Corporal Brown were wrongfully arrested."

The letter was also then passed around the court and again Captain Wallace did not question it, allowing the Major to continue.

"I believe that desertion or cowardice in the face of the enemy must be punished as such actions seriously endanger the lives of those that they are serving with at the Front. Such punishment must act as a deterrent to others contemplating desertion. Corporal Brown though was not deserting and if anyone is at fault here, then it is perhaps me for the slackness of my paperwork.

"This young man, given the chance, can make a real difference at the Front because a good sniper can damage the morale and the operational effectiveness of the enemy. I would respectfully urge that he be released, without a blemish on his character, and allowed to return to his comrades."

Captain Jessop looked at Captain Wallace who shook his head and closed his file and at his panel members who, by a slight nod of their heads, indicated that they were in agreement.

"Corporal Brown, stand up, please. Corporal Brown, the court will adjourn to consider its verdict."

**

The hospital train left Victoria on its journey to Dover to collect another batch of wounded men and Sis had been excited when Aunt Bessie told her that she would be part of its nursing complement.

The nurses' room was in a first-class compartment in the middle of the train, although Aunt Bessie or Sister Hand, as she now had to be referred to, had warned that they would not see much of it on this trip. It was a place to store their few belongings, repair the inevitable tears in their uniform caused by the tight spaces they had to work in with the many sharp edges and nail heads that stuck out, and, if time permitted, to search their hair for lice, have a quick wash and if really lucky enjoy a short nap.

The trip to Dover gave Aunt Bessie and her company of volunteers, the chance to make sure that the train was fully prepared for whatever patients they were to receive.

On arrival they had to wait for the hospital ship from Dieppe and then once it had docked, loading the train was a slow process and carried out to the unmistakeable noise of the guns from the Front. The walking wounded or sit-ups as they were referred to, were ushered eight at a time into compartments that in happier times would have been occupied by families returning from a day out on the south coast. Some of these men had foot problems or wounds to their arms but they never complained as they were only too happy to be travelling away from the Front and some travelled in the knowledge that their war was over as they were confident that their's was a blighty.

Those on stretchers were loaded carefully into carriages that had been adapted to take their sorry cargo. Many of these men had suffered terrible injuries to their heads, chests, stomachs and limbs. Some of these men were unconscious while others groaned and cried out for water, their mothers or both.

Sis had been allocated to such a carriage and she carefully moved among the men familiarising herself with the nature of her patients' wounds. To some of the men who slipped in and out of consciousness, she appeared as an angel while others who had been deprived of female company and despite their wounds, muttered requests that made her blush. As Sis passed one bunk a hand that was still covered in dirt and blood from the Front, gently touched her arm.

"Sis, is it really you?"

She thought she had misheard and feeling flustered she moved on without stopping. Later as she passed that same bunk she heard a voice clearly say, "Sis, it's me, Harry. Harry Tibbins."

A short while later we all stood to attention as Captain Jessop and his colleagues came back into court. As we all sat down, Captain Jessop opened his file and seemed to be tidying up the papers that it contained before speaking,

"Corporal Brown, stand up, please. Corporal Brown having listened to your counsel, this court has decided that there is no charge to answer and that you are free to leave this court and to return to your unit."

With that, the clerk said "All stand" and Captain Jessop led his colleagues off the platform. Once the door had closed behind them, the Major picked up his file and we then walked out of the room. Once outside, he shook my hand. I am sure that he took my ashen face to be a sign of my relief at the court's decision as he would not have known that my father was the police sergeant in Acaster and in my confusion and shame, I was not about to tell him.

"Corporal Brown, there are no certainties in life but something will be terribly wrong if Private Smith is not freed in the next hour. The generals like their blood sacrifices and they won't be happy that you will have slipped through their fingers. I suggest you return to the guard room and collect your belongings and all being well. Private Smith should have joined you before you have finished."

"Sir, thank you, sir."

"Just go and kill Germans until this bloody war is over."

The Major then went back into the court to await Harold.

***

"Harry, is that really you? What's happened to you?"

At that moment it seemed to Sis that the world suddenly consisted of just her and Harry and the groans and suffering around her simply faded away.

"It's my leg – the left one. A machine gun bullet right through the shin bone. By the time I was brought in, the doctors had no alternative but to cut my leg off below the knee. Funny thing is it feels as if it is still there as I feel that I can wiggle my toes or my foot itches but then when I look down or go to scratch it, I remember that it isn't."

***

The Major was as good as his word and within the hour, Harold was back in the guardroom collecting what few belongings he had. The redcaps seemed surlier than ever and were clearly disappointed about this turn of events and so we took care not to provoke them. The last thing either of us wanted was to give them an excuse to lock us up again. They made us wait a long time before we were finally given our orders and travel documents.

Throughout our journey to the Front, Harold barely spoke and he seemed somehow different to the friend I had known growing up and for me the reason was as clear as day. I put it down to delayed grieving for his mother and the knowledge that the father of his best friend and his girlfriend had tried to get him killed. He wouldn't speak despite my many efforts to broach the subject and so I entered into a monologue where I told him everything that I was feeling namely the shame and the anger and I apologised to him. He just looked at me and shrugged.

Eventually, after some poor directions had caused us to get lost and increased our anxiety that we would again be picked up as deserters, we finally presented ourselves to Captain Hargreaves who was in a dugout in the reserve trench. Captain Hargreaves was as good as gold but he had never had much time for small talk, preferring to get straight to the point.

"Good to see you both. The Germans have got some bloody snipers out there and we have taken casualties. Now if what the Major has told me about you two is true, then get out there and make sure the bloody Germans get a taste of their own medicine."

***

Life at the Front had quickly settled down into boring routine, interspersed with our sniping assignments and eventually I forced myself to write the letter to Sis that I knew was long overdue.

Dear Sis,

Hopefully, you will know by now that the charges against us were dropped and we are now back with the company.

I am sorry that I haven't written sooner but I have been so confused by events. At my courts martial, I heard that Harold and I were arrested following information received from Acaster police. That could only have been Father. I know that he disliked me but I never thought he hated me enough to do that to his own son. He must be very disappointed with the outcome. I wonder too how much you knew and whether that was the reason you went off to Aunt Bessie?

Harold has taken his mother's death, our arrest and subsequent trial and the news that our father was the cause really badly. He is very upset that Father's actions deprived him of the chance to be with his mother at her death. When you have the time, please write to him – you are probably all he has now. And, of course, I want to hear all your news too. What's it like living with Aunt Bessie?

Take care and hopefully you will let me take you for a swish tea up in London when I get back.

Love
Jack

***

Having reached Victoria, Harry had been taken straight to the Springfield and Sis would visit him whenever her shifts and his treatment allowed. Almost immediately, Harry had taken a slight turn for the worst and the surgeons decided that his wound had become infected and so they took a bit more of his leg off to just above the knee. Now on the road to recovery, he was sitting out in a chair when Sis paid him one of her regular visits.

"How did it happen, Harry?"

"I thought I was well out of range behind the lines but the Germans had sneakily moved one of their machine guns far enough forward that it could reach the road that my company was moving along."

"What did it feel like? I've seen many wounded soldiers but have never thought it right to ask them what it had felt like when they had been wounded. But, you're different, so, please, tell me."

Harry looked at Sis for a moment deciding how to reply.

"I didn't know what had happened at first except one minute I was marching up this lane and the next minute I was knocked to the ground. For a moment I struggled to get up, confused as to why I couldn't and then the pain came and I have never felt pain like it. I looked down and could see my leg hanging half off below the knee and blood everywhere. I remember a mate putting a tourniquet on, which was painful in itself, but then thankfully I passed out and didn't come around again until they'd taken my leg off."

Sis reached out and held his hand.

"Thank you for telling me. You poor, dear, but you will be all right now. What will you do when you are discharged?"

"I've no idea. I can't see anything for me here. Maybe I'll go to Canada. I've got relatives there."

Harry noticed what he hoped was a shadow of disappointment pass across her features.

"Sis, I've dreaded asking you this but how is Jack? Harold? I am so sorry that I played a part in that business."

"They are both fine and presumably at the Front shooting Germans. They had to go through a court martial but the charges were dismissed."

"Good. Have you seen them?"

"No. Straight after their arrests I came to live with Aunt Bessie, Sister Hand to you by the way and I've not seen them since. There have been the occasional letters but they are becoming fewer as time passes."

When Sis left him that afternoon, she would not have seen the small smile playing around his lips or the look of hope in his eyes.

***

Sis had run out of excuses for not writing the letter that she had been putting off for so long. It felt wrong not to be honest but she had remembered her Father's view on letters to serving soldiers and the part that honesty had played where Harold was concerned. After many false starts, she found what she hoped were the right words.

Dearest Jack,

Thanks to the kindness of Lord Acaster in writing to me. I did know that you were back at the Front and without a stain on your character. I hope that you are keeping safe and that this awful business will soon be over. I have enclosed some socks and gloves that Aunt Bessie has knitted for you.

London is a different, bigger, noisier world but I have settled in well, thanks to Aunt Bessie, who seems to be larger than life – I can't wait for you to meet her. I am working as a VAD with Aunt Bessie at the Springfield War Hospital and sometimes do a shift on a hospital train. On one occasion I came across Harry Tibbins on his way back from the Front with a nasty leg wound – in fact the poor dear has had his leg amputated above the knee.

Dearest Jack, there is no easy way to say this so I will just come out and say that Mum is dead. She hadn't been well and she had a fall down the stairs. I found out from Miss Palfrey when she forwarded my wages. I have not heard anything from Father and despite my love for Mum, going to the funeral would have been too much but perhaps we can visit her grave together one day.

I am so sorry, Jack, but please stay safe and when you come back, we can both take Aunt Bessie out for afternoon tea. And please tell Harold that I will write soon but as you can imagine life is hectic here.

Take care
Sis

***

Harold continued to be withdrawn and I felt both unwilling and unable to jolly him out of it because Sis's letter had stunned me with the news about Mum. It was hard to find somewhere private to think and in particular think about Mum. It is something that comes to us all, the realisation that we will never see our mother or some other loved one, again. Despite everything that had happened, it never crossed my mind at that time that her death was anything other than an unfortunate accident and I hoped that she had not suffered.

In time I realised that Harold had been barely mentioned in the letter while Harry Tibbins was a 'poor dear'. I decided that I would not tell Harold about Harry Tibbins either, who I did not know had joined up. I did tell him that Sis had written and that my mum was also dead and he had just patted my shoulder before turning back to cleaning his rifle.

It was a relief, therefore, to get back out into the field where talking was strictly limited to the job in hand. Our regiment had built a number of cleverly hidden posts that could be used for observation and sniping. The telescopes used were carefully wrapped in sandbags with sunshades to prevent the glass reflecting and therefore giving away the position.

Looking through my monocular, I had observed the head of a German who was in the trench opposite and believing that the early morning was off limits to snipers, had removed his forage cap and scratched his bald head. I hissed for Harold to take up position next to me and he slid across and picked up his binoculars. The German's head was clearly visible and on this bright, clear morning, I knew it was not the most difficult shot that I would ever take. However, I couldn't get an image of Mum lying at the foot of the stairs out of my mind and I hesitated.

"Do it," hissed Harold. But I couldn't for the life of me pull that trigger and then the German was no longer to be seen. Harold looked at me and then indicated that he would shoot and I should observe. I trained the binoculars on the spot on the opposite trench and two minutes later was surprised to see the German's bald head reappear. He might have got away with it once but he had now run out of luck as without a word Harold pulled his trigger and I watched as the German's head seemed to explode in a pink mist.

We carefully slithered in a zigzag pattern back through the undergrowth and settled some distance to the right of where Harold had fired from and behind a small mound to await the Germans angry response and sure enough it came in the form of a random machine gun burst and a mortar round.

"You must stop shooting the most popular German every time because his pals don't appreciate it."

Harold just grunted and turned and lay on his back looking up at the sky.

***

Much to Sis's dismay, Harry was soon well enough to be transferred to a convalescent home and was moved to The Grange a large country residence in Surrey near Croydon. When Harry arrived, he was required to sign his name in what was effectively a visitor's book that stood on the hall table and to add a comment about his wound.

On the first of her infrequent visits, due to the shifts she worked, Harry couldn't wait to show Sis his entry.

"Wounded at Messines. Left leg amputated above the knee. I would like to meet the German who fired the machine gun. We would have words."

By now, Harry was dressed in the blue uniform that was issued to all wounded soldiers with his left trouser leg carefully pinned up. Sis pushed Harry out into the garden in his wheelchair and the two of them sat on the patio enjoying the views.

"What about your father, Sis? Have you had any contact with him?"

"Not since I left that house to come up to Aunt Bessie. And now that Mum is dead, there is no reason to go back."

"I'm sorry. I didn't know that your mother was dead. She was always very kind to me. How did it happen? I mean I know that she wasn't well."

"It was Miss Palfrey who told me. She put a small card in with the wages she owed me. It seems that Mum fell down the stairs. Apparently, my father was out at the time and found her on his return."

Harry heard the catch in her voice and reached out and took her hand, giving it a gentle squeeze. Sis was not used to any young man but Harold holding her hand and instinctively pulled away and was then dismayed at the disappointment on Harry's face.

"No, I'm fine, thanks. It's just that I can't bear to think that Mum died before she knew that Jack and Harold had been released. And do you know the worst thing? I was the one who had to tell Jack."

Before their afternoon could descend too much into the grip of melancholy, a tray of tea and cake thankfully arrived.

"Any more thoughts about what you will do when you leave here, Harry?"

"Walk, I hope. I am not spending my life in a wheelchair having you push me around."

They had not spoken before about any form of joint future and both were shocked that the subject had at last been broached and Sis decided to make a joke of it.

"So you believe that I am going to be part of your life, do you? Where will you take me away to then?"

"Canada, I think. I have family there and I am sure they will find me some sort of position in their business."

"What business are they in?"

"A brewery."

"A brewery – I hope you won't be planning to bring work home?"

It was one of their typical conversations where they flirted and talked about plans that for a while neither believed in, however, from that point onwards, there became more substance to their conversations.

161

Father must have been taken aback when a sharp rap on his office door was followed by Lord Acaster stepping briskly into his office. Father was sitting at his desk with a newspaper spread out in front of him with his jacket off and his braces hanging from his sides and he struggled to conceal how flustered he felt as he quickly closed his paper and stood up.

"Excuse me, your Lordship. I was not expecting any visitors." As he spoke, Father had pulled his braces up and put his jacket on while trying, unsuccessfully, to work out from his Lordship's demeanour the purpose of the visit.

"Please, sit down, Sergeant Brown. May I sit here?"

Playing for time, Father asked, "Can I get you something to drink, your Lordship?"

Lord Acaster politely declined and when they were both seated, he took his time and looked about the room with interest taking everything in as it was somewhere he had never had cause to visit before.

"I thought I would come personally to tell you that your son and young Smith are now back at the Front, having had the charges against them dismissed. You must be relieved."

"I am, thank you, sir. It's a big relief to know that."

"It must be Brown because I understand that the courts martial heard that their arrest followed information received from here."

Father's brain whirred as he formulated his response.

"Yes, sir, it was a bad business. I only found out afterwards that young Tibbins had taken it upon himself to ring up Aldershot. I was shocked. You see, being ex-army, I knew what the penalty was. When you watch your son march off to war, it's one thing if they get shot by the enemy and quite another if they are shot by their own side."

Father was a master-manipulator and he was never afraid of a pause and so he stared down at the floor as if deep in thought although in reality he was waiting for Lord Acaster's response.

"It's a bad business, Brown. Mrs Smith's death on that same day must have been caused by Tibbins's actions. What happened to him?"

"When he realised what he had done, he was off like a scalded cat. Left his uniform upstairs and rushed off to the Junction and was on a train and away before I knew what had happened and could have it out with him. I'm not sure where he went or what he is doing now.

"My Sis was so upset – I think she blamed me just because I was Harry's sergeant – and she went off to London to live with her aunt. And my poor Alice died shortly after. It's a terrible, terrible business."

Silence hung in the air as both men appeared to ponder this statement but Father still had something he needed to know.

"Excuse me, your Lordship, but do you know why the charges were dropped?"

"They were officially on leave it seems. It was a mix-up with the paperwork."

"Ah, right. The army and its paperwork, eh? It was just the same back in my day."

"Well, look after yourself, Brown. I just thought you should know. Put your mind at rest. I'll bid you good day. You must join her Ladyship and myself for a spot of tea sometime soon."

Before Father could reply, his Lordship had taken his leave and walked out of the office.

***

Captain Hargreaves was agitated as he sat in his dugout looking down at the letter that he had started to write when Jack and Harold pushed aside the groundsheet curtain and stepped inside.

"I have another order for you. Young Baines – you know Baker Baines' son – had only been here a couple of days when a sniper killed him. I now have to write a bloody letter to his grieving parents and what do I tell them? The truth or make up some sugar-coated version of an honourable death?

"Do I tell them that he died bravely and without suffering or the truth? You see for some inexplicable reason he decided to poke his head up above the parapet. Unsurprisingly, there was a loud crack and he slipped back and staggered for a pace or two with blood spouting from his mouth before dropping down stone dead. Do I put that in a letter to his mother? Of course, not!

"If I am to be killed out here, let it be when I am doing something and not by a dirty sniper – oh, present company accepted, of course – who waits his chance for perhaps, hours. Now go and get that bastard!"

Father was shaken by Lord Acaster's visit, even though there was no sign that his Lordship knew about the part he had played. Even so it sparked Father into another round of searching for Harry Tibbin's letter. He had been frustrated and angered by previous attempts to find the letter that Mum had hidden.

He knew that she had not left the house, so where was it? In his view, Mum was not overly blessed with intelligence so why couldn't he find it? He had carried out searches of properties before as a soldier in South Africa and as a police officer so his temper was not improved by his continued failure to find it.

Frustrated beyond belief, he decided for the first time in an age to have a brew, a sit down and a think about the problem. It was as he went to spoon some tea out of the caddy that he saw the corner of a piece of paper showing beneath the tea leaves. He pulled the piece of paper out of the caddy and smiled when he saw that it was Harry's letter. When Mum was alive, Father never lifted a finger around the house and would certainly never make a cup of tea and so Mum, not anticipating her death, had put the letter in a place that she was confident that he would be unlikely to look in and as he liked his brew the caddy was always kept topped up with tea.

Strangely enough with Mum dead, he had not been drinking so much tea and so consequently the tea in the caddy had taken a while to get used, preferring instead to turn to whiskey as a source of comfort. Mum must have hidden the letter when he was out and he now regretted not forcing her to give it to him that night when everything had started to go wrong.

Equally strange was the fact that he did not immediately destroy the letter that was the only real evidence against him as he still expected Harry, along with Jack and Harold to be dead, and that Sis would never tell what she knew. In these circumstances, he believed that war could be a force for good. Instead, he decided to keep it as some sort of trophy from what he saw as a victorious campaign. He carefully refolded it and placed it in the back of his pocketbook.

He decided that he would celebrate and so he put his jacket on and headed for the Stag."

***

I had always enjoyed the fact that the German trenches were always presenting a problem to be solved. The German parapet opposite our position was uneven with pieces of corrugated iron and metal boxes with loopholes that could be shut when not required but were more than likely for effect only and sandbags coloured red, black, green, blue or striped which were designed to confuse our eyes. It was a deliberate mess behind which was a higher parapet that allowed a sniper to go about his business with impunity.

Harold and I had started to operate alone, not always though, and so I was lying out in no-man's land hopefully concealed by the long grass and poppies growing there and which moved enough to give me a sense of the wind speed and its direction. I had long gone past being squeamish about shooting Germans as I had managed to convince myself that they were to blame for whatever had happened back in Acaster as they had caused me to go off to war leaving my family behind.

I found my target, an observer, who was also out in front of his lines, took aim and fired. It was a good shot, I didn't need to see the result to know that, but I didn't wait around. Slowly over the course of a couple of hours and believe me on your elbows and toes it takes that long and you know all about it, moved my position about 50 yards further back as the Germans fired wildly in retaliation.

**

On another occasion, Harold and I were puzzled by a particular sniper who was causing havoc in a communications trench. Despite our close observation over the course of a day or so in an attempt to pinpoint his location, we hadn't found him and then I saw him or rather I saw the lark singing shrilly above him. He had settled himself down to wait with great patience to put a bullet in some poor devil behind me.

I watched the spot intently and then I saw something move and it was his head turning slightly but it was enough. He must have become aware of the lark's nest close to him and the danger it had placed him in, however, he was too late as my shot blew his head apart.

**

"What about Harold, Sis?"

Harry was now able to move around with the help of crutches and having gone for a walk in the grounds of the Grange, he and Sis were now sitting on what they had come to regard as their bench with its view back to the house.

"What about Harold?"

Harry knew that she was delaying answering the question in order to give herself time to gather her thoughts.

"How do you feel about him?"

Sis kicked at a stone and looked across to the house.

"I have never admitted this to myself before but as I sit here, I don't have any feelings for him. Look, I know that sounds harsh in the circumstances but he was a boy that I grew up with and he was my brother's best friend and I wanted him to be my best friend as well. I didn't know any better and so I thought that we would just drift through life together with a home and children.

"What happened in Acaster changed everything. I can see now that I was too naïve about life and opportunities. Coming to London was the best thing I could have done and I owe so much to Aunt Bessie because she has opened my eyes to a different world. I understand more and I have found that I can do things that previously I would have thought beyond me.

"Harold and I had played at making plans but then he enlisted without discussing it with me first and I felt all over the place emotionally. I haven't seen him since the day he was taken away. We still occasionally write letters but in all honesty that hasn't happened for a while now.

"And then you and I met again. We could probably have hoped to have met under better circumstances but the important thing is that we met."

Harry had sat quietly, listening intently to not only what Sis said but how she said it but he was not able to contain himself any longer.

"Sis, how do you feel about me?"

Sis looked at Harry and he could see tears in her eyes.

"I can't bear being away from you. I am at my happiest when I am with you. I want to be with you."

Harry tapped his empty trouser leg. "What about this?"

"My experiences over the last months have been horrendous in terms of what I have seen, so I know your situation could be much worse. The loss of your leg does not affect how I feel about you."

They sat there contentedly holding hands for a short time before Harry spoke casually and without looking at her.

"I know how you feel because that is how I feel too. I had better get on then and get fitted with my artificial leg because I want to be able to walk holding your hand and nothing else – no stick, no crutch and no wheelchair.

"I can't somehow see me asking your father for his permission to marry you, so perhaps I need to come up and speak to Aunt Bessie?"

Sis laughed. "She is far scarier than Father!"

"Oh, good! A stiff drink before we meet then? You do realise that going down on one knee is going to be a little tricky, don't you?"

If anyone had passed by and asked them, then they both would have answered that they had never been happier, however, Harry knew that there was something else that needed to be agreed before they could take things further.

"What about Harold?"

"I will write to him but I just want to enjoy this moment and gather my thoughts before I do."

"Just don't leave it too long. I think we owe it to him."

"I will but what about your family? When will I meet them?"

Harry picked at his pinned up trouser leg.

"You won't unless you come to Canada with me as any family I have is there. Dad was a police officer but he died trying to save a girl who threw herself off a bridge into a river near where we lived. He's the reason that I joined the police. Mum had died when I was much younger and sadly I cannot remember what she looked like. I was really brought up by my gran but she died just before I came to Acaster. Gran could be scary too so perhaps she and Aunt Bessie are like two peas in a pod?"

***

Christmas at Aunt Bessie's was more colourful and exciting than anything Sis had experienced before. The tree was big and festooned with all sorts of decorations, mostly hand made by Aunt Bessie herself while beneath lay a number of mysteriously shaped parcels.

The main reason for Sis being excited was the presence of Harry who was still in his blue uniform but he had now been fitted with an artificial leg that saw him walking almost normally albeit with the aid of a stick. Harry was confident that he would soon be able to manage without the stick.

Aunt Bessie had gone out of her way to make Harry feel comfortable and told him to call her 'Aunt Bessie'. Although the happy couple had not said anything, Aunt Bessie had not missed many of the little looks that passed between them or the shy holding of hands and she was happy for them.

They were all sitting around the fireplace after their Christmas meal happy and relaxed and had finished opening their presents. Given his present situation, Harry was genuinely bemused to receive a pair of hand knitted socks from Aunt Bessie particularly as when he held them up, Sis, who was in on the joke and her aunt couldn't stop laughing.

"So, Harry, Sis tells me that you have family in Canada and that you are thinking of going there to work. Have you been to Canada before?"

"No, I haven't but I want to go. The size of the country is massive and I think there will be more opportunities there, particularly if I can get a job in my uncle's brewery."

"But surely the breweries are closing down as a result of prohibition?"

"The family's brewery is in Ontario and although there is prohibition, they are still allowed to make and export beer which they do to the United States. They are also allowed to produce a beer for locals but it has to be below two percent proof or something like that."

"Have you written to your uncle about all this?"

Harry paused and looked across at Sis before replying.

"Yes. I am waiting for a reply."

"Well, good luck to you. And then, what about Sis here?"

Sis blushed and looked down at the floor.

"I want Sis to come with me and to come with me as my wife. She will easily get work as a nurse if that's what she wants. Look, Aunt Bessie, I want to do things properly. Who should I ask to get permission to take Sis to Canada as my wife? I don't particular want to go to Acaster to ask her father but if that's what I have to do, then so be it. I hope though that you will give it your blessing?"

"I would be happy to. I don't think we need to worry too much about Bill Brown. Now who would like a small glass of sherry?"

While Aunt Bessie busied herself with that, Harry looked at Sis.

"Now, will you write to Harold and Jack as well and tell him of our plans?"

1918

The start of the New Year brought about some personal recognition and some changes as we, along with other snipers at the Front, were no longer attached to our company but became part of a battalion sniping section made up of 16 men plus a corporal and a sergeant, under the command of a Sniping Officer, that operated along a designated length of the Front no matter which regiments were around us.

Personal recognition came when I was promoted to sergeant while Harold received his second stripe. Our achievements were further recognised by the Germans who we discovered had placed a bounty on our heads. We only found out when a patrol came back with some captured papers one of which promised the man who knocked us out a week's home leave. We had our near misses as the Germans responded to our sniping with nothing more than the odd scratch or bruise to show for them but after that, it just seemed to us or perhaps we were imagining it that we were receiving a bit more attention.

Promotion had not stopped Harold becoming more withdrawn and miserable. He had used to be easy going and funny, however, it was getting to the point where I really couldn't stand being around him. I had tried everything from a bit of banter to a good bollocking but nothing seemed to get through to him. He would just look at me with eyes that showed that he couldn't care less and I had therefore come to the conclusion that we weren't doing each other any good. It was something that I really needed to deal with but then the letters from Sis arrived when we happened to be out of the line for once. I was sitting in a local, smoke-filled estaminet which although full seemed to afford some privacy and scnsc of normality with a glass of rough wine when I opened my letter.

Dear Jack

I hope you are keeping safe and getting used to the third stripe on your arm.

This is the hardest letter that I have ever written but I need to tell you something so that you are prepared when Harold brings you the news. You will remember Harry Tibbins. Well, I met him some months ago when he was being brought back on a hospital train that I was working on. He had been wounded and as a result he has had a leg amputated above the knee.

I never meant it to happen but I have grown very fond of Harry, who thinks the world of me. Jack, Harry has asked me to marry him and I have agreed. Aunt Bessie has given it her blessing because for obvious reasons, neither of us felt like approaching Father. I know this will be upsetting for Harold but we have hardly seen each other since you both joined the army in 1914. I am sure we have all changed and I know that I am not the girl that I was in Acaster. Although we talked about it, Harold and I have never made a commitment to each other.

Harry and I want a fresh start and all Harry's family are now in Canada, where they run a brewery. They have offered Harry a job near Toronto and we are going out there as soon as we are married. Jack, with the way this war is dragging on, I hope that you will understand that we can't wait for you to get back before getting married. Almost certainly by the time you come back, I shall be Mrs Tibbins and living in Toronto, Canada. You must promise to come and visit us as soon as you can.

Please, feel happy for us and take care of yourself and Harold.

Love
Sis

I assumed from my letter that Sis had hoped that it would arrive before Harold's but the chaotic state of postal services at the Front ensured that he had unfortunately received his at the same time. The first I knew of this was when he came and sat down opposite me with a face like thunder and threw the letter across the table.

"I've had a letter from Sis. Here you read it."

I offered to fetch Harold a drink in an effort to gain some time but he brushed my attempt aside and sat there watching me as I read through the letter. It contained nothing that I had not already read in my own letter.

"You knew about this, didn't you?"

Harold was clearly angry and hurt and his raised voice was attracting interested and amused attention from those around us.

"Look, I have only just found out too. Sis has written to me – here you can read it."

Harold wasn't interested. I had never expected or wanted to hear such bitterness from him but I suppose it was understandable.

"What have I ever done to your family other than become sweet on your sister? My mother is dead because of your father, I was arrested for desertion because of your father and now to top it all off, your sister is dropping me in favour of a man who assisted in that arrest. All of that is down to your family. What sort of family, are you? I thought you were my friend. What have I got left? What have I got left?"

There were things I could and should have said but Harold was already leaving, pushing his way to the door and I didn't see him again until I returned to our billet. As I sat watching him leave, I thought there was not too much difference in our circumstances because what did I have to go back to? Despite everything, we continued to work as a pair as I felt that I had no choice in the circumstances, however, I grew increasingly concerned about what I saw as Harold's risk taking.

***

Harry had been adamant that he would not marry Sis until he could walk her down the aisle unaided. Slowly, and with determination, he had learnt to walk with his artificial leg. In the preceding weeks, he had perhaps tried too hard as his stump had become sore, blistered and then infected putting him back in hospital for a brief period of time.

However, their big day had finally arrived and they stood holding hands as the vicar said the all-important words,

"They have declared their marriage by the joining of hands and by the giving and receiving of rings. I therefore proclaim that they are husband and wife."

Aunt Bessie had been only too happy to make all the arrangements and she had been able to pull a few strings to enable the service to be held in the small, candlelit chapel at the Springfield War Hospital. Their family situations meant that they would have seemed lost and a little sad had the wedding gone ahead in a normal-sized parish church but the hospital chapel with its flickering candles reflected in the heavy silver cross that stood on the altar leant the occasion an intimacy that made it memorable for the happy couple. Apart from Aunt Bessie, who had proudly accepted the chance to give Sis away, the only other people present were Miss Hawking and Millie, a nurse, who had become a friend of Sis together with Sid, a fellow amputee, who acted as best man. It was Sid and Aunt Bessie who acted as witnesses.

"Those whom God has joined together let no one put asunder."

The happy couple, Aunt Bessie, Miss Hawking and Sid then returned to Victoria, Millie having returned to work, for some refreshments and Aunt Bessie produced an as yet unopened bottle of sherry to toast the new Mr and Mrs Tibbins. Later that evening, after Miss Hawking had left, blushing as Sid had offered to see her home, Harry and Sis spent their wedding night in the small bedroom next to Aunt Bessie's. They were both excited but Harry was, to start with at least, inhibited by the fact that Aunt Bessie was in her bed just the other side of the thin, dividing wall. There was a fair degree of muted giggling as he explained to Sis that he had this image of her lying there listening to every creak and groan of their bed before they eventually heard Aunt Bessie's deep snores and then, with some fumbling, the marriage was finally consummated.

***

The following morning, the start of their last full day in England, began with breakfast with Aunt Bessie and then final preparations and packing. Aunt Bessie had told them to be finished and ready to go out by one o'clock as she had a surprise for them.

Aunt Bessie had been fortunate enough to get four tickets to His Majesty's Theatre for a special fundraising revue in aid of the Springfield War Hospital which was also to be attended by members of the Royal Family. Also in the audience was the guest of honour, Captain Bruce Bairnsfather who was well known for his cartoon depictions of life on the Western Front and who had donated a signed picture, depicting his famous character Old Bill, which was auctioned on stage. Afterwards, as a further treat from Aunt Bessie, the three of them went to the Lyons Corner House in Piccadilly Circus. Having given their order to the waitress, Harry and Sis marvelled at their surroundings and then they became aware of Aunt Bessie staring across the room with a look of excitement crossing her face. "It's him," she whispered to them without taking her eyes off the object of her attention.

"Who?"

"Him! Captain Bairnsfather. Over there by that column."

Before they could look around, Aunt Bessie got up and moved across the room. They saw her weave her way through the tables and the waitresses and approach a man sitting alone at a table unnoticed by the other diners. Aunt Bessie stopped by the man and they saw her lean forward to speak to him. Though he looked a little embarrassed they saw him reach into his inside jacket pocket and take out what looked to be a card. He then seemed to search his pockets for a pen but Aunt Bessie had gone armed and had one to hand which he then used to autograph the card.

Having thanked the man, who they could still not identify clearly, Aunt Bessie returned looking a little flushed and excited. She was beaming as she resumed her seat. "It was him. He is such a nice man, although I don't believe he really wanted to be recognised."

"I was watching you and saw him sign some sort of card."

"Two cards actually. Here I want you to have one of them. I am going to get mine framed and it can stand alongside Stephen's photograph – I think he would like that."

She passed across the table one of the postcards which advertised a revue *Flying Colours* at the London Hippodrome, showing a picture of Old Bill which had been dedicated to the 'Happy Couple' and signed 'Bruce Bairn's father' together with the date. Harry and Sis thanked Aunt Bessie and assured her that they would treasure it.

They glanced across to where Captain Bairnsfather had been sitting but he had already left probably, they thought to avoid any further interruptions.

Later that evening, Aunt Bessie wished them good night and *bon voyage*. She told them that she would not see them the next morning as once she had got changed into her uniform, she was going to go to the Springfield having conveniently arranged a night shift. She assured Sis that she and Miss Hawking would keep fighting until they had achieved their goal of equality for all women and in addition an end to the war.

"I hate goodbyes at the best of times but I have grown very fond of you both and I don't think I can face the prospect of waving you off. Today has been lovely, so let's just remember that. Make sure you write to me now as I want to know all your news. Just put your keys through the letter box when you leave in the morning."

With that, Aunt Bessie kissed both of them and then went up to her bedroom. Harry and Sis made sure that they were in theirs by the time Aunt Bessie returned downstairs and left the house.

The following morning Harry and Sis left Victoria and made the long journey to Liverpool to embark on the SS Missanabie and a new life in Canada. Harry was well aware of the dangers of German U-boats but he felt that the risk was worthwhile. He had discussed it with Aunt Bessie and they had agreed that it was best not to say anything to Sis and just let her enjoy her excitement.

***

Dear Jack,

By the time that you receive this letter I will be Mrs Harry Tibbins and on my way to Toronto to a new and exciting life. Harry will start his new job in his family brewery and once we are settled, then I hope that I will be able to start work as a nurse in one of the many hospitals in Toronto.

Aunt Bessie has been wonderful and would be pleased to see you once this war is over. Please take care and you know that you can come and visit us whenever you want. Now that I am happy, all I want is for you to be happy too.

Look out for Harold.
I will write to you again once we are settled.
Love Sis.

I decided that I would not tell Harold that Sis and Harry had got married but over time it became clear that he knew.

A week or so later we were settled down in a derelict house just behind the lines, patiently waiting for a target to appear. We had been there some while without speaking with Harold looking through his binoculars when he suddenly broke the silence.

"Do you ever worry about getting killed or turned into a cripple before you've been with a woman?"

"Can't say. It's something I've never ever thought about. Why?"

"Things have changed. I've no reason to wait now."

"Harold…"

"You should have told me. You're my friend and I wanted to hear it from you but you couldn't do it. Sis had more guts than you as she at least wrote to me."

"Harold, listen…"

"All the time I thought I was going back to Sis, I was happy. It kept me going and I never wanted to go with another. In fact I can honestly say that I never even thought about it because I knew that no woman could be better than Sis. I was happy to wait. Now, why should I? I don't want to die without knowing what it's like."

"Harold…"

"So I'm going to try these places that I've seen others slink off to when we are out of the lines. I'm going to try as many of these women as I can. I listen to the other blokes and they say the women come in all shapes, sizes and colours and I want to try them all. I'm not saving myself for anyone – not now, not ever! If I am going to die, then I want to taste whatever life has to offer. You're a long time dead, Jack."

"Harold, I'm sorry but it's not my fault. I have been out here with you all the time. Sis is her own person. I'm as surprised as you that she has decided to marry Harry Tibbins but it was her choice – I had nothing to do with it. Look, we've been friends for as long as I can remember and I hope we always will be. Let's just get through this and sort ourselves out when we get back. What do you say?"

Harold never answered and continued to look through his binoculars.

He was as good as his word and whenever we were out of the line, he would take himself off. He never told me where he was going although I never asked I could guess.

***

Divisional Headquarters had received information to the effect that a high-ranking officer would be visiting the German lines, 300 yards opposite ours early the following morning and we had been told to see if we could give him a warm welcome.

We had a number of hides that we used, as it was never a good decision to stay too long in one place, so on this occasion, we had made our way overnight into the remains of a Church Tower that had somehow survived the regular bombardments and the ebb and flow of battle. It gave us the height needed to see more of what was going on in the German trenches and it had a number of small holes that enabled us to vary our sniping position to keep any watching German guessing.

If it hadn't been for the war, this would have been a wonderful spot to watch the sun rise and the odd fox scavenging out in no man's land, although it didn't pay to think about what they were scavenging on. In addition to the women and I suspect gambling, one of the other things different about Harold was that he had recently taken up smoking with a relish, which I had taken as yet another example of his desire to experience anything and everything. Consequently, as the time passed, he became fidgety as he grew desperate for a smoke and it was an itch that he knew he could not scratch which only made it worse.

Harold was in his preferred role as our observer and he had his binoculars trained on the German lines when I sensed rather than saw him tense.

"What?"

"There are suddenly a lot of periscopes peering over the top of the trench directly to our front. It could be that this officer of theirs is being given the guided tour. Do you think you could put one through the lens of one of them? Even if the officer isn't holding the other end of it, he will get one hell of a shock. Whoever is holding it could well end up with a shard of glass in their eye. Go for the one in the middle. There's more chance of that being the officer."

"I'd rather wait until we have a definite target rather than waste a shot and give our position away."

Harold muttered and then after what seemed an age later said, "I can see them. You should be able to get one of them now."

I settled down and went through the process of judging the range and the speed of the gentle breeze that blew from left to right. I lined up the shot on a small dip in the lip of the trench opposite and waited. Experience had shown us that no matter how aware of a danger point soldiers on both sides might be, they would still, if engaged in something else, forget and show themselves if only for an instant and I only needed an instant. I didn't have to wait long for a target to appear and in that instant, I fired and saw the body crumple.

With the number of periscopes that had been pointing our way, it was perhaps inevitable that our position should have been noted. The German retaliation was immediate and purposeful and all we could do was to keep our heads down as bullets peppered the stonework in front and above us and chips of stone flew everywhere.

"Shit, Harold. They know where we are. We'll be done for if their artillery fire at us."

Our heads were pressed as far into the flag stoned floor as we could get them. Harold stretched out his hand and put it on top of mine. It was the first gesture of real friendship between us for some time.

"They don't know how many of us there are. They are just looking to hit someone and then they will go back to their breakfast. Now the way I see it, you have more to look forward to than me."

"What?"

"I've got nothing waiting for me back home. Don't you see it's the only chance you have? If they get me, then you have a chance of getting back to our lines when it gets dark."

"Harold, no! No!"

It was too late as Harold lit up a fag and rose up just enough for the top of his head to show above the window ledge. He was looking at me when seconds later the bullet struck and blew a large part of the back of his head away.

Blood and brains showered everywhere and Harold slipped slowly down the wall and lay beside me with his eyes wide open, staring at me. I desperately wanted to close those eyes but there was no way that I could touch him. I had seen the aftermath of soldiers who had been shot by a sniper but this was different. Here was my best friend with an unbelievably small hole just above his left eyebrow but an exit wound at the back of his head large enough to put a fist in. With his blood on my face and hands together with pieces of his skull and brain, I rolled onto my side and threw up. I lay on my back, sobbing as my tears made little pathways through the gore on my face. There is no way that I will ever be able to forget what it felt like to have the blood, skull and brains of my best friend all over my face and hands and to have my best friend looking at me knowing that he was dead. It is beyond words.

Harold was right and the Germans seemed satisfied that they had got their sniper. I lay there with Harold throughout that day, unable to stop the clouds of flies descending on his head. As time wore on, I forced myself to at least reach out and take Harold's water bottle which I knew that I would need as this hot day progressed particularly as I had used a fair bit of mine already. After what seemed an eternity, night fell and I was able to slip away and make my way back to our lines.

I was not able to find out where Harold had been buried. If indeed, he had been buried, as I was quickly assigned a fresh sniping partner and we were regularly tasked with assignments along our piece of the line. I have never and will never tell Sis the circumstances of Harold's death but they will stay with me for the rest of my life.

In the years after the war, I did some research and discovered that Harold's name was on the Tyne Cot Memorial. Sadly, this meant that either his body had never been found or identified. Each year on the anniversary of his death, I have visited the memorial and each time I have stood there blubbing my eyes out at all the names and Harold's in particular. It doesn't get any easier no matter how many years have passed.

***

It had been an eventful year for Father. The old goat had struck up a 'friendship' with a young war widow called Elsie Bromley. Elsie, apparently, was more than happy to dispense favours for cash or kind in an effort to get by. As a widower, Father had not felt the same need to be secretive about his visits to Elsie and he could easily afford, from time to time, the odd half a crown and ten woodbines required and he had enjoyed the banter with his peers at the Stag, many of whom also occasionally visited Elsie.

And then Elsie became pregnant. This sent a slight shockwave around the male community of Acaster and their wives, particularly as Elsie chose not to hide herself away or indeed move away. When the baby arrived, those who saw him were in no doubt as to the Father as apparently, he could not have looked more like Father if he had arrived smoking a pipe and gripping a truncheon. If Father noticed, then he apparently ignored the situation and nobody dared say anything about it within his hearing.

And then Elsie and the baby disappeared. One day they were there and the next day they were gone. Nobody was overly concerned and such questions as there were petered out after a few days. Nobody raised any official concerns with the police and so there were no enquiries, official or unofficial, made. The overwhelming feeling of the Acaster community was good riddance and Father certainly did not disagree.

To be honest, I remember very little of the rest of 1918. I went about my work literally with a vengeance, keen to kill as many Germans as possible and get the bloody war finished. I seemed to live a charmed life, convinced that nothing the Germans did could stop me. I used all my experience and craft to inflict maximum disruption to the enemy at little or no risk to myself. My favourite target was the man who fired the machine gun and I like to think that my actions saved many lives.

The Germans did get lucky on one occasion and I found myself back in England having been caught by a bit of shrapnel in my right shoulder. And then it was all over. I was pleased, of course, I was, but if anything I felt more scared of re-entering civilian life than I had been enlisting in the army back in 1914.

***

There was no lasting damage to my shoulder, however, when I left the hospital, it needed some physiotherapy to get it back into shape. In the meantime, the army didn't really know what to do with me and so on 11 November, Armistice Day, I was living with Aunt Bessie and attending the Springfield for my physiotherapy sessions.

That morning, I decided to go into London and as soon as the maroons went off and the church bells rang out at eleven o'clock, people started to gather in the streets as the shops closed and the factories emptied. The traffic came to a stop but nobody seemed to mind as years of tension over the war could finally be released. People were happily waving Union Jack flags in the streets, from windows and whatever vantage points could be found. Impromptu choirs of complete strangers were formed on street corners and, after minimal encouragement, led many a procession while others were led by bands that happily struck up a medley of popular tunes and all, with me included and without anything needing to be said, headed towards the centre of the city and Buckingham Palace.

As the crowds gathered outside the palace, they started to chant, "We want the King." The excitement was reaching fever pitch when eventually the King accompanied by the Queen, Princess Mary and the Duke of Connaught came out onto the balcony and waved happily to the crowds gathered before them. The people made it very clear that they wanted to hear the King speak and eventually they got their wish, although how they could all hear him was a mystery to me.

"With you I rejoice and thank God for the victories which the allied armies have won, bringing hostilities to an end and peace within sight."

Although it rained that evening, nothing could dampen the enthusiasm for peace. The focal point for revelry was Trafalgar Square, where a number of bonfires had been lit. The glow from these fires revealed the smiling faces of the people who were just happy to be there and happy to be alive among whom were many soldiers and sailors, who were fortunate to be in London on that day. Their happiness manifested itself in song and soon there were competing groups of people variously singing the old favourites – *It's a Long Way to Tipperary* or *Land of Hope and Glory.*

I eventually found myself in Trafalgar Square, where I wandered about feeling lonelier than I had ever felt before, as I accepted pats on the back from unknown men and kisses from equally unknown women. I was struck by how well-behaved, given the circumstances, everyone was and, dwarfing all other considerations, it was almost tangible just how happy they all were.

I felt apart from the celebrations as I could not bring myself to be happy and I was certainly in no mood to forgive as I reflected on what this day meant for me. I had lost my best friend to the war, my mother had died while I was away and my sister had married and gone to Canada.

1919

The New Year started with my discharge from the army. My shoulder was now fully recovered and physically I was in reasonable shape but in my head I was all over the place and I had no idea what I would do next. Sis had invited me to Canada where I think she hoped that I might stay but at that time I felt no great urge to either visit her or to emigrate.

I was still living with Aunt Bessie, who had welcomed me into her home without a moment's hesitation, following my stay in hospital as there was no way I wanted to return to Acaster. Aunt Bessie was a strong character who did not, as she put it, do issues. I got away with moping about for a short time and then she must have seen that I had reached a fork in the road and while one way was shrouded in uncertainty, the other inevitably led to self-destruction and she was not going to allow that, being as she was a firm believer in tough love. One night after supper as we sat by the fire with Aunt Bessie doing a little sewing, we had the conversation that turned out to change my life.

"Well, Jack, how long do you intend to go on like this?"

"Sorry, Aunt Bessie, like what?"

"Wasting your precious, God-given life. You are a young man who has not only survived that awful war but come back unharmed apart from a scar on your shoulder. Millions of young men will never have the chances that you now have and you owe it to them not to waste your life. Am I right?"

If it had been anyone else, I think I would have argued back if only for the sake of doing so but with Aunt Bessie that did not seem to be a sensible option.

"Why don't you go and visit Sis? Her letters paint a picture of a land of space, clean air and opportunities. She and Harry would love to see you. You may like it enough to make a life out there. Harry has said that he can get you a job in the brewery."

"Aunt Bessie, I appreciate your concern but I don't want to go to Canada. I love Sis and I am happy for her and Harry and I will visit one day but just not now."

"Well, what will you do then?"

"I have no idea."

I could feel Aunt Bessie looking at me intently. After a while she put her sewing down and took a letter out of her apron pocket.

"That's what I thought you would say. I am not prepared to see you waste your life and so I took it upon myself to write to Lord Acaster…"

"Aunt Bessie…"

"That's all right. You can thank me later. As I was saying, I wrote to Lord Acaster. Sis had told me when she was here, that he had promised a job for all the men of Acaster who returned from the war and so I wrote to him about you. He has replied to say that he would be delighted to have you back working on the Acaster Estate and he would like to see you the day after tomorrow at mid-day."

"I can't go back. There's Father…"

"It seems to be that your father has blighted your life for too long. I can't possibly know all that happened in Acaster but you owe it to your mother, Sis, Harold and his mother to do what is right for you. You mustn't let your father stop you doing what you want…"

"But, I don't know what I want."

"I believe from what you have told me that you enjoyed working on the Acaster estate."

"Well, yes, I did, but…"

"Jack, it is so much easier to be able to blame something or someone else. It is so much easier to do nothing and feel sorry for yourself than to get up and do something. So, I'll tell you what I am going to do. You can stay here another two weeks. You can decide whether or not you go to see Lord Acaster, however, if you don't, then you will need to find something else because I will expect you to leave here in two weeks' time. Is there anything else that needs to be said?"

"No, Aunt Bessie. I know you're right. I've known it for a while but it needed you to give me the push I needed to sort myself out. I now know why Sis thinks so much of you so, thank you for all your help. I will go to Acaster."

"Your whole future is ahead of you so grab it by the scruff of the neck and move on. Now, how about a small sherry? I always find it helps me to sleep."

It seemed very strange returning to Acaster. Fortunately, the road from the station went past the Acaster Estate before entering the town and so I was confident that I would not bump into old acquaintances. However, just in case, I took the precaution of wearing a hat and turning my collar up.

I made my way up to the house and around the back to the Estates Office. As had always been the practice, I knocked on the inner door and sat down to wait. I did not have long to wait before the door was opened by Captain Hargreaves, who leant heavily on a stick. I had not given much thought to what had happened to him and I was as delighted to see him as he was me.

"Come in, come in and sit down."

As Captain Hargreaves made his way back to his desk, he caught me looking at him and when he sat down, he smiled.

"My friend, Gerry, wouldn't let me go without giving me a small leaving present. Pity the bugger didn't do it a few years earlier as I would have been home sooner. It's just a bit of shrapnel in my hip but no real damage. Some days it's better than others. Now, would you like some tea or something a little stronger? Or would you like something a little stronger in your tea? I'm going to."

I said I would join him and as he made the tea, waving away my offer to make it, he asked me about the last couple of years of my war. I had not spoken to anyone about my war and God knows Aunt Bessie had tried often enough but it felt so easy to talk to him.

"I was sorry to hear about young Smith. He was a good man. What about your sister? They were sweet on each other, weren't they?"

I told him, even though I couldn't explain it, that Sis and Harold had drifted apart. She had married Harry Tibbins and they had emigrated to Canada.

"I was sorry to hear about the death of your mother. Your father seems to have kept going and is keeping well. I assume that you will be visiting him?"

If he registered the fact that I did not answer, he chose to ignore it and continued.

"Now, I suppose we had better talk about this job. Oh, don't worry. This isn't an interview. The job's yours if you want it. His Lordship and I have discussed this at some length and this is our offer to you.

"As you can see, I am not getting any younger. I wish it was otherwise but there you are. His Lordship likes continuity and therefore we would like to offer you the job of 'Assistant Estates Manager'. You will learn about the different aspects of the role and then when I retire, you will be able to take over. How does that sound?"

It was more than I had expected. I thought I would just be offered my old job back and had already decided that I would accept. This was as good an opportunity as I was likely to get and I readily accepted.

"His Lordship will join us for lunch and he will tell you the pay involved. I can, however, tell you that a small cottage on the estate will be provided. It hasn't been lived in for a while but it shouldn't require anything more than a good clean and a lick of paint."

"Thank you, Captain Hargreaves…"

"Don't thank me, lad, thank His Lordship, and I think I can hear him outside."

***

I thought I must be the happiest man in England that day as I set off back to London. I had taken a quick look at the cottage that was to be my new home and Captain Hargreaves was right as to what was required.

Aunt Bessie had spent an anxious day waiting to hear how things had gone and she was very happy for me when I told her that I was to be an assistant estates manager.

"Well, Jack. How exciting. I am so pleased for you. You won't be looking back now. When do you start?"

I explained that I would be moving down at the end of the week to give me a bit of time to sort out the cottage and then I would start work on the Monday.

"I took Sis and Harry to the Lyons Corner House in Piccadilly Circus to celebrate their wedding and as I am a firm believer in equality in all things, I would like to take you for afternoon tea too. How about tomorrow?"

The afternoon tea was memorable not just in terms of the sandwiches and cakes but for Aunt Bessie's company. We talked pleasantly and at length about a range of topics. Some we could agree on.

"Yes, I would like to get married."

"Well, make sure you get out and meet some girls. Remember, the world does not end at the estate's walls. Life isn't going to come to you."

Some we couldn't agree on.

"I know he's my father but…"

At the end of our tea, Aunt Bessie told me to put my hand out. It was the sort of thing I imagined she would have said to me when I was about ten but I did it anyway. She then put her hand out and covered my palm. When she took her hand away, there was a ten-pound note sitting on the palm of my hand.

"Aunt Bessie…"

"Use it wisely. Put it towards something you need for your cottage or use it to start a saving fund to visit Sis. You will pay her a visit, won't you?"

"Thank you, Aunt Bessie. You have been so kind to me. I will visit Sis one day once I have settled into my new job."

"Make sure you do, lad. You will regret it otherwise."

Post 1919

I felt happy to be back working on the Acaster Estate. I recognised a number of the men who I had enlisted with and felt sad when I realised who was missing. I kept myself to myself to start with and then His Lordship decided that he would mark the official ending of the war with a dance for the estate workers and it was there that I met Edith, who worked as a nanny to His Lordship's grandchildren. Even if it wasn't obvious to us, others could see where things were headed.

We married in 1921 and we've been together ever since and both of us have kept working for the Estate. To start with we tried for a family but nothing happened, although I can say that I was not really disappointed. I was worried that the way my father behaved might have been passed onto me and no child deserved that. I made the right noises where Edith was concerned and we adjusted. Edith was a regular churchgoer and she took it as God's will. She never complained and I never explained.

I tried to keep out of Father's way as much as he tried to keep out of mine. When he retired, he had to move out of the Police House to make way for his replacement and his family. Father moved into a small cottage not far from where Harold used to live. Despite his ability to look after himself over the years, a number of the women from Acaster offered to act as cleaners, cooks and general help and all quickly left Father's employment. It was only in the last few years as his health declined that he really needed help. Edith offered but I refused point blank to let her. Edith knew that something had caused the bad feeling between us and in the early days she asked me about it but I had no intention of telling her all that had happened. Eventually, getting nowhere she had let the matter drop.

Eventually, Father's needs were such that we had to find someone to look after him and we were fortunate to come across Miss Galbraith, a retired military nurse of many years' standing, who clearly would not stand for any nonsense. She was a very private person, who appeared to have no family or friends, however, she came into her own when there was someone to care for. She would go in every morning, leave early in the evening and return to put him to bed. If Father still had wandering hands, then we never heard about it and I always suspected that he would only ever have done it once where Miss Galbraith was concerned.

It was impossible to avoid Father completely and when we did meet, it was civil if brief. Edith wanted to meet him and so we did visit him in his cottage, although I made sure that there was never a time when he was alone with her.

***

Father declined physically quite quickly, although mentally he remained as sharp as ever. I told Edith never to visit him unless I was with her. She never asked and I never explained. I worry that it makes me sound like him but I had my reasons and continued to stand my ground whilst being happy to give way on pretty much everything else in our marriage.

I was in the Estate Office one morning when I received a message from Miss Galbraith that Father had been taken ill and that she had called the doctor. Later that day I went to see him and found him in bed with the covers tucked in so tightly that he couldn't move his arms as Miss Galbraith was worried that he might fall out of the bed. The doctor had said that he had had a stroke that had left him numb down one side but his mind and his speech were unaffected. If they had of been then I am sure that matters would have turned out differently.

Miss Galbraith was leaving just as I arrived to visit Father.

"Good evening, Miss Galbraith."

"Good night, Mister Jack. Your father is no better but he seems to be in a bit of a funny mood. Maybe you will be able to cheer him up."

Very much doubting that, I entered the house and went up to his bedroom which smelt of piss and carbolic despite Miss Galbraith's best efforts. A small coal fire, giving off as much smoke as heat, battled to stay alight in the hearth. The room was still cold and Father had several blankets and a couple of his old police overcoats spread on top of him. A small lamp on his bedside table gave some light. He didn't speak when I entered the bedroom, content it seemed to let me lead the conversation. I stood there looking at what was left of Sergeant Brown, my father and it must have been something in my look that finally set him off.

"Don't you stand there pitying me, you bugger! What do you want?"

"I just came to see you, old man…"

"Don't you dare call me old man. I've told you about that before. Show me some respect. It's lucky for you that I can't get up or…"

And that's how it started. "Or what, old man? Tell me, why have you never liked me?"

"Is that really what you want to ask me? Pathetic. Here get my old pocketbook. It's over there on the stand. I'll start you off – have a look at the letter tucked in the back."

I took the letter out and opened it. It was Harry's letter and I couldn't take in what I was reading. Certain bits have stayed with me since that day.

…but I am afraid that I cannot take anymore…at Mrs Smith's house. It has made me feel both shocked and ashamed for the part that I played in it…hearing Ester Smith's shouts and cries and then being told to deny any involvement by Sergeant Brown…I might have played a part…in getting the two of them shot is going to stay with me for the rest of my life.

Yours
Harry Tibbins

I looked at this monster that I had known as my father and almost spat the words out.

"Why? Why would you do that? What had Harold done to you except fall for Sis? What had I done? What had Mrs Smith done besides fall ill?"

He looked at me and then started to laugh. "I have wondered what this day would be like. Telling you everything and watching you in pain. Knowing that once it is in your head, then you will have to live with it for the rest of your life. There is so much to tell you and so little time, according to that doctor, to do it. Think about that and if you are man enough and you really want to know then you know where I am. I'm not going anywhere."

He laughed again before started to cough which only ended when a large ball of phlegm landed at my feet.

With the hatred of him returning in waves, I was determined to lash out and to give him a small measure of pain in return, so I told him something that I was sure he didn't know. I watched his face as I told him that not only was Sis married but she had married Harry Tibbens and they were living happily in Canada. He hadn't known and so a small victory was mine.

I wasn't ready for the conversation that he had offered and so left and the walk back to the cottage helped me to calm down. I knew I would go back and that it had to be soon.

***

Over the next couple of days I could feel the pressure building up inside me to the point where I thought I would burst. Edith had grown used to my frequent bouts of insomnia which I dealt with by reading downstairs or going out for walk and so she never even stirred when I slipped out of our cottage late one evening.

I made my way through the shadows and alleyways until I reached the rear of Father's cottage and slipped in through the side gate. I had a set of keys and entered through the back door. As Miss Galbraith kept the cottage spotless, I made sure that I removed my boots as I wanted there to be no trace of my visit.

As I made my way carefully up the stairs, I could see the weak light from Father's bedside lamp framing the door to his room and I wondered if he would be awake, and he was.

"Come in. I've been expecting you."

He still had the ability to make me feel like a small boy all over again as I stood there looking down at him. The room felt cold as the small fire was no competition for the lack of heat elsewhere in the cottage.

"Time's short and there's a lot you want to ask me so go on. Ask me anything? Where would you like to start?"

His eyes glittered as he looked up at me from a face that had a yellowish tinge. His skin was stretched as thin as paper, tightly across the bones of his face.

"What? Cat got your tongue?"

I stood at the end of the bed considering whether to leave but, as we both knew, of course, I couldn't.

"Let's start with Sis. That night I crept along the landing and saw you sitting on her bed. It wasn't the first time that I had heard you go into her bedroom at night so what was going on? Did you?"

He was determined to enjoy every minute of our encounter. He motioned to the glass of water on his bedside table. It was one of those moments. I knew that as repellent as I found him, I would have to touch him because he needed help to sit up before he could drink and he knew it and enjoyed my discomfort. When he had settled back onto his pillows, he looked at me and smiled.

"I remember that night too. I never forgave you for that."

"Why? You didn't?"

"No. I wanted to. I believed it was my duty, no, my right, to break her in. I deserved it. I had put a lot of time and effort into it. I didn't want her first time being with some boy like that Harold with face fluff instead of whiskers who knew nothing about anything.

"I never wanted a son you know. I'm not like that. I was so disappointed when you were born."

The room suddenly felt smaller and claustrophobic and I felt sick when my mind filled with the full horror of the implications of what I had seen that night and just heard. I felt myself sag back against the chest of drawers disturbing some of the medicines on top of it causing them to rattle against each other. It was only when I heard his laughter that I pulled myself together.

"Did Sis know what was going on?"

"Of course, not! Your sister was never the brightest marble in the tin. She thought and I never told her otherwise, that it was all perfectly natural. She was a little surprised when I first started going to her room but over time I gradually led her to the point where what came next would seem natural and I think she wanted it to. But after you decided to be nosey, it seemed best to go no further."

He was saying no more than I expected but it was still shocking to hear him talk about it in such a matter-of-fact way. The horror of what I was hearing was increased because before he could continue, I had to sit him up and give him another sip of water.

"Come on, Jack, don't look at me like that. You hated me before, so now you just hate me a bit more."

My head was reeling and I seemed unable to get my tongue to work. I could see that he loved every minute of this, drawing strength from the effect his words were having on me while I seemed to be getting weaker. Eventually, I recovered enough to find my voice.

"Why did you get Harold and me arrested?"

"Why not? It seemed to be a way to settle a lot of things in one go. I couldn't stand you and your disrespect. I couldn't stand Harold for coming between me and Sis. And then there was Ester Smith herself.

"A woman like that should not be on her own. It's a waste. She was still good looking and I thought I would give it a try. She wouldn't as it happened because she preferred to let His Lordship have her. Now there was no way I was going to let that go unanswered. I started standing in the shadows opposite, keeping her under observation and having a wank to pass the time. There is something exciting doing it while the woman who is exciting you has no idea she's being watched. I still kept an eye on things when she was ill and then a gift fell into my lap. I saw Harold there and I knew if he was there then you would be too. A quick check with His Lordship confirmed that you weren't there on leave."

"She was ill. She was dying. What you did probably killed her sooner. You knew that Harold and I could have been shot."

"So what? I saw better men than you two shot in South Africa."

"So you caused all that misery simply because you were denied a shag? You really are an evil bastard."

He went to speak but then stopped a moment as if a thought had struck him before continuing.

"I blame your mother. She hadn't been a proper wife to me for years and a man has needs, you know."

"Most men can control themselves. You hadn't been a good husband to her with all your vile abuse."

And then at that moment I knew what had happened.

"You killed Mum, didn't you?"

He looked as if he had not enjoyed himself so much in years and motioned for another drink probably just to prolong the agony.

"Did I? Why would I do that?"

"Because she knew what you had done? She saw Harry's letter, didn't she?"

"The morning you and Harold were taken away by the military police, I was there watching it happen but unfortunately Ester Smith saw me. Somehow despite her being so ill, she was able to get to the police house and threaten me. Sadly, for her, she never made it back to her front gate.

"Meanwhile that young bugger Tibbens was upstairs writing his letter which your mother found after he had run away. There was a big row and Sis stormed off to London. Your mother threatened me and hid the letter. So with you and Harold arrested and likely to be shot, Ester Smith dead, Sis in London, it only left your mother who could make life difficult for me. I never for one minute believed that Sis was any sort of threat and anyway she didn't know everything.

So, your mother had to go as I was not prepared to live the rest of my life with her threats hanging over me. She was very frail at the time and it was easy just to give her a gentle push and watch her fall arse over tit down the stairs. She was dead by the time I walked down those stairs and out the door. What did you expect me to do?"

I thought my head would burst and tears stung my eyes.

"You bastard, I will see you pay for this."

This seemed to amuse him even more and once the racking cough that followed his laughter had subsided, he continued goading me.

"Now a lot of good that will do you. Come on, you are talking to me here. Where's your evidence? It's just your word against mine. And if anyone should believe you then by the time they've finished looking into it, I shall be dead anyway."

I moved towards him. "You are not going to get away with this."

"What do you think you're going to do? There's a big difference between killing a man when you are so close that you can smell their breath and look into their eyes and see the fear there and being a sniper hundreds of yards away from the man you kill. You'll not see any fear in these eyes but you will need to grow a pair because you haven't the balls to kill me."

I cannot be sure but equally I cannot deny that I had thought about this moment. His arms were down under the sheets and he put up no resistance as I sat astride him. He put up no struggle. His eyes bore into me with a mixture of amusement, contempt and pure evil. He was clearly expecting me to put a pillow over his face but I had something else in mind as I needed to look into his eyes and watch the life go out of them.

With my left hand under his jaw, I forced his mouth shut and I then pushed the index and middle finger of my right hand up his nostrils as far as they would go so that he could neither breathe in or out. He was not going to give me the pleasure of witnessing him struggle for life. He was intent only on me seeing the hatred in his eyes. Tears from my eyes dripped onto his face and then he was dead. I waited as long as I dared just to be sure before I removed my fingers, swathed in the snot and mucus from his nose and quickly dried them on my handkerchief. I stood there staring at him and the enormity of what I had done hit me. I had killed my own father and if proof was needed, then this was it – I was no different to him. Like father, like son. What I had always feared had now been proved.

I knew that I had to make sure that there was no trace that I or anyone else had been in that room and so I quickly smoothed his bedclothes and topped up his water glass and then I looked at him for the last time as he lay there with his eyes open staring sightlessly at the ceiling. I am sure it was no real shock to Miss Galbraith when she came in the next morning and found him dead.

**

Early the next morning Miss Galbraith rang me to tell me that Father was dead. By the time I arrived at the cottage, the doctor had been and gone and Miss Galbraith had washed and laid out Father's body. Neither Miss Galbraith, nor more importantly the doctor, had any cause for concern over the cause of death and I made sure that my behaviour did not suggest otherwise. I thought it was important to wait for you to come for his body and so Miss Galbraith and I went downstairs and shared a pot of tea and what was left of a cake that she had made. I paid her up until the end of that week and added a further week's money as a bonus, assuring her that we would give her a good reference.

**

It had now grown dark and Jack and Sam had finished their drinks long ago. Neither had wanted to go for another drink for fear of breaking the flow of what Jack needed to say.

"Sis and Harry have now settled happily in a new and bigger house in Milton. We have always written to each other and bits of this story have come to light as a result. It wasn't easy for them to begin with and after they had been in Canada for two years she became pregnant. Sadly, she miscarried and it was another year or so before Simon was born followed, after another two years, by Kate. She and Harry have seen them grow up and marry and they are now grandparents too. Harry is still enjoying his job in the family brewery and is now a director while Sis has returned to work in the local hospital and is now a sister.

"Invites to visit Canada have come thick and fast and I have always made sure that there has been a good reason to turn them down and with a growing family, it has not been practical for them to visit us. I did put Aunt Bessie's ten pounds in a savings account called my Canada Fund and I have added to it when I could over the years. You know that I intend to retire next year and then Edith and I are going to go out to Toronto. I feel ready and able now to have the conversations with Sis that I know we both need. It's been a really long time, too long, since we have seen each other and I want to go before it is too late."

Sam shook his head.

"I don't think you are a bit like your father. Go to Canada for God's sake. Move out there and enjoy your Canadian family. What's stopping you?"

Jack's face was a mask of desperation as he searched the face of his friend.

"You could stop me, Sam, if you choose to go to the police about what I have told you."

***

12 months later Sam opened the airmail letter that had arrived that morning.

Dear Sam,

I hope this letter finds you well.

I know you will want to know what going to Canada was like, so I thought I would write and tell you.

For what seemed an eternity, I sat rigidly in my seat staring into the confined space that I inhabited along with many others, waiting patiently for the release that I had spent many years anticipating. I had long thought that I would be dead before this day came. If I could be bothered, I could turn my head to see the progress of the day through the small, reinforced windows. I had never been someone who could settle down with a book and thereby block out the realities of life at least for a little while so I found it quite boring and the time was only broken up when either the drinks trolley or meals were handed out.

I had only the anticipation of the moment of release and what came next to occupy my mind and uncertainty had always proved difficult for me to deal with. After what seemed a lifetime, the door to the outside world was opened and I shuffled forward blinking as I stepped into the light. I was with every part of my being an outdoors man and incarceration had been sheer purgatory with little or nothing to break up the time and I felt as stiff as a post from hours of enforced sitting.

We, like the others, made our way as directed and we moved forward from one branch of officialdom to the next, having our documentation checked. I could only have done this knowing that at my side was the one person who over the

194

last years had kept me sane and alive. Finally, the last checks were carried out and we were able to step into the bright lights where others waited. The space hummed with excitement and anticipation.

It had always worried me that when the big day came, she would not recognise me after all the years apart. I stood still and put the bags down by my side. I looked around at the faces in front of me and then I saw her looking little different to the last time we had been together. Smiling broadly yet with tears starting to wet our cheeks, we moved forward and for the first time in decades I hugged my sister. We stood there with Sis almost totally enveloped in my arms while leaving Edith and the rest of the welcoming party feeling excluded but emotional as they could see what it meant to the two of us. Hastily breaking the spell and remembering his manners, Harry awkwardly hugged Edith and introduced her to Simon and Kate, who with eyes moist from tears said, "Welcome to Canada," and gave her a hug too.

Sis took a step back and looked intently at me. "Welcome to your new home, Jack. You've barely changed a bit." She then hugged me again and said quietly in my ear, "We've so much to catch up on and now we have the time, as long as it takes, as long as we want. There's no need to rush and let's just enjoy being together again. Simon and Kate are so looking forward to getting to know you both. Now introduce me to Edith."

So far so good and yes, you are right as I should have done this years ago. When we have settled, you will come out for a visit.

Yours sincerely,
Jack